Every Voice Heard

N.Y. Dunlap,
D.T. Powell,
and
Sarah Hanks

Praise Through the Pain

N.Y. Dunlap

Chapter 1

Alexis slipped out of the practice room and into a wide hallway, as she stuffed a praise flag into her oversized purse. She approached one of the many massive church corridors. Was the exit in this direction? Even after a month of leading the new praise dance team, The Way Church was still a maze.

Time weighed heavily on her chest. The echo of her footsteps along the limestone floors matched the intensity of the thudding inside her chest because, while she navigated this modern structure with hallways like veins on a Tuesday afternoon, she still needed to get to her church this evening.

And then she saw the light.

Glass doors lined the exit, and opposite it, another row of doors led into a stadium-sized sanctuary. Alexis pushed through the door leading to the exit in triumph. Cool April air rushed to her face, and she breathed as though freed from the mega-church's too-tight grip. She dashed down the broad steps, which fed straight into two wide boulevards, boasting San Antonio traffic.

Although she'd made it outside, anxiety cinched her throat like a tight scarf. After helping The Way prepare for Easter, a two-hour drive through Texas lay ahead, which included more Easter preparations at Cornerstone. Her tiny church, with its faded carpet, weary pews, and three brave youths who clung to a ministry the small town seemed to have left behind. *Her* praise and worship ministry.

Alexis's flowing skirt caught the breeze as she tugged her purse higher onto her shoulder. "Welp. Here we go again."

At the far end of the parking lot, Aunt Cherry shut the door of her weathered truck, a Tupperware container balanced in hand. "Oh, good. Caught you just in time." She held the container like a prize.

The rich scent of beef stew floated up as Alexis accepted it, and her lips curved in appreciation despite the knot in her chest. "Auntie, you're gonna make me gain weight. I've gotta stay in shape to praise dance." And the career she lived for. A career that demanded strong arms and a steady heart.

Aunt Cherry rolled her eyes. "Hush. You'll be half starved by the time you arrive at Cornerstone Church this evening. You pass a thousand tumbleweeds to get there, and I won't have you eating fast food, Alexis."

"I . . ." Ugh, so true.

"Mhmmm. I still can't believe you haven't switched churches with me. You drive to that ghost town multiple times a week. How many girls do you lead in praise dance now, or are you going just to practice?"

"I still have three eager girls on my roster. Second, multiple times a week? Hah. That's a stretch." Alexis tried not to laugh. "I attend on Sundays. And literally just once a week if I develop fresh routines. Or a holiday arises, such as the impending one where we worship God's greatest sacrifice. Cornerstone's youth team needs me."

"I'm surprised Pastor Otis still stays awake long enough to give a sermon." Aunt Cherry fell into step beside her. "Bless his heart, he's getting up in age."

Alexis didn't respond right away. The foundation of their church had crumbled. Most of the old faithfuls—like Momma—had already passed on. And the children? Either boredom took over or bad influences led them astray. Only three kids remained and the list of "approved" worship songs was older than her first pair of leotards.

"So"—Aunt Cherry's lips curved slyly—"how did our girls do?"

Alexis hesitated. "Well . . . your Way kiddos are excited. This Easter performance will be their debut review, Auntie. So let's just say, they catch on quickly. Now, I must g—"

Aunt Cherry stopped mid-step. "That's not a performance *review*."

"They . . ." Uh-oh. How did Alexis tell her aunt The Way youth had the coordination of cute—and very blind—pandas? Alexis placed the dinner her aunt had given her onto the passenger seat. "The girls love the song."

Glenda, a close friend of her aunt, descended the limestone steps with a knowing smirk. "Board members say it's too late to start a praise dance team for Easter."

"Christmas," Aunt Cherry muttered. "Start it for Christmas, they said. I've prayed ever since. So, how did the girls really do?"

Before Alexis could break the news, Glenda spoke up. "You know how certain adversities change because of prayer and fasting? Well, we don't have a moment to spare." She offered a sweet smile, and Alexis could tell she hadn't meant to be sarcastic.

"All right, there you have it, Auntie. I really am in a rush." She faced the street and frowned. Traffic was a mess. The freeway would be worse. Cedar Cove was far away, and the last 35 miles were stop-sign purgatory. God had used that stretch of road for a lesson in patience. And she had learned a greater lesson. Thou shalt not try the leader of the

Motherboard. Another wave of anxiety washed her palms in sweat at the thought of incurring Mother Phyllis's wrath.

Then she heard it.

The wail of sirens. A lone police SUV hurried towards the red light, decelerating near the intersection. Alexis instinctively whispered a prayer. As a paramedic, she knew the strain of fighting to keep a critical patient alive on the way to the hospital. And a crash could be deadly to them all. Officers had their own version of that fight—racing toward a disturbance and needing to arrive in one piece. *Please, Lord, keep them safe.*

Most cars slowed or stopped.

Except one.

An F-350 swerved into the wrong lane—just as the officer accelerated through the light. Metal slammed metal. The police cruiser spun like a dreidel. In a flash, Alexis registered the San Antonio Police Department's motto, "Protecting the Alamo City," emblazoned on the side, before it crumpled inward.

The F-350 driver paused—then gunned it in reverse and peeled away.

While the driver sped off, Alexis processed all she could. "Auntie, call 911!"

She bolted to the small trauma kit in her trunk. Long tendrils of corky curls slapped her warm brown cheeks as she yanked the kit free and raced around stopped cars. Alexis rushed toward the wreck. Drivers exited vehicles—some frozen, some filming.

"Alexis, wait!" Glenda shouted. "It could explode!"

Alexis ignored her. Ugh, action movies. *Why do people watch paranoia-inducing action movies?*

Cracks webbed across the passenger-side window of the police vehicle. She yanked the door open. The glass from the driver's side windows had blown inward and covered the seats in jagged shards. She climbed into the empty seat, mindful of the glass.

An officer sat slumped behind the wheel, chin against his chest. Blood trickled from his closed eyes over his dark brown skin. The dashboard pinned one leg, and crushed metal swallowed the other.

Her heart cracked. God's gift—praise dancing—required her to have legs. Officers needed them too. So did the folks who labored from nine-to-five to survive.

Radio static crackled. No chatter about much-needed backup, while she absolutely required assistance.

Alexis checked his airway. Shallow, strained breaths. Possibly a collapsed lung.

"Officer," she used calm, short phrases and glanced at his nameplate, "Hayes, I'm Alexis Carter, paramedic. I'm here to help."

Not a twitch.

She yanked open her kit and grabbed trauma shears. In a second, she sliced through the dark blue of his uniform. Fabric peeled back beneath her fingers. *Abba, Father, give me steady hands. Let this man breathe.*

After dropping the shears into the kit, she snapped open a needle from its sterile package. Her fingers found the right spot—between the second and third ribs. She stabbed fast, angling it just right between his ribs. And drove it to a safe distance.

Hiss.

Built-up air released from the needle in a sharp gasp.

"Thank you, Jesus," she whispered beneath her breath.

The officer's lids fluttered, and she caught a flash of hazel eyes before they closed again. "Jesus?" He murmured, cracked lips curved into a weary, faint smile. "Good Guy."

She laughed softly. "He is. And since you seem familiar with Him, I'd like to make a deal."

No reply, but the smile lingered.

"Oh, before I do," she began in an encouraging voice, "please don't freak out. Your legs are pinned." No response. She sighed, then added, "So here's my deal: I get to pray—off the record—while I stop your bleeding. Deal?"

As she packed gauze against his head wound, she wondered why the airbag hadn't deployed? Horrible how often it happened. Even with the newer vehicles.

But she didn't have time to dwell on technical issues. First responders needed to get the pressure off his legs before the nerve damage was irreversible. Her stomach tightened.

Her hands trembled, but her voice remained calm, her prayers steadier than her pulse. "Jesus, I love You. You know I do. My legs are probably second on that list—after You, Aunt Cherry, my brother, nephew, and the kids at Cornerstone. But please . . . please," she croaked, "please save Officer Hayes's legs."

As she sealed the prayer, sirens screamed in the distance. Finally.

*****

Many hours later, bleach permeated the air in the hospital waiting room. And a melody from singer Dean Martin. The Rat Pack crooners serenaded Alexis through an imaginary speaker in her mind, while she sat, shoulders slumped. Her hand clutched her phone like it held every answer.

Alexis hadn't meant to get so invested that she messed up her commitment. She just wanted Officer Hayes to stand again. Tall as he appeared. Which was what? Six-foot-three based on the way his limbs stretched forever beneath the steering wheel?

A deep inhale of stark disinfectant helped dispel the Rat Pack's version of "Sway" from her mind. Romance wasn't in the cards. She'd given her statement and berated herself for not saving the Cornerstone Kiddos numbers on her cellphone. She'd called her old Sunday school teacher Margaret, who was also the church secretary, and discovered the children had waited for almost an hour. Unusual for her to miss a practice. Well, she hadn't been asked by Aunt Cherry to help establish a praise team at The Way years ago when her aunt had first moved to San Antonio. So this was a first. Still, they'd waited and waited. *Get it together, Alexis.*

Her phone buzzed.

Without a glance, she answered. "Hello?"

"Why aren't you at church?"

Ugh. Phyllis. Of course. Head of the Cornerstone Mother's Board since Moses came off the mountain. Sadly, Phyllis had none of his characteristics—love, patience, kindness. And world renowned doctors would never locate a maternal bone in her body. However, her fashionable hats got bigger and fancier each year. So, there was that.

"Sorry, Mother Phyllis. I had an emergency."

"No, you didn't. I heard you were up at The Way, with their girls. I knew this would happen when you moved to San Antonio."

"Well, I needed a job."

"That's what a car is for, Alexis."

She bit her tongue. Hard. Why would she drive four hours every day to accommodate a demanding paramedic career? "I pick up a few girls from an after-school program, take them to The Way, and we practice for two hours. Once a week." Uh oh. She shouldn't have said that. "They started late in—"

"Two hours? We get one hour. If that."

"An hour and thirty minutes, Ms. Phyllis. Besides, like I was trying to explain, the girls at The Way only started to practice recently." Alexis's anxiety rose to a new height, and blood swooshed in her ears. She served with her whole heart. Every week. Every dance. The youth dancers performed only on holidays or Cornerstone anniversaries. Alexis danced once or twice a month! *God's not counting, Lex.* She cleared her throat. "Can you pray for someone?" She shifted the tone.

"I always pray."

"No, I mean—will you pray for someone? Officer Hayes."

Phyllis paused. "Hayes, you say?"

"Yes, Ms. Phyllis, please pray for him." Alexis's voice was a fragile whisper, and a heavy sigh escaped her lips before she could catch it. She quickly explained how she'd encountered Officer Hayes and relayed the desperate reason he needed their intercession. "I'll try to reschedule with the girls," she added, her mind already in a race because of her tight schedule. Easter Sunday was her next available slot, given that she had Mondays and Tuesdays off to rest and accommodate her Tuesday practices at Cornerstone.

Silence hung heavy between them, filled with unspoken thoughts. As if Alexis's willingness to add another practice had finally swayed her, Phyllis spoke. "I'll pray."

Alexis ended the call, the phone's weight impossibly heavy in her shaky hand. Then she rubbed her sweaty palms against her jeans before pressing the heel of her hand into her chest. Every breath was a pant. Kneading the area above her hollow lungs eased the anxiety dragging her down.

She focused on the officer's voice—such a charming voice—and the wave of panic ebbed a little more. His desperate "Jesus" still echoed in her ears. She couldn't shake the whispered plea for hope. The sound pierced through the chaos and lodged itself deep in her heart.

She didn't know this stranger, but she suspected he had an incredible relationship with the Lord. *Don't dwell, Lex.*

Alexis rose to her feet. She didn't have hours to spend on a stranger. Especially when she needed to get home, find her dance journal, and grab parent contact information for the three Cornerstone kids. She'd call and attempt to wrangle them up for a virtual video practice before the end of the week, a small piece of normalcy to cleave to.

Above all, she desired to pray. Because for all her skills, strength, and stubborn will, prayer was the greatest help she could give Officer Hayes. And that's exactly what she did during her long walk toward the hospital exit.

A few minutes later, Alexis passed through the sliding glass doors. Her eyes blinked at the fading sunlight outside. Woah. She hadn't expected night would greet her as she left.

"Well, I'd better hurry and find that—" Alexis's phone vibrated in her hands. A long series of numbers scrolled across the screen. An overseas call. It had to be her brother, whose love of country often overshadowed his love for his wife and eight-year-old. As she made a beeline for the parking structure, she tapped the accept button. "Hey, Aaron? Did you take leave for East—?"

"Sis, where are you?" The Marine's solid and direct façade cracked. "Go to the VA hospital. Right now."

Her pace faltered. "Aaron, you're scaring me. Is something wrong with Bev or . . . AJ?" Her heart clenched at the idea of harm befalling her eight-year-old nephew and his mom.

"Both."

Chapter 2
Easter Sunday

As part of a three-person paramedic crew, Alexis usually wore her uniform when she provided updates to an ER team. She'd speak in clear, concise sentences and whispered prayers. But Tuesday was a repeat offender. First she'd visited Officer Hayes at one hospital, then her family at another. She'd gone alone. No uniform. No patient. Just a woman carrying hope's weight.

Aunt Cherry, Glenda, and a few prayer friends met Alexis in ICU. The sweet sister she'd inherited through marriage had died on the operating table. But Aaron Junior had survived. The doctor said his specialized car seat, designed for autistic kids, had saved him and left him unscathed. And it had changed the course of Alexis's life forever.

Every morning for the past five days, she'd woken before the sun. Not by choice. Aaron Junior hummed in a low, repetitive tone when his internal clock signaled dawn's arrival. His inner realm differed from the external darkness that might remain outside for other Texans. She didn't begrudge him that, though. The low, rhythmic sound reminded Alexis of how bees might worship: purposeful, focused, and only a little overwhelming.

She'd gotten into a routine and removed frozen waffles from the microwave. She cut them into perfect little bites on the marble countertop.

Minutes later, he sat at the kitchen table in his favorite seat, ready for breakfast. Days ago, it had taken her forever to find the powdered sugar. Smiling, Alexis poured the perfect amount, dusting AJ's waffles in the sugary, snowy concoction. She'd caught her stride in his ranch-style house, where she'd temporarily moved.

"Temporarily." Alexis exhaled that word like a prayer. "Is this honestly temporary?"

Beverly used to say her only complaint about Aaron was that he always chose black-ops missions over birthdays. Over applied behavior analysis therapy sessions. Over them.

Jesus, please . . . let this be temporary. Let Aaron come home.

He had come home all right. In crisp dress blues, he'd buried his wife, saluted his son, who didn't prefer hugs, and thanked Alexis for her support.

With a shake of her head, she returned her attention to her nephew. AJ chewed waffles scooped from his square blue plate—the only plate in the house he used. With every bite, his sneakers tapped the white oak chair legs. The soles lit up in neon bursts. The eight-year-old's army fatigue joggers matched his shirt, which featured a roaring T-Rex.

Phyllis would have a fit.

Alexis could hear her now: "This isn't how a young man dresses for church." Never mind AJ's autism. Never mind the trauma he'd just endured that didn't touch his outward appearance. Phyllis wouldn't see that—only the noise. Their differences.

A gentle stirring in Alexis's gut—the Holy Spirit, maybe—nudged her toward The Way church.

No, she shook her head. She loved Cornerstone, with its quaint, intimate scenery. Her pastor had baptized her, prayed over her after Momma died. That church was family. This other church was . . .

With no desire to entertain harsh thoughts about a church she wasn't familiar with, Alexis lowered her eyes and breathed a quiet prayer while she packed AJ's bag. "Thank You, Lord, for Your help. Aunt Cherry is amazing. And thank You for AJ . . . Even though my brother serves from a distance, I trust You've got us covered today."

She checked the time. 7:20 AM.

"Oh no." Church started at 9:30, but she'd promised to meet the praise dancers early for one last run-through.

The knot of tension returned and pressed against her chest. She prayed harder.

For the next hour, Alexis murmured praises and prayers as she drove toward Cornerstone Church. With every breath, the weight in her chest lightened. It didn't disappear, but it lessened.

Eyes sweeping toward the rearview mirror, she eased off the freeway. AJ sat securely in his sensory-friendly car seat, surrounded by barriers softer than a hug. One she wished his dad could give him, although AJ did not welcome touch. That's why Aaron chased medals and never came home. At least that's what Beverly had said one night when Alexis had stayed over to help after AJ got chickenpox.

She pictured her brother in his Marine uniform—sharply pressed, spotless. A soldier down to the laces. But the same uniform that created a hero had shaped him into a stranger in his own home.

A tumbleweed whipped across the road. She swerved. "Sorry, AJ."

Her eight-year-old nephew stared ahead at the colorful bar spinning on his car seat, unbothered. Another call came. This time she pressed a button on her steering wheel to answer Aunt Cherry's call.

"Hey," Alexis said quickly. "I know plans changed when Beverly passed. But I decided it's best for me and AJ to visit my church today. I appreciate your help with AJ this week. And yes, Easter dinner sounds awesome."

"Girl, I figured you wouldn't visit The Way. Just wanted to know if you had left home yet. I planned to hitch a lift to Cornerstone to hear Pastor Otis's Resurrection sermon, which I also . . ."

Alexis murmured the rest of her aunt's statement, ". . . know by heart." She shook her head. Seriously, when would her aunt leave Pastor Otis be? Sometimes he recycled sermons. Good sermons. "Mhmm," she replied. "Sorry, I'm about thirty minutes away from Cornerstone now."

"Figured as much. Anyway, our pastor decided not to preach today. His oldest son, while nice to look at, isn't—"

"Auntie!"

"What? God created that cute kid. One day, Baby Hayes will be as dynamic a leader as his father."

Alexis braked at a stop sign. "Did you just say Hayes?"

"Yep. Everyone has to learn to preach. Baby Hayes—he's probably in his early thirties."

Early thirties made him a smidge too old to be Officer Hayes. What was she thinking? The cop's last name wasn't uncommon. Still . . . "Is there another"—Alexis cleared her throat—"Baby Hayes. Does your pastor have a younger son? Who is, by the way, a police officer?" She held her breath, remembering how the EMTs hadn't allowed any of the many bystanders near *her* Officer Hayes. *So could they be the same?*

"Oh, girl." Aunt Cherry laughed. "Yes, Pastor Hayes has another son who is a man of the law. I see why you're suddenly interested in The Way. Their youngest son, Elijah, is twenty-eight, twenty-nine? How do you know him? Tell me quickly, and then we can arrange to meet with him after church next Sunday. You'll have to join The Way, y'know."

"Hah. I'm not interested in a Sunday love connection, Auntie." Alexis sighed, then brought her aunt up to speed while the image of a weak smile flashed in front of her eyes.

Officer Hayes's smile.

The man she'd prayed over. The one she'd rushed into twisted metal to save, whose smile had been frail but real when he'd whispered, "Jesus." Gee, she couldn't get over that smile.

A sigh of relief rushed through her as she engaged in small talk with her aunt. She'd prayed for him throughout the week, wishing she had a moment to pop by the hospital for an update on his status. So not necessary now. He wasn't alone. He had a church family. A big one. Why hadn't the thousands rallied in prayer? Why hadn't she seen the prayer chains on The Way's online portal?

Unless they didn't know.

Or worse—unless he didn't belong to that world anymore.

Alexis had a request, but first, she needed to wait until her Aunt Cherry stopped with the small talk. And duty came first. She asked, "The girls aren't dancing anymore?"

"No. We had an additional rehearsal on Friday. What a mess. Kids stumbled into each other. One girl stubbed her toe on a pew. Poor dear needed a bandage. The board members watched and voted—almost a unanimous sweep."

"You held out?"

Aunt Cherry huffed. "Yes. Me and Glenda. She's the secretary, though. So, when she lifted her hand, it didn't get a count."

"I'm so sorry, Auntie."

"Stop that. You apologize all the time."

"Okay, I won't apologize for my next request." Her voice became hushed as she approached another stop sign. "Do you think . . . would you mind watching AJ later today?"

Aunt Cherry didn't skip a beat. "Oh, you wanna offer Sunday dinner to Baby, Baby Hayes?"

"I might." Alexis's smile gave a subtle tremble. It unsettled her that the cop might still be in harm's way. "But don't call him that, please. Officer Hayes or, if he's Elijah Hayes from The Way, that works, too."

Her aunt snorted.

Once they ended the call, she prayed. *Jesus, if Officer Hayes doesn't have a church family praying over him, maybe he's estranged from his family? Maybe the Corrupt Celebrity Pas—ahem. I suppose not all pastors who run large churches are corrupt.*

"Ugh, Lex, this prayer has gotten quite chatty," she mumbled, palm to forehead.

Abba Father, for whatever reason, maybe Elijah Hayes doesn't have a church family. Maybe You're nudging me to be that family today.

Not forever.

Just . . . for now.

Chapter 3

Three broken ribs. A crush injury to his left leg. Rhabdomyolysis—muscle breakdown. Fracture displacement was minor, though shifting in bed triggered reminders of slow recovery. His leg was in a cast. He hadn't tried to walk yet. Wouldn't for a while.

But yesterday, when the doctor painted worst-case scenarios, Elijah had cut him off.

"No, I'm gonna get through this."

And he would.

With Jesus' help.

Now, with the soft click of a remote, Elijah shifted into a reclined position on the hospital-grade bed—set up in the downstairs guest room of his parents' house. Just one of the many guest rooms in one of the finest homes in the Dominion, a lavish neighborhood in San Antonio.

Pain should've met him halfway through the movement. Right from the start, the nurse hadn't bought his story about a lack of pain. Maybe his face had given him away? He desired to avoid lots of drugs, yet he required them.

He glanced at the vaulted ceiling. A breath swooshed out. "Guess I didn't do it Your way, Abba Father."

In law school, he'd gotten hooked on Adderall. Not to party, but to prove he could honor God without standing in a pulpit like his father.

That faith could resemble advocacy, pro bono work, or giving a voice to the unheard.

He'd imagined God walking beside him into courtrooms, not churches. But somewhere between ambition and anxiety, he'd stumbled. Failed the bar. Twice.

A career in law enforcement had been Plan B. To his father? It probably felt more like another dose of betrayal.

And now? Here he was. Injured. Back under his parents' roof. In the home The Way's congregation had built through love and tithes.

"Eight thousand square feet. Is that a dollar for every member?" Elijah had once said, bitterness tucked beneath his sarcasm.

Someone knocked on the intricate doorframe.

"Come in." Elijah shut his eyes for a beat. *Lord, please don't let it be Dad.*

They hadn't seen eye to eye since Elijah was seventeen—back when he'd quoted The Passion Translation during a youth Bible study and was met with Dad's thin-lipped disapproval. Sure, Elijah had later compared the TPT with more established versions like the King James and the NIV and spotted the inconsistencies himself. But the argument over the Bible translations had only scratched the surface. The real divide was deeper. Elijah didn't want to follow in his father's footsteps and become a preacher.

Despite everything, he loved his father deeply, yet he still got sweaty palms when Dad entered the room.

Sure enough, his father walked in with the same hazel eyes. Clean-shaven except for the salt-and-pepper goatee. No tailored suit today. Just a polo shirt and golf pants.

"You're usually in your study at church this time of day." Elijah's brows rose. "Don't you need to prepare your sermon for Easter?"

A faint smile flickered. "Finished my sermon ages ago."

"Then you're usually still *in* your study at church from dawn until you're called to preach at eleven." Where he refused to be bothered.

His father stepped further inside the room. "My son was in a horrible car accident. Can't I be here for him? Your mother tells me you still resent how dedicated I am to the church."

"It's not that—"

"At her request, I didn't inform our congregation of what happened to you on Tuesday. It was just us. Your mother, your brother, and I seated beside your hospital bed. Praying."

Elijah cleared his throat. Looked down. His ribs ached. Not as intolerable as the guilt pooling in his chest. "Thank you for your prayers. And I appreciate that you didn't drag the church into this."

His father nodded, but the peace between them was short lived. "You still insist on loving God on your own terms. Without the solid foundation of the church?"

Elijah let out a sigh. "Please, Dad. Not right now with Hebrews 10:25." Man, even that sounded harsh. "My only point was that the investigation is ongoing. A man fled the scene. Left me for dead. Yet, I am familiar with the verse in every possible manner." He met his father's eyes. Aside from color, their irises were distinct. His father's eyes glinted stern, inflexible. "I have a relationship with Jesus. I really do. Not out of obligation anymore. Not to impress anyone. Just . . . me and Him." Now that he no longer worried about what people wanted.

No response came. Not right away. After a few seconds of silence, his father offered a stiff nod.

Before the pastor could leave, Elijah said, "Someone prayed for me. At the scene. The paramedic." Her voice seared his heart. Beautiful, wonderful, and godly. "I need to know her name."

His father raised a brow.

"I'm not trying to ask her out . . . I just want to send flowers. To say thank you. Her voice . . . it stayed with me."

His father walked over to a paisley chair near the window and sat. "Already done, son. The flowers, I mean. Yesterday."

"What's her name?" Elijah asked again.

Dad offered a peculiar look before he pulled his phone from his pants pocket and scrolled on the screen.

Elijah's heart thundered faster, but he kept his expression neutral. "I'm not looking to date her," he added quickly. Then, after a pause, "Maybe coffee. Eventually."

"Let's see." His father squinted at the iPhone screen. "The floral shop delivered the bouquet to the paramedic team. Olga Butts and an Ezra Dreyfuss."

Butts? That couldn't be right. All right, maybe the woman's face didn't match her angelic voice. He still needed to locate her. And thank her for her prayers.

Elijah closed his eyes and exhaled. *God, I know it's not spiritual to track someone down over a gut feeling . . . but You placed Olga there for a reason. I believe that. Help me find her, Lord, if it's Your will. Her voice hasn't left my heart since Tuesday.*

He looked up again; conviction tightened his spine. "I'll reach out to Olga. Thank her for the prayers."

His father didn't reply, but Elijah caught the way his mouth twitched—just slightly. Approval, maybe. Or resignation. Hard to say with him.

Elijah reclined in the bed, with sore ribs and suddenly a steadier spirit.

One step at a time.

Faith was still faith, even if the first step was a whispered prayer in a hospital-grade bed instead of a shout from a pulpit.

Chapter 4
One Easter Later

Alexis's silver hatch back slid into the driveway of the picturesque ranch-style house she'd called home for the past year. Pastel-colored Easter eggs dotted the manicured lawn. As she sat behind the wheel, her eyes latched onto a vibrant purple wreath adorned with plastic lilies on the front door. So beautiful, and a stark contrast to the hollow ache in her chest. She turned off the engine, and the silence amplified her unease. The expansive bay windows of the house, so clear they seemed to invite the outside in, dwarfed the entire width of her old studio apartment. Okay, maybe that was a slight exaggeration, but shock and hurt lingered. The life she lived now didn't belong to her. She'd dropped into someone else's life—wore their shoes and tried not to trip.

And worst of all? She didn't have the solace of praise and worship at Cornerstone to help her make sense of it.

Warm sunlight glinted off the windshield, and she crushed her eyes closed. The sudden, unwelcome memory of last Easter, vibrant and raw, hit her with the force of a physical blow. A choke gasped up her lips, and she pressed the heel of her hand against her eyelids, as if she could somehow push the images back, erase the mockery behind her eyes. A cruel twist to what should've been a joyous occasion.

The past played in technicolor, anyway.

Alexis had left AJ in the only Sunday school class available. The teacher, Margaret, was sweet enough, smelled like fresh-baked cookies, and claimed to understand Autistic

Spectrum Disorder. She'd even promised to text Alexis if anything went wrong.

AJ had his tools: iPad, noise-canceling headphones, and faithful brontosaurus, Brody. Of course, her nephew preferred the gentle giants one day and T-Rex the next.

She leaned her forehead against the steering wheel and cried, unable to get his expression of sheer terror out of her mind. Wild-eyed, he'd bolted into the church sanctuary mid-dance routine, after a mess up in Sunday school. His panicked expression had etched into her heart.

At first, Alexis was a ball of apologies and explanations before the entire congregation. Disdainful glances and hushed comments about AJ's behavior followed. And instead of nurturing love from Mother Phyllis, the woman's words hit harder than a slap.

Jesus, I can't go back to church. Not with him. Not with all those Phyllis clones in every sanctuary.

The hate ladies. Wide-brimmed, organza hats anchored like Church crowns. No, better yet. Sanctified like armor— nothing said "church leader" like a judgmental side-eye and those self-righteous hats.

"Amen," Alexis sighed, too tired to listen for a message from God. She climbed out of the car. Her sneakers pattered up the rose-lined walkway, one more favorite of Beverly's that she barely kept alive.

The salary Aaron sent home paid the mortgage on a home he should've grown old in. He and Beverly had bought this gorgeous open-plan house instead of maximizing his basic allowance in a military community. They'd had two incomes.

Alexis meandered inside. The fresh scent of enchiladas enveloped her. The comfort food's scent didn't make her feel good, but her blood pressure crept up. The applied behavioral therapist didn't cook.

On the far side of the room sat the kitchen. Behind a large island, someone rummaged beneath the cabinets, singing a soft hymn. An old one. A Momma kind of hymn. The kind Alexis hadn't allowed herself to feel in months.

She blinked hard. *It's not the song. I miss Momma.*

Although she prayed every day and night—Pray without ceasing, right?—truth was, she missed God's house.

A voice interrupted the ache.

"What's with that crooked grin?"

Alexis startled out of the memory as Aunt Cherry stood opposite the island and placed a hand on her hip. "Nothing." Alexis brushed a corky strand of hair away from her cheek and nodded to the stove. "Are those Enchiladas?"

"Yep. My specialty." Aunt Cherry's eyes twinkled.

She wanted to eat the whole pan. Best not to tempt herself. "I'm not hungry. Where's AJ?"

"In his room."

"With his ABA therapist?"

"I let her go early."

And there it went. Another uptick in her blood pressure. Alexis stuttered, "W-why? We pay her too much."

"Alexis, chill out about the money. Besides, even caregivers deserve a break."

"She's salaried, Auntie. This place bleeds money." Alexis dropped onto a barstool with a huff. "I miss the ambulance." The words spilled out before she could wrangle them.

Aunt Cherry stilled.

"My bad for the drama. I should've told Aaron that the last time we talked," Alexis continued, softer now. "Instead, I offered my brother empty platitudes, so he'd feel comfortable seeing his son a couple of times a year." Two times, to be precise. When Beverly was alive, he hadn't been deployed as much.

With a curious expression, Aunt Cherry handed her a fork and napkin. "Wait? You dance every day now."

"Twinkle Toes Dance Studio has a different aesthetic." Alexis forced a smile. "I dance to toddler bop and glittery unicorn songs, not powerful, soul-altering praise dance. Even the rocks cry out, 'holy,' when we cease to offer Him worship."

The older woman sighed. "You've got a point there. So it's not the ideal songs at the moment. Still, you're in the job you dreamed of. You attended college for dance before you came home and switched to the paramedic track. You even taught AJ to dance—albeit weird little moves—while CeCe Winans streams from YouTube."

"Yeah. It calms him sometimes. However, dancing has always been between me and Jesus. Not a dream. A reality," Alexis whispered. She let every thought flow away when dressed in her praise-dance leotards. She didn't focus on the crowds' approval or disapproval. None of it. She focused on God. "It was sacred. Our thing. I used to pray over every movement. Now I'm lucky if I don't get drooled on. And AJ— he's sweet, but he's not mine. And I . . . I yearn to be a mom. One day. Not just an aunt who plays house and offers lies when AJ asks for his dad."

Aunt Cherry's eyes softened, and Alexis spilled out her story. "You come home every night to a boy who depends on you. AJ demands attention."

Alexis stared at her jittery hands. She picked up her fork and tried to balance it on her knuckles as if her juggling act would end their conversation. After five failures, she set it down and sighed. "Is it bad that I want a break?"

"No, you're human. Even mothers need a break. And you stepped into motherhood overnight without the nine months to prepare or process. To make matters worse, you tell your nephew the sweetest, teensiest"—she offered a wobbly smile—"of white lies when he misses his dad."

"Thank you." Alexis smiled through the tears. "I just . . . when I was in an ambulance, I knew God was with me. I heard Him. Every heartbeat, every prayer. He was in it. Now, it's—it's static."

Aunt Cherry stepped around the island to her purse, draped over a stool. "That's it. I'm calling Aaron."

"Don't." Alexis snapped upright.

"He's my nephew, and *my* niece is a mess. You've handled his mess! This house, therapy."

"It's okay. The lieutenant didn't want to work with my schedule, so I pivoted back to choreography."

Aunt Cherry folded her arms. "That's the only paramedic gig in San Antonio? Girl, please. You think God put that fire in you for no reason? You've got more than book smarts. You've got spiritual authority. You lay hands on people. You pray. You intercede. That's your calling."

Alexis rose from her seat.

"Sit." Aunt Cherry pushed her gently back onto the stool. "Don't think we're done with this conversation."

While Alexis groaned in her seat, she flexed her tired feet beneath the island counter. Aunt Cherry removed a casserole dish from the oven. Steam curled into the air from the bubbly tray of green enchiladas.

Aunt Cherry plated one portion, slid it across the quartz countertop, and held it just out of reach.

"Pahlezzz, Auntie, I'm hungry."

Her grip didn't budge. "Convince me you shouldn't be back in that ambulance. When you started, you gave me this whole speech about being God's hands. Can you top that?"

"Yes," Alexis retorted. After a whimper of annoyance she said, "'A man's heart plans his ways. The Lord directs his steps.'"

Still, Aunt Cherry didn't release the plate. "Great verse. I don't get how it connects with this situation though?"

"Which means," Alexis groaned but continued, "that maybe—for now—God wants me here. With AJ. Just . . . not forever."

Aunt Cherry's eyes softened, but she didn't slide the plate those last few inches. "You think God said that. But you already said you don't hear Him like you used to."

That one hit.

Alexis bridged the gap between her and the food and snagged the plate with wobbly hands. "I'm trying."

"I know, baby. Just make sure you don't settle for surviving when God called you to thrive."

After a prayer, Alexis took her first bite. The warmth grounded her; tears pricked the corners of her eyes.

"I don't want to settle," she whispered.

Aunt Cherry's arm, steady and strong, slipped around Alexis's shoulder.

Chapter 5

"'Within my heart I can make plans for my future, but the Lord chooses the steps I take to get there.'" Elijah quoted The Passion Translation while he eased his truck into park in front of the Emergency Medical Technician building. Although he depended on more accurate translations these days, the passion had a nice feel in this instance.

Rows of ambulances sat ready, their headlights dark. They appeared as beacons of hope. He took a deep breath. *Please, Lord. Guide my steps right into Olga's today. Today has gotta be the day.*

For nearly a year, he'd tried to catch up with the paramedic who'd saved him, prayed over him, and vanished before he got the chance to thank her.

He figured Olga attended church. Before he settled in as a regular at The Way, he'd attended church services at every Baptist, nondenominational, and Protestant church in the Greater San Antonio Area. Six months. No solid leads. Only two women had the same name, and their voices didn't carry the same lilt.

This was his last—and only—hope.

With a slight limp, he stepped onto the pavement—just a shadow of the injury that nearly took his life. It hadn't stopped him from passing the department's physical and mental evaluations, but the limp reminded him daily of what he'd almost lost.

What he would've lost, if not for her.

He hadn't showered or changed after work. He didn't want to miss her again. Between swinging by after the hectic hours at the police station or his new job as head of the singles ministry at church, he'd always missed her. Every time he'd visited, the guy with the crew cut at the front desk had given him the same half smile and said, "Almost, dude, almost." He'd Googled ambulance call patterns, studied shift rotations. Still, she'd eluded him.

Why hadn't Olga responded? The flowers he'd sent on numerous occasions, the notes—he'd meant every word. But she hadn't responded. Not a peep. Why?

Elijah strolled toward the open area, still nagged by her lack of response. Not even to his sincere note? *God, did I hear You correctly? You told me not to forget her.* However, God hadn't revealed when they would meet again.

Abraham and Sarah waited.

David waited.

Joseph waited.

Even his Savior Jesus waited.

So he'd waited too.

Elijah strode over asphalt toward Station 138. In the ambulance bay, a man tossed plastic medical packages into a biohazard bin.

Crew-cut guy. "You lookin' for Olga again?"

"Yep. Is Olga here?"

"Dude, you just missed—" The man's face dropped, but then he barked a laugh and pulled out his phone. "Kidding. I'll text her now."

"Thanks." Elijah let out a breath and moved to perch on the low cinderblock wall near the edge of the structure. He glanced at the sky, heart pounding. *Thank You, Jesus.*

Moments later, a woman emerged—short, cropped hair curled beneath her ear, a shade whiter than his mom's graceful silver hair. The woman's biceps could bench press a patrol car.

Elijah's gut clenched. *No, Lord. You've got a sense of humor, but please . . . she can't be my angel.* "Is Olga—?"

"I'm Olga." The woman crossed her arms.

"Elijah Hayes," he said, cautiously. "You're Olga Butts?"

"That's the name on my marriage license," she said with a tight nod, voice defensive.

"Oh? I uh . . ." he sputtered. She figured he wanted to hit on her. A married woman. "There must be some mix-up. I'm not trying to—I thought you were someone else."

Olga narrowed her steel-glinted eyes. "Listen, I didn't mind the first bouquet. My husband wasn't thrilled about the others. And you're a cop? What's your deal?"

He took a deep breath and straightened. "Ma'am, you and Ezra Dreyfuss saved my life almost a year ago this week. Right before Easter. I drove a police SUV. Chest trauma. Crushed leg. You were on the call. Just came to relay my appreciation because more important than two legs . . . is . . . I'd lost oxygen." The words choked up his throat. "I could've died."

She tilted her head, less defensive now. Not by much, though. "I get that. Flowers are welcome. Normal. But it's gone overboard, especially the meet-up requests."

"I apologize." He tried to bow out of the conversation by stepping back. "I didn't mean to come off—"

"As a stalker?"

Jesus, now I know You're up there laughing.

At that moment, a question dawned on him. He'd weeded out the two churchgoing Olgas because of their voices. Now, he stepped forward a bit. "Was there another paramedic, a"—

he cleared his throat, a middle schooler in love—"female paramedic, the week before Easter, when you pulled me out of my police cruiser? A woman who prayed for me?"

"Pray? Definitely not me." Olga's laughter hit him in the gut, worse than his foolish presence.

Of course, he'd stalked the wrong woman. Olga's lack of church attendance made sense now.

His shoulders sagged.

Then she paused and stared at him again. "Wait, I remember you. I haven't worked with Ezra in ages. In fact, he retired last May."

Which was why Elijah had stopped trying to speak with Ezra in order to get to her. Whoever this "her" was? He'd need to ask his boss before he used the company system to find her.

Or an angel? *Lord, was she an angel?*

Olga shrugged. "There was another paramedic. A woman. Off duty. She was on the scene when we arrived."

He stood taller. "Who was she?"

Olga shrugged. "No clue. Think she got canned. Yeah, that must be it. Praying for people. If she's not fired, she will be the second I tell the lieutenant."

Elijah's jaw clenched. "That won't be necessary." He turned and strode away before he said something he would regret.

Inside the truck, his hands gripped the wheel as a memory came back. The doctor had given him a diagnosis, much worse than issues with his leg. Tension pneumothorax. Yeah, that had to be it.

His chest had filled with air and pressure from the crash, collapsing his lung and almost stopping his heart. First responders had inserted a needle into his ribcage to release the pressure.

She had done that.

She'd saved his life.

And then . . . she'd prayed.

He could feel her hand on his knee, warm and steady, as she prayed over his crushed leg. She'd apologized for the touch, while her voice had trembled with something sacred. As she'd prayed—he'd sensed Jesus' presence. Peaceful. Supportive.

Why did she disappear? Who was she?

A few buddies on the force had caught the man who'd hit him almost two weeks later, hiding out at his girlfriend's home. Elijah remembered how he'd rushed to a domestic violence incident. A DV incident at a home he'd been to way too many times. Instead of arriving on the scene as planned, he'd gotten rammed at the stoplight. The assailant had fled a gas station robbery. Unarmed and reckless. He'd stolen a couple hundred bucks, careened away from the scene, and crashed into Elijah. Left him to die.

But she didn't.

He rubbed his knee absentmindedly, still confident he could feel the imprint of her prayer. Now more than ever, he must locate her.

And he knew exactly how. The work incident report, which he had never read. Felt odd to read his own incident report. Now he would. For within him, he knew: she was a piece of the purpose God had started to unfold.

Chapter 6

Supercalifragilisticexpialidocious blared for the tenth time that afternoon, and Alexis was this close to losing it. Her smile held while the five- and six-year-olds linked arms as they giggled and kicked their legs with more heart than coordination.

Sure, they were barely in sync. The kicks were more ankle-height than the Rockettes' eye-high kicks. But today, no one had cried when they stumbled. No one ran off when they accidentally got hit. For once, no tears complemented their tiny triumphs.

Maybe she could love it here. Twinkle Toes Studio. The clatter of tiny tap shoes, the smell of resin, sweat, and Crayola-scented innocence. Maybe Aunt Cherry was right about calling Aaron. She smiled at the children. Their carefree courage gave her the confidence to consider it. She'd force him to come home. Or . . . Not.

God said she needed to wait in this season.

"Good job, Alana." Alexis glided across the polished wooden floor with a dancer's poise. "Allie, smile like you're on the teacup ride."

Allie blinked up at her with big blue eyes and an O-shaped mouth, her Shirley Temple curls bouncing. That reference? Pure gold. Allie loved the teacup ride from her fifth birthday at Disneyland. With a renewed grin, Allie pumped her chubby legs again.

From behind the half-wall that divided the studio, the girl's mother shouted, "Yay, Allie!"

Alexis winced. Parents. Bless their hearts. But could they not?

Sure enough, the rest of the girls faltered, their eyes on their parents in an attempt to earn praise too. The rhythm shattered instantly. And then one of the newer students, a redhead, spun in the opposite direction of the group and crashed to the floor with a soft thud.

As the girl's lip trembled, Alexis moved with speed and grace to her side.

"Oh, sweetheart." She scooped the little one onto her hip. "You're okay. Let's sit for a minute."

Right then, the studio door creaked open and a strawberry blonde in heels, with dagger eyes, stormed in. No death glares yet, just sharp stabbing pricks, so Alexis considered it a win.

She passed the girl to her mother and crouched down to examine her ankle. "She seems okay, but I'll grab an ice pa—"

"How would you know?" the woman snapped, a tight smile in place but her tone sliced deep.

Alexis flinched. Even so, she'd turn into a lioness if her own child got hurt. She bit back a sigh and steadied her speech. "Because—"

"She was a paramedic," a smooth voice interrupted. "A very good one."

Alexis froze.

The mother muttered beneath her breath while she stomped away. But Alexis? Her gaze drifted past the pony wall, past the kids still twirling in uneven lines, and landed on him.

Elijah Hayes.

In uniform.

Rich dark skin and those hazel eyes. Too familiar. Too attentive. They remembered her even when she wished to remain unseen.

No. No. NO. Not today. I'm in a hidden season, caring for my nephew.

Why was Baby, Baby Hayes here? Elijah Hayes was mega-church royalty, and she'd sworn off church. Her practiced smile dropped. She gave him a curt nod, then reached for her phone, tucked into the pocket of her leotard, and pressed play on a button that was connected to Bluetooth. "From the top."

She would do anything to not feel flutters in her abdomen, especially when "Sway" by the Rat Pack played on a soundtrack only she could hear. She hoped he would leave. Maybe he was on break and worked in the area? How did he find her? Why?

Alexis firmed her dancer's spine and strolled back and forth while the girls prepared for the spring recital two weeks away.

"Allie, watch your smile, it's disappeared again," she said.

As the clock ticked past dismissal, parents started to check their phones, gather belongings, and head outside. Alexis handed out her usual affirmations—"Alana's improved tremendously!" and "So proud of your twirls today!"—though most of it was fluff.

This was a beginner class. No one expected perfection. Except maybe the toddler intermediate group, where the moms clutched spreadsheets with dance by numbers and had Super Supreme pageant tiaras on their minds.

As she headed toward the broom closet, the studio emptied out for the night, she heard him.

"Are you avoiding me?" he asked in a deep, curious voice.

Alexis sighed, turned around, and feigned a smile that resembled the easy one on his lips. "You? Who are you exactly? If you'd like to enroll your daughter for—"

"I don't have a daughter," Elijah politely cut in.

"Niece?"

"She's two months."

"Fine. You can sign her up for the winter session."

His thick brow rose, amused. "You train babies?"

"Baby pageants start early." She deadpanned. "Not that I recommend them. But if your brother or sister craves their first victory, then sure."

"Brother," he said with a chuckle. "And I'll pass. No one in my family's about that life. Have coffee with me?"

"No."

"Why not?"

"Because . . ." Alexis hesitated. Gah. The reasons existed somewhere in her brain. And those logical reasons melted fast beneath that amiable smile and calm presence. He didn't push. Just stood there, open. Which only made it worse.

Truth be told, the moment she'd seen him, whole and upright, a worry in her had deflated. Relief rushed in. Swift and undeniable. For a flicker of a second, she'd even praised God under her breath. His recovery from the car accident touched her more than she cared to reveal. Elijah Hayes was a stranger after all.

However, he epitomized the kind of partner she shouldn't fall for. The son of a mega-church pastor? Please. Getting tangled up with someone like him would be messy. Judgmental family. Spotlight. Expectations. A family she had no intention of living up to.

"You know who I am?" he asked softly.

"Conceited much?" She snorted, and sarcasm shoved down the flutter in her chest.

He ran a hand over his short-cropped waves. "That's not what I meant. But you do, don't you?" He smiled. Not in a boastful way, but he appeared to relish their awkward interaction. Or maybe he looked . . . relieved? Why?

No. Discovering why wasn't in her job description. She strolled toward the cotton dust mop.

Elijah surprised her when he grabbed the tiny, old dust mop in the corner that nobody, not even the dance teachers, ever used because of its miniature handle. Maybe someone had used it to punish children in the past by forcing them to mop?

"What are you doing?" she asked.

His over six-foot frame hunched over, and he began on the opposite side of the floor. "The door sign says you close right about now. So, I'll help you close. I'll bow out if your hot date is due to arrive any minute. A date with lots of insecurities and a bad temper." He swept further away from her. "In that case, I'll sweep here. Keep some space between us."

A scoff was her only response.

They glided across the floor in different rhythms. It hit her. She didn't want him to leave. That frightened her beyond measure.

Chapter 7

Elijah hadn't wandered into Twinkle Toes on a hunch. After a year of dead ends and false leads, he'd finally sat down and read the full incident report from the night he'd almost died. The truth had remained within his reach this entire time and sent a couple of hard tears to his eyes. He'd read a handwritten witness statement from the off-duty paramedic who'd worked on him before the ambulance had arrived. Alexis's handwriting had been shaky. Tiny, darkened spots dotted the page. Tear stains, maybe? A smudged signature, but the officer's report clearly stated her name.

Alexis Carter.

He'd searched her online and found Twinkle Toes Dance Studio.

When she turned toward him across that polished dance floor, recognition flared in her eyes. She'd touched his leg, whispered a prayer, and asked God to give him another chance.

Now, there he was, cracking a stupid joke about her date. Real smooth. But the second he laid eyes on her again, after an entire year, a deeper sentiment had stirred. Not just gratitude. Not just curiosity. Hope. As if God still intended to weave their stories together a little more.

Alexis placed the dry mop between them like a boundary, a quiet reminder that hers stood high. And against better judgment, he defaulted to a version of himself who cracked jokes to fill the awkward silence.

Every facet of this moment seemed fragile, like it could all shatter before he got the chance to know the real Alexis Carter.

Then she snorted.

She didn't have a boyfriend. Relief settled in him. Quiet, but solid.

For a while, they swept in silence, mops whispering across the floor like a soft confession neither of them could speak yet. Elijah looked for words. But he'd cornered a stranger. Not really. He knew her voice—the one that had spoken life over him when he'd been so close to death. That voice had stayed with him. And she hadn't seemed repulsed by his presence like Olga Butts. Or if she did, she didn't show it.

Or had he lost touch with reality after falling in love with the sound of her faith.

Then, mercy, she smiled at him. "I'm glad to see you up and about, Elijah."

"I can get around." He shrugged, then swiveled the small dust mop like an old-school microphone while he hummed a few bars from The Temptations under his breath. *Lord, forgive me for the reference. I can't remember any other old groups who danced around a single microphone.*

He was half-joking, half-relieved that God's sense of humor hadn't stuck him with Olga Butts.

Alexis arched a brow. "Okay, maybe don't quit the police force to pursue any dancer dreams. I can't be part of this so—" She walked over and handed him the taller mop. "Here."

"Thanks." He stretched, relieved not to be hunched over anymore.

Another soft snort from her, then she returned to her side of the studio, ten yards away. Their mops swished in opposite directions as they converged slowly toward the center.

He timed it right. When they were parallel, close, but not too close, he risked it. "You have a girl or a boy?"

"What?"

"Who you're rushing home to. I figured maybe someone expected you before the streetlights came on, even on a Saturday."

No smile this time. Just a quiet answer. "No. I raise my nephew. He has ASD."

"Autism?"

Surprise crinkled Alexis's eyebrows, as though she didn't anticipate his knowledge of Autism Spectrum Disorder.

"I've got a younger cousin with it," he said. "We're tight. The world doesn't always slow down enough to meet individuals with ASD where they are."

She didn't speak, but her posture softened. A flicker of trust. Maybe.

He cleared his throat. "Okay, how about coffee? Before your next class on Monday? Or I'll bring some. Just a few minutes to talk." It wasn't a big ask. Just a window. A beginning.

"Or . . ." he hesitated, a smile played on his lips as their mops touched in the middle of the dance floor. "We meet right here after we finish polishing, Monday night?" Ugh. That sounded awkward. Like he was laying it on thick. Maybe he was. That year long search had really gotten to him. Also, he'd read her statement—riddled with tear stains—and now heard her voice again. The whole situation had cracked him open.

A laugh bubbled from her. Honest and warm. "Okay, Elijah. Quite presumptuous, but you know how to dust a floor. So we'll call that a start." She placed a hand on her hip. "Besides, I have your badge number."

The laugh came, and his heart softened, lighter than it had been in a long time. Maybe this was the beginning of something. God had written this meet up long before either of them saw it.

*****

Over the past two weeks curiosity drew him to the studio to meet with Alexis. They swept. Talked. And circled sentiments he couldn't name. He hadn't seen Alexis outside of the studio. But these quiet moments—shared in a hush of mops swishing against hardwood and the hum of old praise music played faintly from the office speakers—felt set apart.

Tonight, like every other, they found themselves paused in the center of the dance floor. The light caught the curves of her face. She always looked tired by this point, but a gentleness settled in her eyes when she was at rest. He'd learned the subtle shifts in her mood, even if she said little.

Elijah leaned on his mop's handle. "Do you give adult dance lessons?"

She shook her head and laughed. "Why do you keep asking the same questions?"

"Because you and your nephew should've met me at church last Sunday. Hello, kids love Easter at The Way. It's their favorite. So"—he shrugged—"payback."

"So I have to hear you ask for dance lessons every day. Okay, got it." She shook her head. "Why church?"

"The Way. It's perfect neutral ground," he replied, voice bright, but heartbeat uneven. "I could prove I'm not a stalker. Just a man saved by grace." He gave a sheepish grin and set the mop down. "Besides, since Resurrection Sunday last week, The Way started a praise dance routine. Brand-new everything. The girls performed well, so they dance monthly now. Every first Sunday. Full production—music, movement. You'll love it. Not just the wiggle." He raised his arms and attempted a flowing wave, a poor imitation.

She squinted. "Was that . . . the wave of surrender?"

"Exactly!" Elijah laughed, but part of his chest ached.

He didn't know why the church had waited until now to launch a praise dance team. If they'd had one back when he still lived under his father's roof, before the arguments about theology and God's gifts, maybe it would've kept the door open between them. Maybe he would've stepped into ministry instead of running from it. To him, any connection to his dad seemed uptight. Strict.

He pushed aside the ache, focused on the woman in front of him. Did his attraction stem from her passion for God, music, and dance? Besides, the fact that she'd saved him? But what caused her church opposition? He had, until a year ago, avoided church, prioritizing his personal relationship with Christ. So he couldn't be prejudiced toward her. Had they shared a similar experience? Did unmet expectations from someone lead her to give up on the environmental aspect of encountering God at church?

"Anyway," he said, "Bring AJ."

"He won't like it." She reached for his mop.

"Allow me." Gently, Elijah removed the mop from her hand and returned them to the corner. "AJ's got options. We designed Bobby's room for kids with special needs—trained staff, calm light, soundproofed walls."

"We?" Her soft sigh almost dissolved into the air.

"It was my aunt's idea. She fostered. One of her girls had Down Syndrome. That's why The Way hired staff and upgraded the room. If AJ doesn't feel safe there, we can still make it work. We'll sit in the back. Or in the nosebleed section."

She winced. Just slightly. Like the words themselves caused her pain.

They were getting somewhere. Elijah licked his lips and figured church, as a whole, wouldn't bother Alexis. Not with her relationship with Christ. "It's Big Church Syndrome? Too loud, too many people?"

She didn't respond right away. Her eyes fixed on the mirror wall, then drifted down to her sneakers.

"Elijah . . ." Her gaze turned glassy, and her eyes never rose to meet his. "I've enjoyed our chats, but can we not do this anymore?"

He stilled. Man, he'd hit a chord. So it wasn't Big Church Syndrome. She detested the whole caboodle, which didn't make any sense after her faith-filled prayer. He needed to understand her.

"Do what?" he asked, barely above a whisper.

"This." She gestured vaguely between them. "The sweeping. For almost two weeks, we chat like we've been acquainted for ages."

Her words hit harder than they should've.

Twelve evenings. Twelve chances to feel hope he hadn't asked for. And now?

"Okay," he said, though the breath went out of him like someone had knocked the wind from his lungs. He started toward the door, as if the blow hadn't landed deep. Before he reached it, a tenderness pulled in his spirit.

A poster near the entrance caught his eye. Cutesy typography on an image of a happy toddler for the Spring recital Saturday night. He'd walked back into her world on a Saturday night. Two weeks ago. It appeared ordinary on the surface, but he knew better. God didn't do ordinary.

As he looked at the poster, a quiet whisper stirred in his chest. *God, is this Your new plan?*

Maybe the door had closed here. Maybe she needed more time to figure she was safe with him.

And maybe, just maybe, he had to stop expecting ministry to resemble his father's wishes and follow the path God laid in front of him.

Chapter 8

Supercalifragilisticexpialidocious's last notes faded, and Alexis groaned in relief. She loved these kids, but if she had to hear that song one more time . . .

From her position behind the curtains, Alexis stood with a side profile of the tiny dancers on stage. The girls softly, slowly, and just a tad fearfully, collapsed onto a mat with exaggerated exhaustion. Their joy warmed the dim-lit convention room.

The curtains swished closed to her left with heartfelt "awes" and a standing ovation.

"Quietly," Alexis whispered as the stage lights dimmed.

With renewed energy, the girls popped up and rushed toward her. Alexis crouched to give out high fives and shoulder pats. "Allie, you smiled brighter than the sun." She slapped the palm of the Shirley Temple lookalike.

Alexis addressed the redhead. "Bluey would be so proud." She hadn't expected Laney's mom to return after the ankle incident and thought for sure they'd demand a refund.

"Guadalupe, do not take off your pantyhose."

"But it's itchy!" The cute brunette whined, stomping a foot.

Other kids chimed in.

"I itch all over!"

"I feel ants on my legs."

"Okay, kiddos, run." Alexis laughed. She and the girls bolted toward the dressing room, giggling. "Safely, kids. Safely." She didn't have the emotional capacity for another incident report. But her heart fluttered, young and free in this moment.

This was always the happiest day for parents, even the ones who normally couldn't be bothered. Before they reached the door, she called out, "Freeze!" in the silly dance voice she used when they warmed up.

*****

Alexis departed the event center an hour later, after promising to have dancer videos personalized within seven days. She massaged her sore shoulders and envisioned a hot bath and sleep.

She scanned the crowd for Aunt Cherry and AJ. They'd agreed to leave the area before it got too crowded. It had been her one favor to help AJ avoid the gauntlet of extended family and vague acquaintances who thought their toddler was the next Misty Copeland or Marianela Núñez.

Her eyes locked on her aunt, who stood outside her van in the lot. And beside Aunt Cherry stood someone else.

Alexis's heart caught in her throat.

Elijah?

He wore a fitted suit with a slim tie and laughed at whatever Aunt Cherry said. AJ was at his side, calm and focused, headphones on, tablet in hand.

Naturally, Elijah knew about the recital. Yesterday, she'd asked him not to meet her after class anymore. He'd fallen silent, and her chest had ached. Their conversations had become a slow waltz, every step taking them closer to something neither of them had choreographed.

Alexis's heels clicked across the pavement as she approached. Arms folded to guard herself, she couldn't stop the tight, hollow ache pressing against her chest. Cold, heavy. The kind that made every exhale a chore.

She hadn't wanted Elijah to disappear.

But the moment she'd said, "can we not keep doing this" the light had dimmed in his eyes. Not angry. Not accusatory. Just dim.

And now, here he was. Less than twenty-four hours later, he stood outside the recital venue, smiling as if she hadn't taken an ax to their tiny spark.

She looked away so she wouldn't mirror his smile or apologize for her steel-plated walls. This was why he'd taken a second glance at the Spring recital poster. His hurt hadn't lasted thirty seconds.

He was fine.

"Hello, Mr. Hayes."

"Elijah," he corrected gently. "Your aunt said you've been choreographing our church's praise dance team. Since Easter, right?" He tilted his head, confusion alight behind the admiration in his voice. "So you choreograph worship songs. That's . . . wow."

Alexis waited for a hint of judgment. A barb. But that didn't exist, only respect and genuine esteem.

Maybe he thought she attended The Way just to teach the kids? She could understand how that confused him. Especially, after what she'd said at Twinkle Toes.

The truth? She hadn't stepped foot in a sanctuary since the Easter when she'd promised AJ they'd never return. Aunt Cherry was the sole link to the church for her.

Months before this past Easter, Aunt Cherry had been the lone voice on the board advocating for kids' ministry. She'd begged Alexis for the old Cornerstone Church dance tapes, ones Alexis had stored away.

Aunt Cherry was persistent. Sweet and fierce. She'd pushed, prodded, and subtly coerced Alexis into offering feedback on the girls imitation of her old rehearsal videos. Even if her correspondence came through a simple email based on video links from Aunt Cherry and her helper at The Way. Even if it hurt to watch said videos.

Elijah's voice brought her back. "The Way is expansive. I hope to see you on the first Sunday. Or even before. If you attend the service for a reason beyond supporting your girls."

His tone was light. Casual, even. Although his eyes lingered, she could tell he still wanted her to connect the dots.

She couldn't help the tiny smile. He was impossible. Not in a bad way, because when he'd mentioned church in the first place, he'd shown compassion and respect.

"He just shared how much you know each other." Aunt Cherry bumped shoulders with Elijah as if they were old friends. "Why didn't you tell me?"

"We don't know each other," Alexis spoke too fast. "Not well, anyway."

"Not well yet." Elijah's grin deepened. "Still debating if your favorite interpretive dance song is 'Yeshua' or Tamela Mann's version of 'Take Me to the King'. Although, based on the way you warm up to Whitney Houston's 'I Wanna Dance with Somebody', I lean toward Whitney."

Alexis stared at him. He'd seen her warmups?

Aunt Cherry laughed and threw her a familiar, bossy look. "Whatever you two know about each other, get to know more. Go to dinner. Celebrate the recital. I'll watch AJ."

Alexis's knee-jerk reaction was to say no. Rehearsals, costumes, and toddler tears slammed her schedule all week. She needed rest, not matchmaking. However, the real reason sat heavy in her chest.

Alexis couldn't afford to fall in love with someone like Elijah. A pastor's son. She avoided pastors, their families, and the churches they preached in. Even her involvement with The Way's praise dance team was distant. She limited their correspondence to behind the scenes communication and emailed tips based on The Way's practice videos. Also, she forwarded her old Cornerstone practice videos, rather than attend rehearsals. Over the past year, Alexis had built a life around safety, predictability, and control. A close relationship with someone like Elijah would unravel all of that.

Elijah wasn't chaos—but he made her feel again. And she wasn't sure she could survive that. AJ couldn't survive another church after the way Pastor Otis and Phyllis had treated him either.

No, I won't be bitter. I've forgiven them. I just can't do this.

Elijah scanned the street with a quiet protectiveness she'd recognized while they swept together. "If you wouldn't mind"—certainty thrummed through his voice—"I'd like to take you all out to dinner."

"Not necessary," Alexis and her aunt replied in unison. Yet Aunt Cherry's protest hinted at mischief. Alexis's held logic. She didn't want to inconvenience him, his budget, or risk heartache with every decline of his church invitations.

"I'll take AJ home." Aunt Cherry wrapped an arm around AJ's shoulder, but stopped, likely recalling he wasn't one for touches. She took a step closer to him. AJ didn't react, still immersed in the rhythm of whatever played through his headphones.

"Awe, that's so sweet of you, Auntie. You've had him all day." Alexis crouched in front of her nine-year-old nephew. AJ got his height from both sides of the family, while Alexis had inherited her mom's height. She caught his eye before she gently slipped one headphone off. "Hey, kiddo. Let's go home."

"Home," he echoed. "Go home."

"Sounds like a plan." Aunt Cherry winked. "I cooked. Elijah has the address."

Alexis straightened. "You cooked?"

She and AJ had talked about pizza, maybe. She'd mentioned it under her breath earlier. And any promises to him were set in stone.

Now she'd have to explain why dinner wasn't pizza . . . and why her heart beat a little faster every time Elijah smiled her way.

Chapter 9

Alexis possessed layers, and Elijah yearned to explore them all. Why did she choreograph the praise worshippers' dance routines without showing up to see the fruit of her labor? Why hide behind the curtain—literally and emotionally—when her fingerprints pressed all over the beauty on stage?

He'd watched her with the kids at the studio, seen her light up when they danced without an audience. He hadn't been able to watch her while the Twinkle Toes performed earlier. The toddlers needed her nearby, yes, but he'd seen her during practices before and the other studio's performances. Passion had blazed in her eyes as she'd watched the stage, evidence of a heart devoted to God. She gave it her all—as if she did everything for the Lord. An audience of One.

Now, her presence surrounded him, yet she remained hidden.

Why didn't she admit she led the Praise team? Another young woman led them. Come to think of it, at The Way board meeting at the end of April, the Dance Team Leader had only smiled when offered all the credit. It had seemed like humility to him then, but it was all Alexis Carter. A woman he yearned to know.

Elijah pushed away his empty plate. Not a trace of red beans and rice, collard greens, or pot roast remained.

He reached for AJ's plate. "How did you like dinner, little man?"

AJ blinked at him, unreadable.

"AJ is higher on the spectrum and has limited speech. Be more direct," Alexis offered, taking her aunt's plate, since they'd sat directly across from each other.

"Okay?" With a grin, Elijah made another attempt. "Chicken fingers good?"

"Good," AJ replied simply.

Alexis smiled. "It's chicken fingers and applesauce or pizza."

"He's a simple man." He winked at her, and a red blush crept over her warm brown skin. "My favorite kind of guy."

"Mhmmm," Elijah trailed behind her to the sink. Nice house. Warm. Lived in. Full of life.

"You're wondering why I choreograph the dances for your church but don't actually go, right?" Her voice was calm, but the way she said "your" church was a blow to his chest. Specifically, the portion that housed his heart. Because he'd fallen in love with her voice.

Yeah, he'd fished for information earlier. That much was true. But not because he wanted answers just to tick the boxes. He just wanted to know her. To understand what made her walls erect so high, what pain sat just beneath the surface of her gentleness. He wanted to dissect the passion that helped the kids praise dance at The Way.

She'd done that.

But a woman like Alexis. Nobody pushed her. They waited.

So he shrugged. "Nope. I'll wait until you tell me."

Her brows pinched. That flicker of surprise made his chest stir. Elijah lifted a quiet prayer to Jesus. *Help her feel safe enough to speak. No pressure. No rush. Just peace.* Taking it slowly for now, he added, "I have a gift for AJ after we knock out this kitchen."

She flipped on the farmhouse faucet. "I've got it."

There it was again. The way she shut him out. The same way she smiled when she wanted to end a conversation or handed him a mop to maintain emotional distance.

Elijah tried to brush it off with a half-grin. "You are one cold woman, Alexis."

He meant it playfully. But the words landed too close to the truth, and he regretted them the instant they exited his mouth. Because underneath his light tone, she'd wounded him. No, maybe not her. Their circumstances had wounded him. He'd done so much to find her. Had stalked Olga—ugh. Not that he'd meant to. Then he'd followed her tear-streaked penmanship to a dance studio.

Elijah hadn't planned on it being anything more than a "thank you" but somehow it simply was more. He hadn't even known her name the day she'd prayed over him. Still her voice had stuck with him like scripture in a dry season.

And now, after one year of effort, twelve quiet evenings, a meal, and a spark he couldn't deny—she still pushed him away?

Not just with the dishes.

With her heart.

Elijah understood not to take it personally. Growing up, he'd witnessed people pretend church was a cure-all. He'd watch his father force a smile while shepherding a room of broken people. Elijah didn't hold his dad's strictness against him. Not exactly. He knew leaders could unintentionally cause pain. Or worse, with full knowledge of their deceptive or vile behaviors.

Pastors often put up walls. Only later, after growth, did Elijah realize those walls could manifest as strictness. A natural product of being as a shepherd, where a pastor needed to stay strong and in some ways distance themself.

Maybe Alexis had seen that. Maybe she'd lived it. But why would she distance herself from him?

After rinsing a dish, Alexis spoke, "I'm not. I'm . . . just careful."

That answer made more sense to him than she seemed to realize.

Cherry waltzed into the kitchen. "AJ has his PECS."

"That's the Picture Exchange Communication System?" Elijah asked.

Alexis paused, sudsy dish rag in hand. "You know what that is?"

"He uses images to build words and sounds."

"It's his favorite after-dinner hobby. Now, the two of you go kick rocks. Enjoy your downtime." Cherry nudged them both out of the kitchen. "Go on. I've known your brother for two years longer than you, Alexis. So, that means I'm familiar with his son. I can handle AJ."

As they stepped around the quartz-topped island, Elijah lowered his voice. "Did she raise you?"

"It takes a village, so I'd say yes. Momma passed when I was at Columbia."

His heart sank. "I'm sorry."

"Car accident. She"—a fissure of raw emotion webbed her voice—"coded on the way to the hospital. I was a dance major on a full ride, but that night changed everything. My brother spiraled. I moved in with my aunt. Maybe that's why . . ."

"That's why?"

"I've tried to live up to the past. Support AJ the same way Aunt Cherry did for me after Momma." A shake of her head erased the emotion and vulnerability. "Anyway, I left college. Took an EMT program while Aaron enlisted."

"Speaking of." At the table, he retrieved a tiny figure from his blazer pocket, which was draped over the chair. "Toy soldier. For AJ."

Less than a minute later, they entered AJ's room. Part dino jungle, part chill zone, T-Rex decals stenciled the wall. A brontosaurus lamp sat on the desk in the corner. AJ occupied a fossil-printed couch. Uh-oh. Elijah should've bought a toy that was scalier with razor-sharp teeth. Like a raptor.

Alexis leaned against the doorframe while he approached the kid.

AJ didn't look up from his tablet as he swiped through picture cards. "Ap . . . apple," he said. A soft trumpet note rewarded him.

Elijah crouched beside him. "Hey, AJ. This is Joe. Joe the Soldier."

AJ didn't raise his eyes.

Elijah placed the figure on the couch arm and stood. "I'll leave him here. No pressure." *Lord, help me have a good relationship with AJ. He's important to Alexis.*

"I think he likes it. Well . . . you'd know if he didn't like it." Alexis straightened up. "Wanna walk?"

He nodded.

Outside, they strolled down a quiet path lined with rosebushes. A Monarch butterfly danced between them. Alexis chuckled, a carefree sound.

Out of nowhere, he mumbled, "I didn't mean to sound rude."

Her chuckle became a hearty laugh. "Oh, yes you did."

He grinned. "Okay, I meant it. A little." He scrubbed his jaw. "You don't know what I went through to find you."

Her brow corked as they meandered along another street. In no time, he told her about Olga Butts. A chuckle bubbled out of her. "Oh, I remember Olga."

Elijah tilted his head in mock annoyance.

"It's okay. Some men like older women." She kept walking.

When Elijah caught up with her, she stopped. "While I won't apologize for the Olga joke, I have a teensy confession. I've declined your invitations to church for nearly two weeks while I choreograph dances for the same stage I avoid."

Her admission stung. How could he argue with such a bold admission? "Touche."

She floated up the steps of a white gazebo. No. Danced. That was what she did: danced her way in and out of his reach. She moved with swift grace, then leaned over the rail, giving him a smile he could cherish. "But I also meant what I said in my nephew's room. If AJ didn't like the toy, you'd have bigger issues on your hands than little ol' me. He likes you."

Elijah inched closer to the steps that led up the gazebo. "That's good. But what about his favorite aunt? Does she like me?"

The side of her mouth lifted in a smile—and though she didn't answer, she didn't dance away from him this time.

Chapter 10

Oh, this guy likes you lots. Alexis's heart thumped off rhythm in her chest as she stared down at Elijah. The man she should push away.

God, what's my other option? You and I have such a great relationship without cluttering it with church. And I've seen The Way on television. He'll need a wife who sits beside him every Sunday, untriggered by church hurt. "Of course Aunt Cherry likes you." She played it off.

Elijah shook his head and ascended the steps. "You know she's his great aunt."

"Yeah. I spend most of my time with him, though. His bad dreams are the worst. So, he probably likes her more because I have to take his behavior from here"—she held her hand above her head—"to here." She dropped her hand to waist level. "It makes both our days pretty cranky."

"You're still his favorite aunt."

"His only aunt. But you know that. So, let's see. Does his aunt like you?" Against her will, a crooked grin tipped up one corner of her mouth. Gah, she was flirting with him. Leading him on. How cruel. "If you learn to dance, sure, she'll only have eyes for you."

For a long beat, he captivated her with an unbreakable gaze. "Teach me your favorite song, Alexis. Your favorite moves. I'll learn them all."

Smooth! "Wrong answer. Suave but wrong. As I've told you, my clientele is under a certain height for beginner dance.

Advanced dancers are jazz and tap. I don't want you to break your hip."

"Let me be honest with you." Elijah propped against the gazebo rail four feet away. She mirrored his action on the other side. "I have a good number of left toes, and two left feet to accompany them."

Alexis chortled.

"Was that a snort laugh?"

Her cheeks turned pink.

"C'mon? Please give me dance lessons, or I'll tell everyone that Alexis Carter, The Gorgeous One with The Most Rhythm, also snort laughs."

"Everyone?" She gave a fake gasp. "You have a wide network if you count all your friends from that massive church."

"How . . . how did you create those praise dances if you're not a member?" Inquisitive illumination warmed his hazel eyes.

Uh-oh. She'd walked right into that one. Despite all his church visit requests, she could've been honest earlier. For some reason, she felt connected to Elijah. She needed to get around to her terrible day.

Jesus, I'm gonna do it. Help me? Please don't change his view of me. I really like the way he looks at me. It's warm, supportive. Alexis's hands curled and her fingernails pricked her palms, and her shoulders tensed. Her stomach had that too-familiar twist.

She hadn't even told Aunt Cherry the entire story.

Her voice came out steadier than she felt, while she fixated on a non-direct opening. She had to warm her way up to the story. "The Way members vetoed Aunt Cherry's request to start a praise dance team a year ago, when I first started helping there, I . . . couldn't commit much time to it."

"A year ago. As in last April? When I had my accident?"

And here was her opportunity. To pivot or tell the truth. Alexis swallowed. She licked her lips with a tongue drier than sandpaper. "Yep. Aunt Cherry tried again a few months ago. The All-Powerful board members agreed to give the girls another chance to look like—" Alexis faltered. She wanted to speak truth, though it might not sound nice.

"Like the dancers were future Juilliard pupils instead of kids filled with joy for God?" he offered.

"You said it." She was relieved she didn't have to sound too bitter. "I only agreed to help again because Aunt Cherry begged me. Bullied me, actually. I gave her old videos from when I instructed youth at another church. She has pecan pies and peach cobblers in her arsenal. So, that's the extent of my connection with The Way." She stopped there. She wasn't finished, but digging deeper meant identifying her pain.

Elijah offered a thoughtful sound. "SAPD has an excellent negotiator, but I doubt the use of sweets is ethical."

"I know, right?" She grinned, but the smile wavered, and her legs folded. Alexis sat on the gazebo's bench, aware she was about to face the unknown with the man who wanted to see her. The real her.

The air between them stretched, thick with silence.

A thousand fears hummed beneath the silence. Alexis walked her fingertips over the bench's surface. *He's gonna think I'm angry, faithless. Too complicated.*

Still, she'd pushed him away before the recital. Tired of the mental fatigue of not sharing her story, she just hoped his love of God was bigger than his love for the church.

*****

Thirteen Months Ago

The tambourine in Phyllis's—and her old lady crew's hands—jingled in time with the swell of *How Great Thou Art*. Alexis danced with reverence. Her arms reached upward, white chiffon sleeves fluttering like wings. Her bare feet glided across the small altar. The three girls in the praise dance team moved behind her in perfect synchrony—every turn, bow, raised hand a simple, yet powerful, living prayer.

The seventy-five person sanctuary was full, air thick with the scent of lilies, perfume, and expectations. Phones rose to record the dance. Sunday school classes had been full today too. Her friend's class had maxed out early to accommodate AJ, so extra late-arrival children fidgeted on hard pews in Easter suits and pastel dresses.

Alexis concentrated on what she was offering to God. Her worry about tomorrow and how to be a good auntie after caring for her nephew for only five days faded as she raised joyful hands.

The double doors to the sanctuary burst open.

A sharp wail shattered the rhythm.

"AHHH-AHHHH!"

Heads whipped around. The pianist faltered but didn't stop.

A small boy ran in, shoes lighting up with every panicked stride.

AJ!

The T-Rex on his shirt bared scary teeth. AJ's eyes revealed wide and glassy tears. He flapped both hands hard at his sides and cried out, louder this time, as he stumbled toward the front of the church.

Sensory overload.

Alexis froze mid-movement. The rest of the dance team stumbled to a halt, confused.

AJ barreled past an usher; the woman's face twisted in anger. His sobs echoed in the hush that fell over the room.

"Spoiled . . ." someone muttered.

The first statement struck up a chorus of murmured questions.

"Whose kid is that?"

"Somebody needs a whoopin'!"

Alexis rushed down the steps, long white skirt fluttering behind her. "AJ, baby—hey, hey, what happened?"

AJ collapsed into her arms at the bottom step. His small body shook violently as she dropped to her knees.

He couldn't form the words—his usual simple, matter-of-fact language disappeared. He never could articulate himself while overwhelmed. Alexis held him close, rocking gently. While whispers rose, she tried to calm him.

A sharp voice overshadowed the others. "Alexis, how will you handle this disruption?"

Head of the Mother Board herself, Phyllis, propped her fisted tambourine on one narrow hip. "That child shouldn't be runnin' wild through the sanctuary. This is the Lord's house, not a circus!"

Shame burned in her chest.

"All right, Mother Phyllis, you've said your piece." Pastor Otis reached Alexis on the ground. The look on his face begged her and AJ to vanish.

AJ shrieked again, burying his face in her neck. The sound echoed along the pitched roof.

"I-I shouldn't have brought him here," Alexis murmured, more to herself than anyone else as the pastor rushed her to her feet. She'd have to tell Aunt Cherry that Otis was stronger than he looked. Still, her brain buzzed with thoughts. "I considered staying in today. But"—she looked up, voice unsteady—"But I knew y'all would talk if I missed it. You all would talk. I can't please you."

Phyllis gave a derisive snort.

"My nephew's mom died a few days ago. Tuesday," her voice cracked. "The wounds that will never quite leave, trust me, I know, are so fresh! I still came here. Performed today."

While her shoulders slumped under the weight of their disdain, she lifted her chin. "Against my better judgment, I showed up. Hours away from all AJ knows and loves, to perform. I can love God on my own time."

The silence that followed wasn't heavy with grace, but tighter. More rigid.

The pastor's brow furrowed. His mouth a judgmental line, but he paused as if to bite his tongue. "Alexis . . ." his whisper didn't hold a soft note. More like caution. "That's enough."

"I'm not done." She picked up AJ, who clung to her neck, face buried in her shoulder. Tears streaked her cheeks. "Beverly must be crying in Heaven right now over how you've treated her son." Shocked, she scanned the rows of familiar faces glaring at her in annoyance. This place no longer appeared familiar.

"I'm not allowed to skip Sunday service, even when I've spent the whole day before trying to keep someone alive. Do you know how hard that is?" She gave a thick swallow and rubbed AJ's back to comfort him. As she struggled to hold the tall eight-year-old, she continued, "When CPR starts on the scene, we don't stop. Not until we're at the hospital. I'm drenched in sweat, praying they'll make it. And if they don't— I've watched someone's life slip away in the back of an ambulance."

Her voice cracked. "If I cried myself to sleep for a few hours, I still have to wake up. Beat traffic. Pass another hour of stop signs. Be pleasant. Perfect." She gave a bitter laugh, then dropped into an impression of Phyllis's nasal tone. "'God has given His life for you Alexis, don't be mannish while you praise Him. Don't frown.'" The sneer didn't leave her voice as she continued, "I'm not allowed to be tired. Or angry. Or human."

The pastor fidgeted next to her. "Alexis," he repeated, this time firmer. "Please. That's enough."

"I suppose it is." Her voice cooled. "Mother Phyllis said her piece. And against your wishes, Pastor, I've said mine. I'm sorry."

Phyllis leaned forward from her seat with a stiff smile. "Don't forget to remove the dress before you go. It belongs to the church."

A groan slipped from the pastor, too quiet to scold, too late to matter. His hand pressed lightly at her back, and he guided her down the center aisle. The touch didn't comfort her, just held a firm and final note.

As she walked with AJ heavy in her arms, tears stung her eyes.

Her performance was over.

Not the one she'd designed with the encouragement of the Holy Spirit. But this one. The walk of shame.

The congregation parted as she passed. Eyes followed her. Whispers trailed like shadows.

She blinked through the tears and ignored a judgmental grunt.

Deacon Samuel held the door open then stepped outside with her. His gentle hand touched her shoulder, and his weathered face softened with compassion. "Don't worry about them. Jesus sees your heart. And that boy's too. You did right."

Chapter 11

Lord, how did this happen? Elijah didn't remember where in Alexis's story he stood up, but he couldn't sit down. Not while red-hot outrage rushed through his veins.

She swiped away a tear. "A praise dancer came out as the deacon went back inside. Her cheeks were so red. Embarrassment, maybe? She brought a water bottle for AJ. Her, the deacon, and my friend who taught children's church were the only ones who offered kindness."

"What happened to your friend? She should've watched him, right?"

Alexis offered a weak smile. "Mother Phyllis forced Margaret to take extra kids. Miss Margaret had agreed to cut down on how many she took for AJ's sake, but Mother Phyllis didn't care. Miss Margaret rushed out of the church when I got into the car. A kid with a peanut allergy got ahold of a Reese's Easter Egg." Alexis swiped away a tear. "AJ slipped out while she was scrambling for an EpiPen."

Alexis stood.

Elijah followed her down the gazebo steps as the sun dipped behind the trees and bathed the park in golden light. Birds chirped, and the occasional ripple of wind rustled the leaves. They strolled side by side along the path, hands lightly brushing now and then. Her long corky hair concealed her face from his side profile of her.

"You okay?" he asked.

"Yeah." Alexis nodded weakly. "It's nice out here."

Not what he meant. He desired to address this and reach the core of her pain. Not discuss the weather. *Jesus, is this incident why You made me wait to find her? The wound was too fresh before?*

Confidence firmed his shoulders. He had his answer. "I get it now. Why you no longer attend church."

She didn't respond. Just kept walking, eyes forward.

"You don't owe anyone an explanation for your decision. Still, I appreciate you telling me."

"I'm glad we understand each other now," she murmured. "AJ won't get those pity smiles from me like your church might offer. He won't sit quietly for two hours. I remember you said the Bobby room can accommodate him. But church has triggered him enough already."

Elijah's heart clenched. "I hate how that happened to him." He stepped in front of Alexis, met her eyes and gave her hands a soft squeeze. "I hate what happened to you." The disaster hadn't just hurt her nephew. It had wounded her too.

"Look, I have a great relationship with Abba Father, Yeshua the Son, and the Holy Spirit." She sounded only slightly defensive.

"You know God." He offered a lighthearted laugh, even though he didn't feel it.

"Yep. I can't live off someone else's faith or testimony, so I have a personal relationship with God. He's my Shepherd, and He watches over me through the darkest valley and whatever season I'm in."

He took her hand. "I'm glad to hear it. Just so you know, I'm not like that. I left the church in college. While I won't compare my reason with yours, I struggled with my decision too."

The sun slanted across her tresses, shading them a lighter brown. "Why?"

"My dad and I fought about what a prestigious college really means. I wanted to go to law school. He asked me in so many ways and on so many occasions to attend Bible school. The pressure got me hooked on Adderall."

She winced. "Sorry to hear that. But . . . you're back in church now?"

"Leader of the single's ministry. I might have had selfish reasons when I started."

Her brows rose. "Your search for Olga?"

He laughed. "I enjoy it now, though. I've incorporated The Passion Translation into our different activities. My father abhors the TPT."

Her brow raised. "Which you loved since inception?"

"How did you know?"

"You've got a lot of fire in you, Elijah, even if you can't dance. So, if we do dinner, like next Friday, will you be bummed if I don't visit The Way?"

A little. "Pray on it?"

"Sure."

"Alexis, I know in my heart that you're not less faithful because you've been hurt in God's house. And I won't pretend every action that happens in those pews reflects Him. 'Coz it doesn't."

"Well"—she rubbed a palm over her forearm—"sometimes I feel guilty, like a bad Christian for not attending on Sundays."

"No, you're a good sister. You're raising your nephew in a world that barely makes space for kids like him. That's the heart of a servant, Lex." He rubbed the back of his neck. "Can

I call you Lex? I heard Cherry say it at dinner. Now that you've told me your story. It sort of slipped out."

"Yeah, thanks for hearing me out, Eli."

"Always," he whispered.

They resumed their walk, slower now, fingers interlaced. Somewhere nearby, a church bell rang.

*****

That night, Elijah sat at the kitchen table in his parents' home, a mug of herbal tea in hand, as his mother rinsed dishes at the sink. The smell of lavender dish soap filled the air.

"Momma?" He set the mug down.

"Hmm, baby?"

"I have this friend," he began. He'd swung by to talk to her about this, but in his family, dinner came first.

"Does she go to our church?"

"Technically."

"Oh! The girl you've been seeing for the past few weeks?" His mom went from asking to a near scream of excitement, as if she knew what came next.

"Which is it, son?" His father stepped into the room.

Elijah groaned into his tea.

"Is she the girl your dad might've mentioned? After you asked him about the thank-you bouquet?" His mom's curiosity wouldn't be sidelined by his father's stern face.

"Mhmmm," Elijah replied. "He probably spilled the beans."

"Guilty." His dad sat across from him and placed his forearms on the marble counter. "Does this girl attend church? Don't tell me she's like . . ."

"Like me?"

"Not the current version of you." Dad reached over to pat his hand.

The touch surprised him. His father had never embraced physical affection.

Lately, a shift had occurred between them. His dad had softened, just a little, ever since Elijah took an interest in the singles ministry. He just hoped his next line wouldn't widen the wedge between them. "My friend stopped attending after an incident a year ago at an Easter service. Her nephew AJ— he's autistic, limited speech—had a meltdown in the middle of service. Right after his mom died in an accident."

"His mom died during Easter week?" his mom murmured.

"Irrelevant," said his father.

"I beg to differ," Elijah replied. "His mother died. He went to a new church—"

"And had a Wal-Mart meltdown?" His dad snorted.

"No!"

"Elijah, don't you yell in my hou—"

"This is my house too, honey"—his mother broke in— "and you don't know what autism is." After her retort, she explained.

"Oh?" His father fell silent.

"Please tell us the girl's name. So we can pray for her." His mom winked as she placed tea in front of her husband.

"Alexis," Elijah sipped his tea, then shared how the childcare attendant had lost AJ during a separate emergency. "He ran into the church crying for Alexis. Forget Easter best, he didn't even wear his Sunday best."

"Mm-hmm, people have higher standards for Easter," Mom said.

"Yep. People weren't kind. Especially the Leader of the Mother Board. Alexis didn't feel like she belonged there anymore. Especially not with Aaron Junior."

"That breaks my heart." His mom's face softened, and Dad patted her hand. "Some people are so prepared for heaven they're useless on earth. Although maybe there's a better way to say this. What I mean is, those who are heaven-minded see others more clearly. They encourage and uplift each other."

"I agree." Dad locked eyes with Elijah. "In Alexis's case, it seems she doubts that church is a safe place for AJ. I don't blame her."

"Thanks." Elijah rubbed a hand across the back of his neck. "I love church. You have to understand, she loved church too. She was in church multiple times a week."

"Can I get a last name?" Mom asked.

"Momma," Elijah groaned.

"What?" she asked innocently. "I need a full name while praying for her."

He and his dad exchanged glances in an unspoken code they used when they'd determined Mom wanted to play matchmaker. Elijah downed his tea. He hadn't been on the same page as his father in ages. "I care for her. Plus, she's the woman who saved my life."

"Ms. Butts?" Mom chuckled. "I thought her first name was—"

Elijah shook his head. For the next hour, he told them all he'd done over the past year to find Alexis. After the story settled, his dad confirmed that God hadn't wanted him to find her sooner.

His mom smiled, giving him a friendly shoulder nudge. "I'm proud of the man you've turned into."

"Really?"

"Absolutely. You just said church doesn't define faith."

His dad let out a breath. "Do you know how many times someone comes into my office asking if they've done enough to please Jesus? I try to clarify that we cannot work our way into Heaven. But I pray about the ones who don't come and ask that very confused question. The deceiver wraps them up in falsehoods. They swap grace for performance-based faith, and then they quit! They say, 'Jesus, I can't handle Your standards. I can't be perfect. Bye.' Don't give Him a chance to remind them"—he shook his head—"He did all the work on the cross. That's what hurts my heart."

Mom laid her head on Dad's shoulder in silent solidarity.

Could he someday have what his parents had with Alexis by his side? "So, what do I do? Alexis is comfortable with her relationship with God, and who am I to tell her she'd be closer to the Lord in the sanctuary?"

Dad surrendered the conversation to Mom. "You keep loving her. Show her the church—the one Jesus built—starts with compassion. Not criticism. Welcome, not judgment. And when she's ready, maybe she'll come back. Maybe you'll get her to come by Christmas." She giggled.

"Don't you go trying to speak that into existence, woman." Dad put an arm around her and planted a kiss on the crown of her head. "Elijah, this mother of yours is prophetic on occasion. With those hearts in your eye, son, I believe waiting until December might be more than you can bear."

Elijah laughed with his parents, elated that he and his father were getting along better these days. Though his parents made light of his desires, he had to agree. Christmas couldn't come soon enough.

Rubbing his hands together, Elijah determined not to place his will above God's plan. "Whether it's a week, or a month, or half a year from now—I won't rush her." *God, please don't let the wait last any longer.* "I'll try to reflect God's love."

Chapter 12
Fourth of July

"Girl, you're not ready yet?" Aunt Cherry leaned against the doorframe of the guest bedroom Alexis had personalized throughout the previous year.

Though she'd sold her secondhand canopy bed because of the move, she hadn't been able to condemn the pillow-top mattress where she sat. She slipped into a pair of peep-toe heels. "Hello? I am ready."

Aunt Cherry eyed her flair skirt. "What happened with the red dress?"

"Pft, you want me to wear red? All red for the first time 'meet and greet' with The Way's singles group?"

"It's an off-property event."

"People haven't seen me at church. They'll stare. And wearing scarlet won't help."

"First"—Aunt Cherry held up a finger—"the red maxi dress goes to your ankles."

"This does too." Alexis stood up on the wooden floor and spun for emphasis.

"Second"—Aunt Cherry added a bit of grit to her tone—"the church is so big. If someone says they go to first service, you go to second. And that's not a lie because you usually watch around 10 am, once AJ is done with his breakfast and all washed up for the day. Third . . ."

After a few beats, Alexis beamed. "Is there a third?"

"I'm thinking, I'm—"

The phone buzzed on the cedar-wood dresser. "Aaron." Alexis reached for it.

"Don't answer, you'll be late to your Fourth of July cruise. I'll catch him on my phone."

"I won't be late." Alexis answered the FaceTime call, and her brother's mocha complexion and sharp facial features appeared on the screen. "Hey, big brother." *Do you want to apologize to AJ for not coming home for the Fourth like you said you would?*

"How's AJ?"

"He's added a handful of additional words to his repertoire. Hard ones to pronounce. I bought him a few more GI Joes and even a couch cover, which he helped me put over his dinosaur-print couch. We might have to swap the nightlight. Our dino days are over."

"You're a remarkable little sis—" Aaron cut short his praise, narrowing his eyes. "Nice necklace," he said, but it sounded fishy.

"Thanks?"

"Where are you off to? AJ isn't a fan of Fourth of July fireworks. I've told you that already. Don't tell me you've decided to take him out."

"No. I'm . . ." *Wait. This is my reason to bow out. Again.*

"Hello, nephew." Aunt Cherry appeared over her shoulder. Her smile was sharper than the bothersome bobby pins that once stuck in Alexis's head during performances. "We expected you yesterday. We really miss you. Once every blue moon isn't enough."

"Aw, Auntie. I miss you too. Had a situation, which I'm not at liberty to discuss." Aaron addressed Alexis now. "You're gonna stick around?"

Aunt Cherry retorted, "She's not, I am."

Aaron rolled his eyes. "With that preacher's son!"

"Okay, that tone of voice is out of line, Aaron Carter," Aunt Cherry said.

"I'm sorry."

Alexis nodded, her palm suddenly sweaty. She held the phone tighter, worried she might lose her grip on the smooth plastic. "Yes."

"You're leading him on, Lex. After what happened to my son—to you—at church. Why waste your time on that guy?"

"Listen, I have to go," Alexis said. "If you'd like to speak with AJ, can you call back on Aunt Cherry's phone?"

"Alex—"

She tapped the off button. A sinking sensation crept into her stomach. While they had gone on dates, Elijah had also invited her to countless The Way Singles' excursions since she told him her story in May. She'd missed singles' charades. Then he'd brought his church friends to the same pottery place he and she had visited in June.

She found AJ in his room, wishing he'd give her an excuse to skip the cruise. One time, Elijah had joked about another woman at the singles' events. And that woman had believed him to be single. Maybe he should be single?

*****

Parking downtown was as close to war as she ever wanted to get. Her blue sandals pounded the cement and masonry concrete of the San Antonio River Walk. She rushed past crowds in sundresses, button-ups, and every other imaginable getup—all in shades of red, white, and blue. She needed to reach the opposite side of the river, which glimmered under

78

the sunset. The faded sunlight danced over the river. She inhaled the water's earthy algae scent and hoped Elijah hadn't been disappointed in the past when she'd bailed on his church stuff. *And if you don't hurry, Lex, you'll have one more disappointment to heap onto the pile.*

She squeezed around a family crossing the bridge and nearly ran into another group. On the opposite pathway, Elijah stood in a navy-blue short-sleeved shirt near the electric-powered river barge. He hadn't seen her. Probably thought she'd parked in the other direction. Couples and singles chatted around him. White lights twinkled along the awnings. Their soft light highlighted the worry thickening his brow.

Who amongst them would suit him best?

As she reached the end of the bridge, Elijah spotted her. A smile broadened his face. The kind that made her chest flutter, whether she liked it or not.

"Sorry." She chewed her lip. "Couldn't find a place to park."

Her nerves spiked. Was she supposed to hug him? They'd shared a few incredible kisses recently, but here—at a church event, where he led the singles ministry's Fourth of July event—seemed loaded. Too intimate might raise eyebrows. Too formal might rebuff her heart with rejection.

Before she could overthink it, Elijah's powerful arms surrounded her, and he pressed a kiss to her forehead. Soft. Sure. Perfect.

"You made it." He held her at arm's length, as if he were proud she'd come.

And just as Alexis let herself exhale in relief, another presence entered the moment. Seamless, graceful, and entirely too poised.

A woman with stylish glasses and neat Sisterlocks folded like a crown on top of her head stepped forward, hand extended. "Priscilla."

Ugh. She had a smooth way of introducing herself, and her smile seemed rehearsed. Alexis wasn't usually the jealous type, but the subtle way Priscilla looked at her knotted her stomach. Ugh. Let the unspoken comparisons commence.

The worst part? This was not her world. Not any longer. And Priscilla seemed to fit into it a lot better than she did. She'd be perfect at Elijah's side. Probably passed his parents a time or two. *Jesus, what am I gonna do?*

Chapter 13

Thank You, Jesus. Please make this event a success and show Alexis she's welcome here. With his fingers entwined in hers, Elijah hoped his prayer melted into her soul.

Minutes later, mellow Gospel-infused jazz played on low. Since The Way had chartered the boat, the music was a big hit with everyone. Elijah stood near the bow, the ocean behind him, mic in hand. A wide but slightly nervous grin stretched across his face. He focused on Alexis, and how her small diamond studs caught the last rays of sunlight. She looked as bright and fresh as the first day of summer, though he knew it hadn't been easy for her to attend.

He caught her eye and offered a subtle wink. She shook her head, betraying hints of amusement.

Elijah spoke into the mic. "Good evening, folks."

The gentle chatter and laughter paused.

"I'm glad you're all here. Thanks for spending your holiday with The Way Singles! Tonight is about levity and laughter, honest connection, and the faith that grows when we get together to support each other."

Sometime later, an explosion of vibrant gold, red, and sapphire cracked above the cityscape. Brilliant reflections shimmered in the water. Elijah found Alexis near the edge of the boat, lightly gripping the rail.

"Thank you," he whispered as the river swayed beneath their feet. "I appreciate you trusting me to be here . . . with these church folks."

"I almost backed out a couple times. Even had a solid excuse."

He raised a brow.

"Aaron."

Fingers crossed, Elijah might meet her brother, eventually. "You pinky promised this time. So, I would've asked the boat operator to extend the cruise. Maybe offer to work out an unpaid parking ticket if he gave us another hour."

That made her laugh, and his heart fluttered.

Hand to her chest, she gasped, "Officer Hayes, you can't do that." While fireworks glittered in her eyes, her gaze met his. "I came to see you, not the church. How you lead your ministry. How they respond."

"And?"

She hesitated, arms folded, guarded. "You were great. Still . . . I also expected judgment."

"Why?" He laid a forearm atop the rail.

"I get the vibe that today isn't the only time you've looked for me at one of these events." She smiled. "The others probably suspect you're not single."

He rolled his eyes. "You weren't the only latecomer. I wasn't looking just for you."

"Yeah, you were. You waited for me. While I've gracefully offered excuses to miss day trips. No one asked which service I attended, though, so I didn't have to resort to my aunt's suggestions." She shook her head. "I don't know how Aunt Cherry is a board member."

"From someone who almost became an attorney"—he wiggled his brows—"I bet Cherry's brilliant suggestions included the admirable use of loopholes. Still, I want you to know that when people see you in church, they should see what's standing right in front of them, a beautiful, strong, black woman."

"If they see me at church," she emphasized the first word. "And I don't think everyone sees me as beautiful, Elijah."

"I didn't say everyone was smart. If they don't see what's right in front of them, that's their problem."

Another firework exploded above, painting the sky with deep golden sparks.

Elijah let the silence settle between them. He didn't reach for her hand. Not yet. But his shoulder brushed hers, and she didn't move away.

As the last firework faded into a haze of glitter, and the boat rocked gently beneath his feet, singles clapped. A few people cheered.

Elijah maintained his spot next to Alexis, his voice quieter now, more personal, since they didn't have the explosion's buffer. "I was thinking about what today actually means."

She leaned against the rail.

"Independence Day, Alexis. It's about freedom. Gotta ditch what once held us back to embrace the future. Which can be risky, but worth it."

Her head tipped to one side. "This isn't just about 1776, is it?"

He smiled. "Not exactly. Come to think of it, I probably could've given the first part of the speech to everyone. Tie it into how God makes all things new."

"Maybe your dad was right about your calling? You'd be a fantastic minister."

"Verdict's still out. But for you, Alexis, I will always minister to your heart."

Her eyes twinkled brighter than the fireworks display.

"God has given us the same freedom of choice. Freedom to act. To heal. To forgive. To belong again."

Alexis seemed to freeze.

Had her mental paradigm shifted? He wanted to believe that. Even a little.

Alexis murmured, "You're good at that, disarming people."

He chuckled, but his gaze held steady. "I'd never try to disarm you, Lex. I just want to remind you that you're already free. Nobody gets to chain you to their opinions or religious expectations. Not even good ol' church people."

Alexis pushed away from the rail and glanced across the deck where members mingled. "I'm not ready for a pew."

"It doesn't have to start with pews. Suppose it kicks off like this?" He nodded to the crowd. "Laughter, conversations. Surrounded by food and happiness. Praying with people who love Jesus."

Her brow rose. "The singles ministry?"

"It's not just matchmaking and bingo nights," Elijah said. "We show up for each other. We don't expect each other to be flawless. If you have to skip a time or two, the team will send you the most hilarious GIF texts."

"I love a good GIF war."

"So, belong again. You've been through fire, and they have too."

The boat moved, slow and smooth under the moonlight. A saxophone's soulful notes emanated from somewhere along the riverbank.

"Okay. No pews," Alexis agreed. "No choir robes or sermons. But . . . maybe I'll come to the next singles ministry event."

Elijah smiled. Not wide and triumphant, but soft—a whispered Thank You to God.

"I'll save you a seat."

"Just don't be awkward, Elijah."

"Just a little?" he teased.

She nudged his shoulder. "You're lucky you're cute."

As the boat curved back toward the Riverwalk's colorful lights, Elijah favored the peace of the moment. He prayed this was Alexis's return, not just to church, but to hope.

Chapter 14
December

Alexis sat in the ensuite bathroom. After a year and a half, Aaron's guest room almost felt like home. It had become her sacred place—her daily rhythm started and ended here. Each day and night, she approached God with her Bible and heart open. She prayed, waited, listened.

And tonight, He'd answered, *"Where are you coming from, Alexis, and where are you going?"*

That question settled around her shoulders, gentle, yet weighty—just like the voice she'd come to know as her Heavenly Father's. He was speaking to her again. And He didn't ask questions for His sake. He already knew. Throughout Scripture, God's inquiries helped His children face the truth.

When Adam and Eve hid naked in their shame, He asked, "Where are you?"

When Elijah fled to a cave, He asked the prophet, "What are you doing here, Elijah?"

And when Hagar fled in Genesis 16:8, God helped her ponder her past actions. "Hagar, Sarai's maid, where have you come from and where are you going?"

Alexis wiped a tear as it slipped down her cheek. Like Hagar, she'd emerged from a bitter place.

She exhaled slowly. "Lord, I've asked You to search me, to know my heart, test me and know my anxious thoughts." While her voice wavered, her spirit steadied. "I've enjoyed The Way singles' events for months. Turns out, Priscilla and I have become fast friends. The others are great too. I can breathe again." She paused to gather her thoughts. "It's time, isn't it? Please help me to walk in the Spirit."

*****

The next afternoon, Alexis stood at the base of The Way's front steps. Behind her, the intersection stretched across San Antonio—the very place she'd once rushed to without hesitation to rescue a stranger. One who had become important to her. She loved Elijah.

She clutched a two-cup tumbler of coffee. Cold air flared from her lips in white puffs. *I'm really doing this.*

She took the steps two at a time and entered the massive front doors. The foyer loomed wide and bright with a long row of double doors that all led into the stadium-sized sanctuary.

Left. Aunt Cherry had told her to go left. She passed a cafe and Christian bookstore and headed down a long corridor with sleek, glass-walled offices. Polished but hospitable. Transparent.

"A church that doesn't hide behind walls," she whispered, the crushing anxiety finally gone. *Thank You, Jesus. This is a good sign.*

A small flicker of nerves remained . . . because of him.

She wouldn't run from Elijah anymore. But what would his family and church friends outside the singles' group think? She'd only encountered his mother on television.

She bit her lip, grounding herself as she approached the office on the left.

Elijah pushed away from his desk. His leather chair swiveled toward the window, phone to his ear. Sunlight caught the slope of his jaw. "Take a deep breath, Win."

87

Ah, Winston from their singles' group. The guy with social anxiety had joined after Thanksgiving.

She stepped inside. "Tell him to pray about it. Whatever it is."

Elijah spun to face her. His eyes lit up.

Without removing his gaze, he relayed to Winston what she'd said, bid the man a blessed day, and tapped the end call button. "You're here."

"Yep." She placed the coffee on his desk. Grinning, she backed away. "And I'm late, sor—"

"Oh no, you don't." He stood, rounded the desk, and took her hands. "You're supposed to jump up and down. Squeal a little. And then I'll do a masculine version with a lot more finesse."

"You mean fake nonchalance?"

"Precisely."

He pulled her into a firm embrace as if afraid she'd disappear again. She didn't dance or squeal, but she leaned in. Just a little. She controlled the urge to inhale his incredible mix of pine and Dylan Blue.

Elijah released her. "You're here?"

"I'm late to choreograph the girls for this weekend, Mr. Smarty Pants. Priscilla haggled me into helping her at the Christmas event. She signed us up for the hot-chocolate stand."

"She did?"

"Yep. And since you still look shocked, yes, I want to watch the girls practice the new routine for the event this weekend and Sunday. Did you have your heart set on hot-chocolate duty? Because I can take my name off the list."

"Oh, no." He raised his hands in surrender as laughter bubbled out of him. "I wouldn't survive the avalanche of sugar rushes—from the kids or the adults."

"Didn't think so."

He laughed harder, shoulders shaking as he murmured, "Christmas."

"Yes, this Sunday is Christmas. What's so funny?"

"I can probably answer that," said someone with a graceful voice from behind her.

Alexis faced an elegant woman with a silver-streaked bob and a smile full of warmth. Instantly, she recognized this poised, beautiful, older woman.

"I told him you'd come back for Advent Sunday." The woman stepped forward.

"You're Ilette Hayes."

"Yes, and you must be Alexis Carter."

Alexis offered her hand. "Nice to meet you, Mrs. Hayes."

While Elijah wiped tears of laughter from his eyes and attempted to make introductions, his mother flashed him a playful smirk. "Please forgive my son. I'm grateful you're here. I hear you've got two practices lined up this weekend."

"Sort of." Alexis relaxed under her friendly gaze. "The little ones will repeat the same routine at the Christmas event and Sunday. The older girls wanted a challenge."

"Let's go check out our girls."

Elijah wiped one last tear of laughter. "Yeah, let's go."

Moments later, Alexis stood just inside the practice room, hands tucked into her cardigan sleeves. On the floor, the older girls moved in unison to a soft instrumental version of "Holy Forever." Their arms arched like wings. Their feet stayed in a precisely imperfect rhythm, though a few lagged a half-count behind.

But the minor faults didn't matter. They danced with the Spirit.

A lump rose in Alexis's throat. These were her girls. This was her calling. She hadn't meant to make this moment sacred, but this was more than a practice. Her purpose had started to blossom again.

From the corner of the room, Elijah watched her silently.

Not the dancers. Her.

This time, Alexis no longer wanted to run from him or the God they both served.

Chapter 15

The church lot was jam-packed on Saturday night. Elijah climbed out of his truck trailing after bundled up families. Christmas lights twined through every tree, barrier, and post and lit cheerful faces.

Elijah took in the scents: roasted cinnamon almonds, kettle corn, and gingerbread. He stuffed his hands into the pockets of his dark peacoat. He found Alexis at the hot chocolate booth in a sweater dress that fell to mid-calf and overlapped high boots. A knot of four kids climbed over each other to drop a fistful of change on the table. While Priscilla counted their coins, Alexis struggled to fulfill orders of chocolate with all the fixings. Whipped cream, marshmallows, candy canes, or all of the above.

AJ sat in a corner, his hoodie concealed the sweater Elijah had gotten him. He'd recently learned some folks with autism hated tags. This sweater was cashmere, tag-less, and Elijah's great grandma would've called it "sharp as a tack."

AJ rocked back and forth, tension elevating with each repetitive movement, while his eyes darted around the crowd.

Alexis placed three hot chocolates on the counter near Elijah. Her eyes brightened when she spotted him. "Oh, thank God, you're here. I need you. I—AJ needs you."

Her needing him sounded nice, but she'd already explained why. Earlier, he'd heard the disappointment in her voice when she'd said Aaron had missed his flight. Her brother had slept through his red-eye.

Tomorrow was the first Sunday Alexis would attend church *and* Christmas. Aaron had to arrive before his son opened gifts, right?

Elijah said, "Beanbag toss?"

"Yes." She sighed. "AJ loves textiles. Even if he doesn't toss the beanbag—"

"—see if he'll stand in a corner and hold it," Elijah finished what she'd told him twice on the phone earlier that day. "I remember. Take a deep breath, Lex."

A few minutes later, Elijah stood beside the beanbag booth. The game wasn't as popular as balloon darts or the dunk tank. Who thought of a dunk tank at a winter church event?

Even though the attendant at the beanbags said AJ could hang around all day for free, Elijah paid. The funds for the event went straight to a prominent toy store that had agreed to provide vouchers to parents, so they could pick gifts for their children. While The Way always hosted a toy drive, this personalized method allowed parents to reclaim some dignity. Parents knew exactly what their children's eyes clung to the longest when toy commercials ran rampant around the holidays.

So, his money would go to a good cause. Plus, AJ was a legend at the beanbag toss.

By the time AJ had tossed enough bean bags to cover Mount Everest, the sun's last rays had disappeared, and stars cluttered the sky.

"I'll have to give you all the biggest stuffed animals." The attendant grinned at AJ from the opposite side of the tent. While AJ made his choices, Elijah removed the beanbags from the netted hole. A single hole. The one with the highest point value. The kid hit the 50-pointer once, and muscle memory took over.

Now, he started all over again. AJ didn't stop his slow throws, even when Alexis and Priscilla strolled over, their work for the day finished. Priscilla watched for a few minutes, then hugged Alexis, waved to Elijah, and wandered off through the crowd of festive churchgoers.

Elijah winked at Alexis.

Together, they watched AJ in amazement until the very last beanbag disappeared into the 50-point net.

Elijah raised his hands as if to make a touchdown call. "We're gonna need a trophy here!"

AJ turned around and smiled proudly.

Past the beanbag toss, the twinkle of lights around the ice rink glowed. Children in puffy coats shuffled across the ice. The goofing around and chatter made it all chaotic—magical.

Elijah traced her gaze to the ice rink.

"I know what you're thinking, Lex," Elijah said.

"I don't ice skate."

"You don't ice skate yet."

She raised an eyebrow. "Are you gonna drag me out there?"

"I hoped you'd fall into my arms. Gracefully. You know. For dramatic effect."

"Oh, you're the choreographer now?"

"Yes, he is." A familiar, bossy voice emanated from behind them. "And I'll watch AJ."

Alexis laughed. "This is just like my Twinkle Toes Spring recital, Aunt Cherry. You tried to make me go out to dinner with a guy. See how that ended?"

"You did go to dinner with me."

"Oh, yeah." Alexis scrubbed a hand through her hair. "I've given away a billion pounds of marshmallows today. I'm tired."

"You don't look it," Aunt Cherry said.

"I agree."

Aunt Cherry took AJ's hand and directed him back toward the beanbag station.

Elijah's heart stirred. The music rose. People twirled. The ice rink was a stage where he'd be the one with moves. To lead.

He took her mitten-covered hand.

She squeezed his leather-gloved hand and whispered, "Don't you dare let me fall."

"Never."

After they rented and laced skates, the grip she'd given him during her muted threat intensified. Terror flashed in her eyes as they wobbled onto the ice. She gripped his forearm, and her legs shook as she eased into a clean glide. Yeah, it was a little clunky and romcom-ish at first, not exactly flawless romantic. But her movements were also hilarious.

His steady arm slid around her back as he helped her glide across the ice.

The cold air whipped around their faces, tinting Alexis's clear mocha complexion with pink as they fell into a rhythm.

"Move it!" a little girl chided good-naturedly.

"Yeah, you're in the way," another voice called, with a similar childish inflection.

He shook his head as an eight-year-old girl and her twin brother from church zipped around them like human Formula 1 racers. Faster than Ferraris. Their custom skates—not the standard white color most people borrowed—were neon orange. The bright, well-worn skates blurred in the night. He knew the kids because their mother had been called to the seven- and eight-year-old class a time or two. They were tiny terrors, but Elijah would never call them that. Besides, tonight they had a positive outlet. "Little showoffs."

Alexis chuckled.

"Enjoying yourself?"

"Maybe." One side of her mouth curled into a grin he knew and loved. "Elijah, I l—"

Someone screamed.

Not a laugh. A real scream.

The girl twin fell near the rink's far perimeter. Her leg twisted in an eerie direction. Adults shouted while the little girl's brother cried out for her to get up.

Alexis was already moving. Her paramedic instincts must've kicked in. She let go of Elijah's hand and ran for the chaos.

He raced after her toward the scene.

"I'm a paramedic," Alexis told the older teen boy she'd used to stop herself.

The kid helped her to her knees just as Elijah caught up. Small bits of ice flew like a fallen snow cone as he stopped.

Chapter 16

Alexis's exhale fogged in front of her face as she knelt next to the girl. A winter coat puffed around the child's body. Unfortunately, the extra cushion hadn't softened her fall. One neon orange skate twisted at an angle that made Alexis's teeth hurt.

The girl's brother wailed louder with every wordless shriek of agony from his twin. "Get up, get up," he moaned.

"Sweetheart, don't move," Alexis said, voice low and steady.

The girl whimpered. She reached for her leg with a mittened hand.

Alexis gently redirected the girl's gesture before placing her hand on the child's chest. "Stay still. I know it hurts."

One leg lay dislocated. Painful and unstable. A tear rolled down the girl's cheek.

"What's your name, baby?"

"Zoe."

"You're doing great, Zoe." To the onlookers, Alexis directed, "Someone call 911. We need paramedics now."

"Already did," a man said, clutching his wife's arm tightly.

The woman stuttered, "Her sk-skate clipped . . ."

"I know," Alexis cooed. She scooted around to shield Zoe from the chilly wind. She couldn't stabilize the girl, not without gear.

The girl needed to stay warm. Alexis shrugged an arm from her jacket before Elijah quickly offered his.

"Breathe with me," she said to Zoe as Elijah draped the peacoat over her. "In through the nose. Out through the mouth."

The little girl's tears fell slower while she matched Alexis's pace. Tension faded from the contorted line of her lips.

Moments later, a young paramedic in navy gear ducked under the rope around the rink. "Ma'am, we've got it."

Alexis stood with Elijah's help. "Left leg, high break or dislocation. Guarding her chest, but no apparent signs of head trauma. She's breathing steady."

"Thanks." The woman gave her a respectful nod. "You a paramedic?"

"Used to be." Alexis smiled, but it felt tense.

She brushed frost from her jeans, and Elijah helped her off the rink.

The crowd dispersed as EMTs loaded Zoe onto a gurney. Her brother, who had wandered off during the breathing exercises, ran back with their mom. Pastor Hayes and others followed the pair.

The memory of a few seconds ago warmed inside Alexis as the mother met the paramedics near the ice rink exit.

As she sat on a bench with Elijah, the training-induced calm lingered. It had all come back. The clarity. The focus. The desire to serve.

After a few beats, Elijah stepped away, as if he understood her need for reflection.

How she missed this. More than she would admit, even to Aunt Cherry all those months ago. Her dream of returning to emergency response hadn't died. Just gone dormant, buried under months of survival while she learned to raise AJ.

Now? *Maybe things are different. If I can convince Aaron to stay past Christmas. If . . . he even comes.*

Elijah thanked the teen who'd helped Alexis. That same boy now handed him his peacoat.

A man roped off the skate rink's entrance. Given the accident, that was for the best. Everyone dispersed to other activities.

As Elijah slipped back into his peacoat, he smiled at her, a glow on his face. The way he looked at her made her feel known. Honored.

Alexis walked toward him, heart in her throat.

He hugged her, ran a hand over her back. "That was—"

"I know," she said before he could finish.

In the beat between words, she glimpsed how invitation lit his eyes. The quiet awe, like he couldn't believe she was really here. Like she'd walked out of his prayers and into his arms. The way the cold brought a red undertone to his powerful jaw only made the moment more vivid, more real. His hand still rested on her spine. Steady. Warm. Possessive in the gentlest way.

He hadn't let her go.

Alexis's heart, guarded for so long, thudded wildly.

Was this it? Was this the instant everything shifted?

Her hands moved before her mind did. One rested on his chest; the other rose to his face. His skin was warm despite the chill, smooth beneath her touch. Her fingertips, feather-soft and tentative, traced his jaw with affection. This touch—this moment—offered him her steadfast trust.

With one hand, he cradled the side of her face, and the other pressed gently against her back, drawing her closer until there was no space.

Then he kissed her.

And she answered without hesitation. She leaned into him. Her hands slipped behind his neck. It wasn't a kiss of fire and frenzy, but warmth and wonder. A promise. Love.

When they finally pulled apart, their foreheads rested together, breaths a mingle of clouds between them.

"Didn't think we'd share our first kiss on church grounds so soon," she whispered, unable to compress her smile.

"Neither did I," Elijah admitted, his voice rough with emotion. He pressed a tender kiss to her forehead, lingering as if he never wanted to let her go. "I love you, Alexis."

Her heart skittered a beat, then burst with feeling. The words long buried in her heart surfaced. "I love you too, Elijah," she whispered.

Familiar laughter at the dunk tank caught her attention. Aunt Cherry. She was supposed to be watching AJ. Instead, she stood before the dunk tank with Glenda. Both women doubled over in hilarity.

The line for the dunk tank had tripled. Pastor Hayes sat over the water in a three-piece suit.

"My mom went to the hospital with Zoe's family," Elijah said. "This is how Dad tries to boost morale."

Her heart thundered. An avalanche in her chest.

Where was AJ?

She rushed around the long line that blocked half a dozen tents housing other games. Elijah was at her heels when she stopped in front of the beanbag toss. No AJ.

Alexis couldn't breathe. Families, booths, and twinkle lights melted into one jumbled mess.

How long had she sat on the bench, lost in thought? Long enough for Ilette Hayes to follow Zoe to the hospital and her husband to create a crowd at the dunk tank. Long enough to delight in her first kiss with Officer Elijah Hayes. Long enough for Aaron Junior to disappear. Why had she left him?

"AJ's gone." Her voice broke. "He was, he was…"

Then she spotted him. At the ring toss. His green camouflage jacket. Tablet pressed to his chest with one hand, he threw a ring with the other. Flawless movements.

And next to him—tall, lean, broad-shouldered, and shaved head—a man she knew as well as her own reflection.

Aaron.

Her brother.

He stopped short of clapping his son's shoulder and played it off, his hand fist pumped the air. "This is my son!" he shouted to a church member walking by, voice raw with pride.

Elijah followed her gaze. "Is that?"

Throat too tight to speak, she nodded. Her hand clutched her chest, and slowly all the breath she'd been holding poured out.

Tears of relief and soul-deep peace gathered in her eyes.

AJ was safe.

Aaron was home.

And for the first time in forever, Alexis would return to her home tomorrow.

Not just a shelter from the elements. A place where she once found rest and, after an extended, painful wilderness, learned to rest again.

She'd praised Him through the pain. Kept her faith when it was just her and the quiet—no sanctuary, no choir, no welcome committees, just whispered prayers and tear-stained pillows. And even when she didn't feel Him, God had never stopped moving. Never stopped calling.

He knew how to reach her. Not through pressure. Not through perfect people. But through Elijah. His patience, gentleness, the way he listened when she finally told the truth and didn't flinch was all she needed. No. Elijah hadn't saved her. But God had used him.

Used his warmth to thaw her hesitancy. Used his steadiness to rebuild the trust she thought she'd burned forever. He showed her that faith didn't thrive in isolation.

She'd tried that. Elijah nearly broke her.

But love? Real love. God's love moved through people. Through connection. Through community. More trials lay ahead. Life wasn't suddenly easy. But she knew she didn't have to face them alone. Not without God.

She rested her head on Elijah's shoulder. If he had chased her for a year, she figured he wouldn't suddenly pull his support. A smile broadened her face because she could also include church. As she inhaled, peace settled inside her.

Tomorrow, she'd walk through the doors of her new church. Her new family. And this time she'd walk in knowing she didn't have to prove anything. She was simply . . . home.

THE END

Author's Note

Fortunately, by God's grace, I haven't endured church hurt. But I wanted to contribute to the Brave Authors anthology. Because of my love for music, I went to YouTube and popped in Church Hurt songs, and lo-and-behold, I came up with one.

If you haven't listened to *Church Hurt* by Hannah Kerr, regardless of whether you've endured pain at the hands of the pulpit or not, I suggest giving the song a chance. Then I went to the comments, and I just love how God's children write their testimony and how we overcome. So, this story is loosely based on a few comments, and eight years as social worker. I worked with the Extended Foster Care unit in Southern California. For those unfamiliar, EFC is a relatively new program that helps keep foster youth in the system past age 18. Instead of kicking them out! They receive services until age 21. I truly enjoyed assisting youth in finding employment, vocational training, and even encouraging some to pursue top-tier universities. Nonetheless, I witnessed EFC's grim nature while carrying sex trafficking cases. And I also had a youth who aged out of the system at age twenty-one, who is nonverbal like Aaron Junior, and thank God he had those additional services. So, here is how I came up with *Praise Through The Pain*. Oh… and I always wanted to be a praise dancer as a child. I grew up in Long Beach, Ca, and none of the churches I knew had this opportunity. I, however, did "force" my daughter to join the praise dancing team for about two years, muhahahaha. She got pizza parties out of it, and now she's part of the choir. She's fine, LOL. I hope you enjoyed my story.

About the Author

Learn more about N Y Dunlap at her <u>website</u> where you'll discover her debut novel, new endeavors into Christian Romantic Suspense, and her Christian/Clean book reviews. She loves reading Christian and clean romantic suspense, thrillers, romcom, and an occasional historical romance.

Please spread the word about Alexis and Elijah. Share it on social media and/or leave a review.

Rapha

D.T. Powell

Dedication

For R. L. S. You were one of the first to believe I could do this. May Jehovah Rapha, the Lord Who Heals, make Himself known to you.

Chapter 1

Rebecca hurried toward the unmistakable shrill of an irate customer. It was only 8:30 and already, too many people had crowded into tight lines in front of customer service. She squeezed between two shopping carts, both manned by middle-aged women staring at shiny new iPhones. "Excuse me. Sorry."

Neither shopper acknowledged her.

Better than being railed at.

She couldn't wait to get out of here and go home to Chelsea. The golden retriever always galloped to the door to greet her, tail wagging. No grumpy comments. No outrageous demands. Just loyal love.

Her chest pulled tight, but she hauled in a few deep breaths to loosen it and stave off the dampness sneaking into the corners of her eyes.

The tired strains of a Christmas carol, playing for the hundredth time this week, sprinkled the air. If corporate really wanted to cheer people up, they'd staff stores better instead of relying on irritating songs and pennies-off sales.

A woman in her sixties leaned over the customer service counter and shook an opened package of socks in the service-desk man's face. Her rose-pink lipstick clashed with red earrings and a neon-orange sweater. "I bought these here two days ago. They won't fit my grandson. You have to take them back!"

"I'm sorry, ma'am, but this store doesn't carry those." The service-desk guy—his name tag read "Josiah"—kept his posture neutral and tone even. Rebecca had never seen him before, but he clearly wasn't new to this. He must be the Georgia transfer.

The customer slammed the package onto the counter. A half dozen red and black checkered socks flew from the plastic bag and showered both customer and employee. "Get your manager over here, right now."

That was her cue. "Yes ma'am." Rebecca slipped behind the desk and stood beside Josiah. "What can I—"

"This stupid idiot"—the woman shook a finger at Josiah—"won't return these socks. How hard is it to scan one thing and give me my money back?"

Pretty hard, if the item wasn't even in the system.

"Do you have the receipt?" Rebecca checked the ever-growing line.

"I lost it."

"Okay, let me see if we have these on file." This was the store brand for Humphrey's Dollar and Dime a few blocks up the street. But telling this woman that would only end with more yelling.

Chelsea's lopsided doggy grin came to mind and lowered Rebecca's irritation level from rolling boil to a simmer. Why did the holidays have to bring out the worst in people?

She made brief eye contact with Josiah, offering him a look of comradeship. Hopefully he'd take it that way. His more salt than pepper beard and the wrinkles spanning his forehead marked him as more than two decades her senior. Probably could retire in a few years. If he'd been in customer service any length of time, he'd seen his share of confidently incorrect, and just plain rude, people.

After scanning the half-empty package of socks, the anticipated error message popped onto the register screen. "I'm sorry. Durham's doesn't sell these. I'd love to help you get a refund, but since the computer can't even tell me how much I should give you, I'm afraid I can't." She slipped the few still-packaged socks into a plastic bag and retrieved stray ones from the floor. "If I have a receipt, I can look up anything you bought at any Durham's location. But without one . . ." She tied the bag shut and held it out to the woman. "Again, I'm really sorry."

The customer stared at the bag in Rebecca's outstretched hand. Her gaze slid to Josiah then Rebecca before she snatched the bag and plopped it into her empty shopping cart. "Fine. I'll take it to the store across town. They always give me my money back." She turned away from the service desk and fumed as she shuffled toward Housewares.

Rebecca wanted to tell the woman she'd have no better luck anywhere else. But if a person wasn't willing to listen to the truth, there was no point saying it. "I'll get somebody up here to help thin out this line," she said as Josiah reclaimed his place behind the register.

"Thanks." He motioned the next customer forward.

She picked up the landline phone mounted on the wall a few steps away. "Natasha, shut off your light and come to the service desk."

The girl didn't even bother to disguise her irritated groan.

Muffled scratching said Natasha had her hand partially over the receiver. "—warmth of a glacier," she muttered. More rustling. "Whatever. Be there in a minute." The line went dead.

Maybe the girl was right about her being cold. But better to wall off emotion and be thought unfeeling than let people in only to spend years salving wounds that would never go away. She'd cared once. Believed people when they claimed to care about her—said they were there to help. Not anymore.

An alert on her handheld said register six needed fives. She hung up the receiver and headed for the cash office.

*****

At lunch, Rebecca searched for an empty chair in the break room. It was already almost one. Only a couple more hours and she could go home. See Chelsea and not have to deal with disagreeable shoppers and uncooperative coworkers.

Every table near the door was packed. The few cashiers on break glanced at her and quickly looked away. That's how it always was. No one wanted to spend their break with a supervisor—especially not one who was all business. She preferred it that way though. Over the past several years, she'd gotten especially good at protecting herself. Getting hurt wasn't just reserved for ill-fated romances. It could arrive from the source someone least expected.

She slipped past the sink and counter, avoiding a knot of rowdy high schoolers clustered around the single microwave and coffee maker. Probably part-timers and temps. Once mid-January hit, they'd be back home playing video games and irritating their college-age friends for rides to parties. As usual, they hadn't bothered to wipe up their crumbs or toss stray fast-food wrappers in the garbage. At least with this lot Maintenance had job security.

At the table in the far corner, one unoccupied chair was crammed next to the water dispenser. She grabbed her lunch—a soda, chips, and a turkey sandwich—from the fridge and bee-lined for the empty seat.

Squeezing into small spaces wasn't something she'd ever been good at. Her leg wedged uncomfortably against the cold plastic of the dispenser. A trail of moisture ran down the machine's side and left a dark patch on her faded black uniform skirt. But the relief of sitting down? Heavenly. The familiar ache in her feet from standing all day throbbed, and her hips and back pleaded with her to not get back up. Unfortunately, if she stayed here too long, she'd be stiff when it came time to return to the floor. That would make for a miserable rest of her shift, and with the weekend fast approaching, she didn't need anything else to deal with.

"Colorful bunch we've had today," said the person beside her.

She whipped around at the unexpected voice.

There sat Josiah from the service desk, fork poised over a Tupperware container of spaghetti. Judging by how stiff the noodles were, it was probably cold.

Rebecca tucked away her surprise and opened her lunch.

She never knew what to say to new employees. Usually, she preferred to avoid them altogether. They'd learn everything important soon enough: the time clock by the sporting goods' desk didn't work; Ron on third knew all the locker combinations—though he vehemently denied it; and the cardboard baler jammed whenever someone crushed banana boxes.

Without a clear escape route, she was locked into this conversation. She'd avoided making the first move in social situations ever since . . . "It'll stay this way until January, then die for a while. Everybody's happy to empty their wallets at Christmas, even if it means ignoring January's bills."

"Same story everywhere." Josiah sipped a Gold Peak sweet tea. "That's how it went back at my home store. It's funny how people end up stuck in ruts—even when the patterns they're living are destructive."

She held back a snort at how right he was.

"How long have you been a front-end supervisor?" Josiah said.

"Couple years. Been at customer service long?" Best to keep the conversation focused on him as long as possible. Personal questions were the enemy here, and she had no intention of engaging them.

"Six weeks or so. They'd just moved me when my transfer request went through."

"Really?" She looked up from her Fritos and Dr. Pepper. "With the way you handled that woman this morning, I thought for sure it had been a lot longer."

"Well, I was in management for a while, and I've been dealing with people for almost twenty years." He dipped into his spaghetti again.

"Sounds exhausting." She checked her handheld, just in case her fellow supervisor, Luca, needed help managing the cashiers while she was on break. Plus, her shifting attention might dissuade Josiah from continuing the conversation.

"It can be. But in my experience, it's worthwhile."

Great. He was a talker. Maybe she could shut him up quickly.

"Can't say I agree," Rebecca bit into her sandwich. A tomato slice slipped from between the turkey and lettuce and plopped onto the table. She wrinkled her nose. No telling what had been on this table before she got here. Setting her sandwich atop its plastic bag, she grabbed a napkin from her lunch box and mopped up the defiled tomato slice, careful not to get any on her sleeve.

Instead of contradicting her assertion, Josiah kept eating spaghetti.

Neither of them resumed the conversation until Josiah packed up his empty Tupperware box. "Have a good weekend," he said before slipping out of the break room.

The weekend good? Only if they invented a way to skip Sunday.

"Yeah." She corralled the word's sarcastic edge just in time. Josiah was just being polite. No reason to saddle him with personal issues. "You too."

Rebecca checked her phone. Email and text notifications, she dismissed, along with click-bait news articles.

Just as she was about to set her phone down, a reminder from her Calendar app dinged. "Look at church list." That wasn't supposed to go off for another six hours. She must've set the time wrong.

Her finger hovered over the notification, poised to swipe it away. But if she did that, she might forget. Lately, once she got home, she was ready to eat and get to bed. Probably better to just look at her list and be done with it.

The address for yet another new church stared up from her Notes app. Five other addresses hung beneath it, along with the dates she'd visited them. Had it really been almost six months since she'd finally left Newton Hill Baptist?

She took a sip of her Dr. Pepper.

If her dad were still here, would he be disappointed? Her parents had attended the same church since before she was born. Even gotten married there. That kind of history was hard to leave behind. But staying somewhere you weren't wanted was a special brand of misery.

Across the break room, one of the temps slammed the microwave door.

Rebecca snorted. That was exactly what she'd felt like doing the day she walked out of her old church for the last time—slam the door and turn her back on the mess inside.

She ate the last bite of her tomato-less sandwich. If only her conscience would let her leave church altogether, it would make life so much less complicated.

Chapter 2

Rebecca slipped into the little church's small foyer. A table with bulletins sat beneath a simple wooden cross, mounted on the wall. She could take off her coat, but the wind's chill still gripped her. Besides, it was more unobtrusive than the deep-pink shirt she wore under it.

Her phone said it was a few minutes after the hour, but the soft murmur of voices still filled the sanctuary.

Newton Hill never started late. As soon as the clock hit 10 a.m., it was like someone had flipped a switch. There, conversations died mid-sentence as both piano and organ loudly announced the arrival of the pastor and his staff, all of whom took their seats on the platform before announcements and the Sunday School dismissal.

Here, a lone piano underscored everything with the familiar, elegant notes of "Near the Cross."

"Is this your first time with us?"

Rebecca bit back a startled squeak. A fifty-something woman in a floral print blouse and dark skirt stood six feet away. Her silver hair was swept into a thick braid.

"Yes," Rebecca said, barely reining the tiny adrenaline rush.

"Would you like help finding a seat? I know how nerve wracking it is being someplace new."

"No, thank you. I'm okay." Rebecca snagged a bulletin and pretended to scan it as she slipped through the open doors leading into the sanctuary. Thankfully, the woman in the foyer didn't follow her.

Three ladies, sitting together a few pews away, turned toward her and smiled. Two of them started to get up, and Rebecca swallowed dread. The standard inane chatter about "Looks like rain today," or "Hope the crock pot doesn't dry out that roast before we get home" always set her teeth on edge. Inevitably, people expected her to join in, and sharing about herself—or worse, her former church—was dead last on her to-do list.

The song leader stepped to the pulpit, hymnal in hand. "Let's stand and turn to 335."

To Rebecca's relief, the women heading her way offered apologetic smiles and went back to their pew. Everyone who had yet to claim a spot straggled to their seats, singing along as the congregation made it through verses one through three of "Beneath the Cross of Jesus."

Rebecca sang the first part of verse four, keeping her eyes glued to the hymnal, just in case anyone looked her way again. "I take, O cross, thy shadow for my abiding place." If she didn't see them, they couldn't make eye contact.

She kept singing. "Content to let the world go by, to know no gain or loss." If only that could be true for her. But walking away from the only church she'd ever known was proving harder every week. Leaving behind the constant whispers and bitter comments was one thing, but abandoning the place that held so many memories of her parents . . . It was like tossing family photos into a bonfire.

Once the last notes of the hymn faded, the song leader shut his hymnal. "I know the past few months have been hard, and I'm grateful God has filled this pulpit every week without fail—sometimes through members of this church family. And today, I'm glad to introduce our new pastor." He nodded to a man seated on the front row before stepping aside.

The sign out front hadn't said anything about this.

Shoes thumped across thin burgundy carpet as the new pastor approached the platform. An indistinct exchange of quiet words ensued between the song leader and new preacher, who still had his back to the congregation. He must not have a mic—or it was off.

Hopefully he wasn't nasally. She'd had more than enough of that at Newton Hill. If this guy's voice reminded her of her former pastor, she wouldn't be back. Whoever this man was, he couldn't erase what she'd been through, couldn't right the wrongs of a man he'd never met. Not that he had any reason to care about her problems. This wasn't her church, and these people weren't her friends.

She flipped open the hymnal and scanned the familiar words and music of "Abide with Me."

"Thank you, Quinton. My wife Essie and I—there she is, in the back—are glad to be with you here at Oak Grove." Rebecca froze. The woman who'd spoken to her in the foyer stood at her seat, across the aisle and two pews ahead of Rebecca.

But that wasn't what made her nearly drop the open hymnal.

At the pulpit, the new pastor held a worn dark-blue Bible as he continued to address the congregation. "I'm Pastor Josiah Hughes."

Chapter 3

Rebecca kept her head down, praying Josiah—should she call him Pastor Hughes?—didn't see her. The last thing she wanted was to come in Monday to an avalanche of questions about her and all things church. Friday, when he'd mentioned "dealing with people" for twenty years, she'd thought he'd meant as a store manager. She'd never suspected this. Now, she was doubly glad she'd left her coat on. Black blended in much better with the dark oak pews than pink.

At the pulpit, the song leader—Quinton—shook hands with Pastor Hughes. No. Josiah. He wasn't *her* pastor. They were just coworkers who happened to be at the same church today.

"My wife and I would like to invite all of you to our home next Sunday evening after the service," Josiah said. "But I'll say more on that later. We're looking forward to what God has for Oak Grove." Josiah bowed his head. "Lord, this is Your church, not ours. Build it for your glory." He closed with an Amen, which several congregants echoed.

As everyone dispersed for Sunday School, Rebecca shifted in the pew. Should she leave? Maybe Josiah was a decent preacher. She'd never know if she didn't stick around through part of the morning service. Indecision rooted her in place until Josiah's wife, Essie, approached.

"Would you like to come to the women's class with me?" Essie scanned the emptying sanctuary. "I don't know anyone here yet, either." The wrinkles around her eyes—it didn't seem right to call them crow's feet—said she smiled often. Even now, one side of her mouth tipped upward just a little.

Staying for Sunday School couldn't hurt. After all, Josiah wouldn't be in the women's class, so there was no danger of being seen. As long as she steered conversation away from work, she should be safe.

Josiah had just disappeared through a side door, hopefully headed to the men's class.

Rebecca gathered her Bible and purse and followed Essie to a room with four tables surrounded by chairs with deep-green padded seats. Two landscape paintings, one of sunrise at Paris Mountain on the far wall and the other of Myrtle Beach at sunset near the door, gave the mid-sized room additional splashes of color.

A woman who could have been in her eighties stood behind a skinny podium. She kept one hand on a four-footed gray cane and used the other to page through notes while everyone found seats.

The instant Rebecca and Essie claimed chairs, the three women Rebecca had spotted before the service sat opposite them.

"We're so glad to have you and your husband here," said one of the three. Gray-streaked brown bangs ended just above her eyebrows. "I'm Jillian. Nice to meet you." The woman's green eyes stayed on Essie, which was fine with Rebecca. The less she had to talk, the better. Hopefully their attention would remain on their new preacher's wife.

Chapter 4

With Sunday School safely over and Essie trapped in a lengthy conversation with multiple church ladies, Rebecca slipped out of the Sunday School classroom unnoticed.

Once in the hall, she again considered sneaking away—before anyone decided to make her their next social target. But her phone said temps outside remained in the low forties, and her Prius was all the way at the other end of the parking lot. Besides, it was so pleasantly warm in here.

Staying another hour wouldn't hurt. As long as she could avoid Josiah and questions involving her church history.

A door down the hall behind her squealed open, and an intense jumble of heated words tumbled out.

She risked a glance over one shoulder.

A man, only inches shorter than the door, barred the way out of the room he'd just left. His crunched brows, ramrod posture, and unflinching stare said he was likely an aggressor. "We don't want you here," his stern baritone filled the hall.

"Brother Shaw." Josiah's steady tenor leaked past the imposing hulk blocking the door. "I'd be happy to talk with you, but this isn't—"

"You're not putting me off, Hughes," Shaw interrupted.

Essie picked that moment to come out of the ladies' Sunday School room.

If the other woman had been a fellow employee, Rebecca would have doubled-back—pulled her out of the line of fire.

Shaw spotted Essie before anyone could intervene. "This includes you."

Rebecca knew that tone. And it made her want to find the nearest closet.

Multiple women hurried past, keeping their eyes purposefully forward, as if looking at Shaw might get them pulled into the conversation too.

Another door, this one near the far end of the hall, opened, and at least a dozen kids flooded the small space with boisterous voices, animated hands, and far too much energy. Seconds later, multiple teenagers emerged from the same room, followed by two couples, probably in their late twenties.

Despite multiple kids nearly running into Shaw, the man wouldn't move. Essie stood frozen too, attention fixed on Shaw and her husband, who was just far enough inside the room to be invisible from where Rebecca stood.

If she were Essie, she'd be terrified. Last time she'd faced an angry man that much taller than her, she'd endured a tirade, then gotten out of there as fast as possible.

Jillian, the woman who'd introduced herself at the start of Sunday School, merged into the chaotic river of children and teens, but the second she noticed Shaw, she stopped and laid a hand on Essie's shoulder.

At Jillian's touch, Essie started. Her heart had to be hammering even faster than Rebecca's.

Chatter, tromping feet, and the rustle of loose paper masked part of what Jillian said, but Rebecca caught, "—you okay?" and "Come with me," followed by a stern glance at Shaw. Though the man said nothing, he met Jillian's gaze with hostility. But Jillian held her ground.

Rebecca wished she had the other woman's fortitude. If she did, maybe the past six months wouldn't have happened. Or, she'd have left her former church sooner.

A gap opened in the stream of people, and Rebecca jumped into it before anyone caught her staring. Though Shaw's wrath hadn't been directed at her, every bone in her legs seemed made of Jell-O. The stream of kids pushing her to her intended destination was a godsend. If she'd stopped walking, she'd have wilted right there in the hall.

By the time she made it to the pew she'd occupied earlier, it was three minutes till eleven, and Josiah hadn't made it back yet.

Whatever Shaw's problem was, it didn't appear widespread among the congregation. A few members wore thoughtful looks, but no one had that peculiar, pinched expression people used to hide being upset. Though Rebecca wasn't naïve enough to believe no one knew Shaw was disgruntled. His rant a few minutes ago would have clued in anyone paying attention.

Seconds after Rebecca sat, Essie and Jillian entered the sanctuary. Jillian accompanied Essie to her pew and sat beside her. At least she wasn't alone.

Unwilling to completely redirect her attention, but even less enthusiastic about getting caught staring at strangers, Rebecca pulled a months-old bulletin from the hymnal rack anchored to the back of the pew in front of her. She pretended to read the folded paper, interspersing mindless scanning with glances toward the door to the Sunday School rooms.

At 11:10, Josiah, Shaw, and multiple other men still hadn't returned.

The song leader, Quinton, stepped to the pulpit. "Let's turn to 197 and stand to sing 'The Church's One Foundation.'"

Rebecca stayed seated until others nearby stood. This kept her partially hidden from anyone at the front of the sanctuary.

It wasn't likely Josiah would spot her back here, but best not to test that theory today. Especially not after the debacle she'd just witnessed in the hall. She'd rather not reveal she'd seen that particular exchange. Or how close to home it had hit. Even now, the hymnal in her hand wasn't completely steady, and her coat had grown uncomfortably hot.

The congregation sang all four verses of the chosen hymn, one of which she'd never heard before, because at Newton Hill, they'd always skipped it.

"Just across the page, let's continue with 'A Mighty Fortress.'" Quinton's eyes kept darting toward the side door all through the first two verses. His timekeeping slowed at odd intervals, and once, the piano had to quickly speed up to compensate for irregularities. When Josiah finally came in during verse three, Quinton's shoulders straightened, and some of his enthusiasm returned, along with more consistent timing. His face, however, maintained hints of concern.

Shaw entered moments later and sat in the front pew so heavily, the entire bench wobbled and screeched. Another older man and six more men filed in behind Shaw. They silently took seats among the congregation.

Whatever had happened, Rebecca sympathized, but she was glad not to be involved.

*****

After announcements, an offering, and a pleasantly engaging forty-minute sermon, the service ended.

Just before everyone stood to leave, Josiah said, "One more thing. As I mentioned earlier, my wife and I would love to have all of you over to our house next Sunday evening, after church. We'll provide everything, and all ages are welcome. I know it's getting close to Christmas, and we're all busy, but Essie and I would love to spend an hour getting to know you and your families. Our address is in the new bulletin. We look forward to seeing as many of you as can come."

Josiah surrendered the pulpit. Just as he stepped off the platform, two couples intercepted him, offering outstretched hands, but blocking his view.

Rebecca soaked in a few last seconds of warmth under the heating vent before heading outside, passing several knots of conversing church members.

As soon as she shut her car door and turned the key, she cranked up the heat. Cool air blasted her face until the engine warmed enough to thaw her.

Both Josiah and Essie seemed well-meaning. Whatever the conflict with this Shaw guy was, she hoped it could be resolved. But there was no way she was getting dragged into something that wasn't her business or her problem. Last time she'd opened her mouth regarding church stuff, it had ended with the pastor shouting at her and then spreading lies. Old anger boiled in her chest. She gripped the steering wheel until her hands ached.

No matter how much it hurt to think about, Newton Hill and its power-hungry pastor were in the past. Leaving them there proved a daily—sometimes hourly—challenge. Shaw's outburst earlier had reminded her of what she'd escaped. But Josiah had given no sign of being shaken by the bigger man's antagonism. No one came through an incident like that completely unscathed. How would he respond once he'd had time to think about what had happened?

Chapter 5

Rebecca walked a cashier to register four and waited while the girl set up the till. Two more cashiers, including Natasha, would be here in an hour, to cover the usual influx of early-bird shoppers. Her fellow supervisor Luca was due in at ten, and they had three maintenance people on the schedule today. Hopefully no one called out.

Customer Service didn't open for another forty-five minutes. She checked the schedule on her hand-held. Josiah would clock in soon to straighten up before opening time.

She stepped into the accounting office for a moment alone. The door automatically locked behind her.

If Josiah asked her what she did this weekend, she'd give him as vague an answer as possible. Lying was off the table. She knew too well the destructive power of being two-faced.

To make sure they had enough change on hand for the day, Rebecca approached the cash recycler. The chest-high metal box boasted a computer monitor and coin tray on top and dispensers on the front. Its bulk filled two thirds of the small space, and the monster's periodic clanks and whirs permeated the tiny office. A floor-to-ceiling set of shelves beside the recycler housed empty tills.

On the screen atop the machine, a "Currency Low" indicator flashed red.

"How on earth do we use so many pennies?" Rebecca muttered as she pulled out a ten-pound bag of one-cent coins and poured half of it into the sorting tray on top of the cash machine. She set the bag aside and pushed pennies into the recycler. Each coin rattled as it fell through a quarter-sized hole and disappeared inside the big machine.

A firm knock resounded over the clatter.

"Just a second," Rebecca called. She emptied the rest of the bag before checking the peephole to see who'd knocked.

Josiah. The clock above the recycler said it was only 6:25.

As the last penny clinked through the cash machine, Rebecca took a deep breath and opened the door, praying Josiah would be too occupied with Sunday's incident to ask her anything.

"Morning," he said as he took an empty till and set it atop the recycler. Faint shadows lingered beneath his eyes.

Yup. That Shaw guy must have gotten under his skin—kept him up late. Josiah had maintained a good front yesterday, pretending nothing was wrong through the entire sermon. But after an altercation like that, she couldn't blame him for losing sleep. After her confrontation with her former pastor, she'd sat on the couch all night, trying to process what had happened. She'd even forgotten to feed Chelsea.

"Hey," she replied before scanning the barcode on the side of Josiah's till and checking out the appropriate bills and coins.

As she worked, Josiah studied the recycler monitor, but his eyes remained unfocused.

The words, "He's not worth it," perched on her tongue, but she didn't dare say them. What she'd gone through wasn't Josiah's business, and even though he seemed decent, his problems didn't need to become hers.

She walked Josiah to Customer Service in silence. If he noticed her unease, he gave no indication. Within minutes, they'd parted ways with nothing more than a polite nod.

It was one thing to be targeted and yelled at by a customer. Half the time, the screamers just showed out for attention. But when someone claiming to be a fellow Christian did it, the barb wedged deeply. And left scars. Ones she knew the pain of all too well.

If she were Josiah, she'd be making plans to go back to Georgia.

Chapter 6

The break room was almost as crowded as it had been Friday. This close to Christmas, they needed all the help they could get. Seasonal was a wreck, toy shelves bare, and Apparel had to keep extra eyes on the changing rooms.

Just last week, they'd caught a teenage girl wearing eight shirts, two sweaters, a coat, gloves, and a hat. Her pockets were stuffed with lipstick and nail polish. The way Nevaeh, one of their assistant managers, told it, the kid had looked like a walking snowball as she'd headed for the door. Security had a harder time not laughing than they did catching her.

Rebecca took a Marie Callender's Salisbury Steak meal out of the break room freezer. She popped it into the microwave before one of the temps could shove in a half dozen chicken enchiladas. Those had been in the fridge since the Monday before last. She gave the kid a look that incorporated both horror and disgust. He side-eyed her and stalked back to his table, suspiciously colored enchiladas in hand.

Surely, he wasn't planning to eat those. This place had enough problems without another employee getting food poisoning.

She put a step between herself and the crumb-speckled counter. Two ants skittered from beneath the microwave and headed for the coffee maker.

Josiah pushed through the break room door ten seconds before the timer hit zero. "Hey Rebecca." He stepped inside and let the door squeal shut. His eyes jumped from her to the high schoolers, and back. "Have you seen Natasha? It's slow—for a few minutes at least—so Luca sent me to look for her. She's supposed to cover my lunch, but she's been on break for two hours."

"Nope." The microwave dinged. Rebecca retrieved her food, careful to be polite but not show interest in a true conversation.

"Any idea where she might be?" His voice was heavier than it had been this morning, and if she wasn't mistaken, he held back a sigh. Lack of sleep would drag anybody down. Add Natasha's antics, and you had a recipe for exasperation.

Rebecca slipped a paper towel under the still-hot white plastic meal tray. "Have you checked the freezers? Sometimes she hangs out in there—since there aren't cameras and management putting on a cold suit would be a sign of the apocalypse."

"Guess that's not just a Georgia thing then." Josiah laughed, but his eyes didn't spark. "I'll head that way." He turned to go.

How often had she looked in the mirror and found that same false composure he wore in this moment?

"Hey, Josiah?" Rebecca said.

He stopped, door half open.

What was she thinking? This wasn't her problem.

"Let me know if you can't track down Natasha."

"Sure."

Once the break room door thunked shut, Rebecca claimed a seat at the table farthest from the temps.

Enchilada Guy darted to the microwave and shoved in his prize. He and two others clustered around the unfortunate appliance for a solid three minutes until a loud *pop-splat* exploded against the inside of the microwave door. The boys collectively cheered before exchanging fist bumps and expressions of congratulation over the revolting display.

Thank God, she'd made it to the microwave first.

Chapter 7

Wednesday night, Rebecca sat in her car outside Oak Grove Baptist. She left the heat running as she gathered Bible, purse, and a half-empty thermos of decaf. It was already ten after, and most everyone had gone inside, including that Shaw guy from Sunday.

During her last three shifts, unless Josiah was dealing with a customer, he hadn't said much. At lunch today, he'd offered a distracted "hello" in the break room and then absolutely nothing else. The subtle tightness in his smile and too-hunched shoulders betrayed just how much Sunday was weighing on him. If he—or Shaw—didn't resolve this, it would eat through him, leaving an empty, bitter shell. Or a numb ghost.

Maybe that was why she'd come tonight. To see what he would do.

She shut off her Prius. Cold air seeped in through ill-sealed doors.

Wednesday night was usually the smallest crowd at her former church. Based on the handful of cars in the parking lot, that was true here too. She'd have to be more careful about blending in tonight if she wanted to remain unnoticed by Josiah.

With already-freezing fingers, she buttoned her coat and popped the car door, elbowing it open so she didn't have to set anything down. Winter's chill wrapped her fingers, but the warmth of the thermos kept away the worst of it. Despite her mittens, her other hand, gripping her leather Bible case, wasn't so fortunate. By the time she'd crossed half the parking lot, her fingers were cold enough to dunk in fresh deli mac n' cheese without getting burned.

The forecast hadn't called for it to be this cold today. Christmas wasn't for another two weeks. Temps this time of year hadn't been so low in a while.

When Rebecca slipped into the church foyer, the bright notes of "Praise Him! Praise Him!" spilled from the sanctuary, and blessed warmth began to thaw her icy fingers.

She left her coat on and took a sip of coffee before sneaking through the doors that separated her from the rest of the congregation. The instant she settled into the same pew she'd occupied Sunday, she laid her Bible next to her. Careful not to spill anything, she settled the thermos onto the floor beneath the next pew up. A cluster of teenagers were already seated ahead of her, providing cover. If Josiah looked this way during the sermon, it was unlikely he'd see her. She clasped her cold hand in her warm one, thankful for the overhead heating vent.

Shaw sat on her side of the sanctuary, but much further up. His full head of white hair stuck out among his peers' thinning combovers. At least he wasn't yelling at anyone for the moment. Multiple other adults near him shifted uneasily, but a man who could have been around Shaw's age sat beside him with no hint of discomfort. Probably one of his supporters. Even in a church as small as Oak Grove, there was bound to be one person—and maybe a few more—backing this bully. If Josiah remained on their bad side, dodging them would be a challenge.

The music pastor—Quinton, if she remembered right— stepped to the pulpit. Two songs later, he sat with his wife in the third row, and Josiah took his place.

Rebecca scooted a few inches to one side, making sure a gangly high school kid was between her and the pulpit.

Essie sat near the front tonight, across the aisle from Quinton—and Shaw. Jillian sat with her again and kept shooting steely glances at Shaw, who didn't seem to notice.

"Open your Bibles with me to 1 Corinthians 13." Josiah repeated the reference as he turned. "This chapter is famous for its discussion of love. God's love is something none of us can fully fathom. But in John 15, Christ commands us to 'love one another' as He loved us. Paul, in Ephesians 5 challenges us to 'walk in love,' and in 1 Corinthians chapter thirteen, Paul, through the inspiration of the Holy Spirit, gives us the most thorough description of selfless love in the New Testament. Let's read, starting in verse one."

Chapter 8

The sermon went long, so when Josiah finally said, "Let's bow for prayer and be dismissed," Rebecca was ready to go home and sleep. Whatever the drama between Shaw and the Hugheses, it would wait until Sunday. The only thing left to do tonight was get out of here unnoticed.

"Lord, we thank You for all Your blessings," Josiah prayed.

Someone on the other side of the room shifted, sending a resounding creak through the sanctuary.

"Guard the people of Oak Grove Baptist, and show Yourself to them in a mighty way."

The kid sitting directly in front of Rebecca dropped a hymnal. It hit the floor with a loud smack and flutter of pages.

She winced and cracked open one eye.

The offender leaned forward to retrieve the book, completely exposing her.

Josiah picked that instant to glance her way.

Rebecca ducked. Maybe he hadn't seen her. She *was* all the way in the back.

After a half-second pause, Josiah kept praying. "There are many wounds in this congregation. Some physical, others spiritual, mental, emotional."

The kid who'd dropped the hymnal picked it up with a rustle and slipped it into the rack.

"You are the Great Physician, Jehovah Rapha. Heal us as only You can." The slight dip in Josiah's cadence said the prayer was ending.

If only she had time to leave before he looked up again. But there was no way she'd make it to the door in under two seconds. At least, not without letting the entire sanctuary know.

"Make us—make *me*—an instrument of Your healing, Father."

Once people started leaving their pews, she'd use them as cover and sneak out—hopefully avoiding conversations along the way.

"In the name of Jesus, we pray this."

She gathered her Bible, purse, and now-empty thermos as quietly as possible.

"Amen."

Through the barest gap between two teenagers, Rebecca caught Josiah glancing her way again. Just for an instant. He blinked, brows crunched together, as if overwhelmed by the lights pointed at the pulpit. But that flicker of curious uncertainty in his posture—the way he turned not just his head, but his shoulders too—said he'd definitely spotted her.

The duck-and-camouflage routine was over.

Now she'd have to consistently avoid him at work or fess up to visiting his church and risk fielding personal questions, including church-related ones.

People stood and headed for the doors.

Just like Sunday, Rebecca waited until someone close by got up. She hated how narrow the gaps were between pews here. Unless she wanted to hip-check people in the back of the head, she had to employ an awkward side-shuffle to escape the row.

Josiah scanned the room a second time, starting with her corner.

Only three more steps, and she could slip into the aisle. She took one long, shuffling stride, trying to close the distance quicker.

His eyes landed squarely on her. He started her way.

Rebecca's skirt caught on the hymnal rack she'd just passed. Precious seconds flew by as she freed her trapped hem.

He was almost to her when Shaw, accompanied by a man with a walker and a piercing frown, stopped him. This was the same guy who'd sat with Shaw during the service.

"A word?" the man with the walker said, a distinct edge to his voice.

Josiah's attention reluctantly shifted to Shaw and his crony.

Walker Guy didn't give Josiah half a second. "What do you think you're doing, taking an offering on a Wednesday night?"

Rebecca's jaw pulled tight in sympathetic trepidation, and her pace slowed. Was this really how petty Shaw's supporters were? What did it matter if they passed an offering plate during the mid-week service? If people wanted to put something in the plate, they would. It wasn't like Josiah had guilt-tripped anyone into giving. He hadn't even brought it up after the single usher finished a brief circuit of the auditorium early in the service.

Josiah's response was too quiet to make out, but the angry man's next words carried.

"This church pays you more than enough. Too much, if you ask me. We could have gotten a better deal with the man we *wanted* here."

This time Josiah spoke more loudly, though he didn't match the old man's volume. "I'm grateful for everything God provides. I only wanted to give people a chance to—"

The old man raised a hand to interrupt Josiah. "You should've just let things be instead of weaseling your way into our pulpit."

"Brother Reinhart, I assure you—"

"I don't want your assurances." The old man leaned hard on his walker as he stared down Josiah. "I want your resignation!"

Shaw stood by, arms crossed, wearing a curiously smug expression as more people took notice of the altercation.

If Josiah was working at Durham's full-time, how much could this place be paying him? This wasn't about money. Something else had to be going on.

"Thank you for taking time to talk, Brother Reinhart." Josiah's voice was far more controlled than hers would have been.

"Oh, I'm not done." The old man's words now carried far enough to reach the back of the sanctuary. "Where's your tie? We wear ties here on Wednesday nights."

Rebecca slipped into the foyer as Reinhart continued listing frivolous grievances. Even though her legs hadn't threatened to dump her on the floor this time, her heart pretended not to know that. Before she reached the glass double doors leading to the parking lot, she tucked her thermos into the crook of her elbow, so her unsteady hands didn't drop it.

Jillian and Essie stepped into the foyer.

"I've told Lincoln over and over that he isn't helping anyone by doing this. My brother can be—" Jillian stopped the instant she noticed Rebecca.

"It's okay. I was just leaving." Rebecca reached for the front door. This wasn't her business, and she didn't intend to change that.

"No." Jillian crossed the distance between them. "I'm sorry. I didn't mean to drag anyone else into this." She glanced from Essie to Rebecca. "Lincoln Shaw is my older brother. He . . . just really wanted his son—my nephew—and daughter-in-law to come back to Burnsville. When the pastorate here opened, he thought that was the perfect solution. But then"—she sighed, and though her eyes flickered briefly to Essie, she mostly stared at the thin burgundy carpet—"the church voted *you* in."

That explained why Jillian had been so forward with her disapproval of Shaw on Sunday. This was a family squabble that had gotten way out of hand.

"I . . . need to let my dog out." Rebecca reached for the door again as other people trickled into the foyer.

This time, Jillian didn't stop her from leaving.

She refrained from making eye contact with anyone as she stepped outside.

Once she reached the parking lot and shut her car door, she sank into the driver's seat, relieved it hadn't been Josiah who'd caught her in the foyer.

Though Oak Grove seemed to have fewer problems than her old church, the most obvious issue kept pulling her back to the incident that had upended her life.

Maybe she should start looking for another place to attend.

But where?

The list on her phone was already too long. None of those churches had been right for her—often for multiple reasons. Going back to any of them seemed a waste of time. Plus, they were all farther away than Oak Grove. At least here, a lot of things were familiar, the preaching sound, and no one groused at her for something she hadn't done. Or spread lies behind her back. Not yet, anyway.

Chapter 9

When Rebecca got up the next morning, all she wanted to do was get breakfast, sit on the couch, and do absolutely nothing. Traffic coming home last night had been bonkers. Two accidents, plus a whole line of cars waiting to go through that Christmas light place up the road. And it would only get worse over the next two weeks.

By her feet, Chelsea, the eight-year-old golden retriever Rebecca had inherited from her parents, stared at her, tail wagging in anticipation of food. The dog's big brown eyes never wavered.

"Come on, girl." Rebecca wrestled free of tangled covers. One leg of her dark green pajama pants was pushed up to her knee. When her bare feet hit the hardwood floor, she regretted not wearing socks to bed.

Chelsea stayed glued to her leg as she headed downstairs.

On the way to the kitchen, Rebecca rubbed bleary eyes. Her dad's recliner—almost the same green as her pajamas—stood ten feet away, facing the TV. She'd only used the overstuffed chair a handful of times during the past six months. Sitting in it in her father's absence still felt odd. He'd loved that chair.

Pictures of her and her parents hung in the living room. Even Chelsea occupied several framed photos. The golden's auburn fur always reminded her of sweetgum leaves in the fall. Mom had enjoyed picking just the right photos to display every season. The ones up now had been there for three years.

"Time for breakfast." Rebecca led Chelsea into the kitchen. She refilled the metal dog bowl from the sealed plastic bucket of Ole' Roy in the pantry.

When Rebecca set the bowl beside its matching half-full water dish, Chelsea sat, eyes on her, waiting obediently for the cue to start eating. The dog's tail thumped the linoleum.

"Good girl," Rebecca praised before setting a Beef Milk Bone on top of Chelsea's food. "Okay." She pointed to the bowl.

The dog daintily ate her treat first, then dug into her kibble. Her tail never stopped wagging.

With Chelsea fed, Rebecca checked the freezer and excavated a ham and cheese Hot Pocket from its half-empty red box.

Her mom had loved making from-scratch meals, especially breakfast. The bread maker—which Rebecca hadn't used since before her dad's funeral—still sat in the corner by the sink, unplugged. Cake and muffin pans filled the drawer under the stove, and the cast iron skillet was somewhere in the pots and pans cupboard. Especially this time of year, even if Rebecca wanted to spend more time in the kitchen, she didn't have the energy.

As the microwave droned, she grabbed a glass of ice water and a fork. Room-temperature drinks made her gag, so ice was a must, even during the winter.

The microwave beeped.

She dumped her steaming Hot Pocket onto a plate without burning her fingers. She'd learned a long time ago that eating these things while they were still in the crisping sleeve always ended in disaster.

The couch in the living room would give her ample room to stretch out, but the recliner was closer, so she sank into it. It still smelled a bit like her dad's favorite aftershave. She half expected him to walk in from the kitchen and ask if she was going to let him sit in "his chair."

But he wouldn't ever have to ask that again. If she knew him, he was probably gardening, cultivating the best flowers Heaven had ever seen.

She swiped damp eyes with the back of her hand and set her ice water on the TV tray. That old thing had been perpetually beside the recliner since the chair was delivered, sometime during her junior year of high school.

The recliner creaked comfortably as she settled in.

When Rebecca had put up the footrest and pulled a crocheted blanket across her lap, Chelsea hopped into the chair and plopped on top of Rebecca's legs. She buried her fingers in the dog's warm, soft fur.

As an old episode of MasterChef played, she dug her fork into the still-smoking Hot Pocket.

By the time she'd finished eating, Chelsea was nosing her arm, demanding attention.

Rebecca set the empty plate and cheese-crusted fork aside and stroked the dog's glossy coat.

Cooks scurried around on screen, grabbing plates or finishing last minute details for their dishes. That's exactly how she'd felt just over six months ago—harried, needing to just be done with the insanity in her life. Her dad's funeral, her former pastor's anger, the lies about her racing through the church gossip chains: all of it had hit at once. If her parents hadn't instilled in her the importance of church and spending time with fellow Christians, she'd have stopped going—probably well before her dad's passing.

While she'd planned and attended the funeral, her whole world had ground to a halt. She'd missed a full week of work and two weeks of church services. When she'd finally stepped back into Newton Hill Baptist Church, the first thing anyone had said to her was, "Oh. We thought you'd left." Not "Sorry about your dad," or "Do you need anything?" Just stares and whispered lies.

A few church members had gone to the funeral, but most of the attendees had been her dad's friends or co-workers he'd known outside of church.

Whether the people of Oak Grove were that callous was yet to be seen. At least *someone* had stood up to Lincoln Shaw—and it had been his sister, of all people. There was something to be said for a person willing to tell their own family, "No." If Jillian had acted in defense of the new pastor and his wife, maybe others would too.

Chelsea rolled to face Rebecca and tucked her front paws into the gap between Rebecca's side and the chair arm. The dog's head draped across one armrest.

"Wish I could bring you to church." She patted Chelsea's head. "Everyone would be too busy with you to even notice me." Another layer of protection against being dragged into the drama with Shaw and the Hugheses.

Once New Year's was over, she'd have more time and energy to keep church hunting. Until then, she'd wait and see how Josiah and Essie handled their two disgruntled members.

Chapter 10

By 9:45 Friday morning, Durham's check-out lines already spilled into Apparel. With only four cashiers on the clock, Rebecca would have to grab someone from another department and hope they could at least count change. Otherwise, she'd have management on the radio whining about lines instead of hopping on a register to help.

Everybody was quick to give opinions on how to fix problems, but no one wanted to actually do anything.

As she passed the service desk on her way to Electronics, Josiah came up beside her.

"Customer Service is dead right now. Send people to me," he said. "I can't weigh produce, but I can handle anything else."

Rebecca's handheld buzzed.

Wet spill cleanup at Self-check.

Probably another Ragu container. Whoever decided to put spaghetti sauce in glass jars should have to mop up all the broken ones for a solid month.

She didn't have time to come up with another solution to the overabundance of shoppers needing to check out. Besides, maybe Josiah was trying to fill the downtime, so he didn't have to think about Oak Grove. Understandable. "All right. Help whoever you can. First shift Maintenance isn't coming in today, so I have to take care of a cleanup."

"No problem." He hurried to the longest of the four checkout lines to wave people over to Customer Service.

*****

Once the spaghetti jar and sauce were safely inside a trash bag, Rebecca hiked to the compactor at the back of the store and took care of the now-dead Ragu.

As she headed back to the front-end, a shopper—a thirty-something man in hiking boots, jeans, flannel, and a thick coat—rushed past her, headed for Sporting Goods. Three boys, all under ten and dressed much like the man, herded after him, chattering about worms and bugs and how you could shoot grasshoppers off fences with rubber bands. As if to demonstrate, one boy snapped a fat rubber band at another, which started a wrestling match.

"Knock it off," called the man. "At this rate, the campground will be closed by the time we get there."

They must be homeschooled. That, or their private school had started Christmas break early.

The boys grudgingly broke up and plodded ahead obediently, but it wasn't ten seconds before one kid pulled the rubber band out again, and all three grappled for control of it.

Rebecca sighed and kept moving. As long as they didn't knock anything over, it wasn't her problem. She had to make sure everything was under control at the front before the next wave of shoppers arrived.

She passed the bait and tackle aisle. The tops of fishing poles jutted above the uppermost shelves. Across the aisle from the poles, metal hooks stuffed with bagged lures filled a pegboard.

The sporting goods counter—unmanned—sat nearby. Paul was probably in the parking lot smoking. Not four feet from the desk, a red fire extinguisher was strapped to a support beam that reached all the way to the ceiling. Somebody had partially unlatched the clamp holding the extinguisher in place.

Her handheld buzzed. A cashier needed pennies.

Paul could fix the extinguisher clamp when he got back from break.

Jumbled footsteps clattered behind her. The three boys and the man supervising them—probably dad to at least one of the kids—passed the fishing poles and lures.

One boy stopped, digging curious fingers into a box of bagged fishing hooks. He picked up one package and fiddled with a hook, trying to poke holes in the bag.

"Tyler, put that back. We're not here for—"

A loud clank and hiss, followed by a scream, cut him off.

Fire extinguisher fumes billowed into a cloud of white and obscured the sporting goods desk.

Rebecca pulled her vest over her nose and mouth even as the airborne chemicals made her eyes water. She held back a cough. The fumes scratched her airway. She had to get out of here and find a manager.

Five or six other shoppers ran out of the fog, coughing into hands, sleeves, or shirt collars.

Slowly dissipating fog hid the boy who'd knocked over the extinguisher.

"Jordan!" The man coughed as he waded through curtains of thickened air, waving it away with wide, two-armed sweeps.

Rebecca snagged the walkie from her vest pocket and coughed a half dozen times before hitting the talk button. "Management to—Sporting Goods. Code White—knocked over—fire extinguisher." She coughed hard into her elbow. "A guy and—three kids—are over here."

Calling a code was the fastest way to get management to do anything, and, sure enough, half a minute later, the store manager and one assistant thundered past, headed straight into the fogged-over back corner of the building.

By the time Rebecca made it to the front end, the irritation in her eyes had eased, and she'd stopped hacking. Hopefully the guy and those kids didn't have any complications. Guilt wormed through her stomach. She should have locked the fire extinguisher as soon as she'd seen it wasn't secured properly. Now, she had to live with the consequences of not acting.

Ironic. The whole reason she'd been run out of Newton Hill was because she *had* acted. Spoken up, actually. When the pastor had made it clear he'd be the final word on all church decisions, alarms had gone off for her. She'd tried to say something about it, broach the subject as cautiously as possible. But instead of giving her the civil conversation she'd asked for, he had resorted to character assassination.

Rebecca had thought about the whole ordeal far too much these past few months. Pushing away thoughts of Newton Hill, she hurried to the front-end supervisor's area and grabbed a bottle of store-use water from the stash they kept under the counter. The small, closed-in section featured neck-high metal walls and a swinging gate. It wouldn't keep out anyone determined to snoop, but it provided an out-of-sight nook to keep schedules, a few personal items, and any out-of-date cigarettes they hadn't ferried to the back of the store for disposal yet.

Her throat itched. Once she'd gulped half a bottle of water, though, the lingering tickle disappeared.

Her handheld buzzed multiple times. Four notifications sent from the same place. Self-check.

She hiked to the far end of the registers.

"Yes, Natasha?" She did her best to keep her tone even as the twenty-something girl poised to tap yet another code into her register's keypad.

"I haven't been to break yet, and I got here almost two *hours* ago. Erica just went to break, and I came in before she did."

Maybe by five minutes.

Would this kid ever quit complaining? She'd disappeared for two weeks last month, only to turn up again with vague excuses and a wild story involving the police. Rebecca might have believed Natasha if she hadn't pulled the same thing at New Year's and then again after Easter. HR should have terminated her ages ago.

"That's because Erica is leaving in two hours, and you're here for a full shift," Rebecca said. "You can go as soon as someone else clocks in."

"But *when*?" Natasha whined.

Rebecca held back a smart retort and checked the schedule on her handheld instead. "Ten minutes." She started back toward the supervisor's station. "And don't make me page you four times before you come back. You're covering Josiah's lunch again. I'm not making him wait an extra two hours like he did Monday." She couldn't fix whatever problems Josiah had with his church members, but she could make his work day a bit smoother.

Natasha muttered something under her breath.

"What was that?" Rebecca said.

The girl's sigh was heavy enough to tip over a full dump truck. "Nothing."

Lunch couldn't arrive quickly enough. Rebecca happily handed the walkie off to Luca, the second-shift supervisor, and hurried through thickening crowds of customers. She passed Sporting Goods, where a thin veil of fog still clung to the air. It was enough to make her blink a few times, but not to induce coughing.

Paul stood behind the desk, open bag of Dill Pickle Lays in hand as he stared into a cardboard box brimming with mixed fishing lures. A paper taped to the box read, "Sort and restock ASAP." Today's date was underlined and circled beneath the note. Paul picked out a single lure, wiped oily fingers on his pants, and scanned the UPC with his handheld. After a few seconds, he set the lure aside, ate another chip, and repeated the process.

Hopefully, whoever wanted those lures put away wasn't counting on Paul getting done before Easter.

After wading through a few clogged toy aisles, she reached the break room. The kid who'd microwaved those gross enchiladas loitered in the corner with two other teenage guys. Thankfully, the few remaining open chairs weren't anywhere near them. She didn't have time for their nonsense right now.

Before anyone could take the closest open chair, Rebecca claimed it with an unopened bottled water.

Chapter 11

When Rebecca got back to the registers, post-lunch shoppers scrambled through packed aisles. Near the door, two women grabbed wrapping paper tubes and glared at one another as if dancing reindeer and Santa eating gingerbread were worth war.

Just as Luca handed her the walkie, the unmistakeable screech of the fire alarms pealed through the building.

Rebecca turned to Luca. "Please, tell me that's a test." They really didn't need this right now.

"Not that I know of," he said.

Rebecca hit the talk button on the walkie. "Management?"

"What?" Nevaeh—one of the assistant managers—growled back.

"Should we head for the parking lot?"

The radio went silent for three long seconds before Nevaeh replied. "Yeah, tell everybody to go outside."

"We'll get things moving up here." Rebecca sighed as she pocketed the walkie. "Everybody, leave your carts where they are and head outside. Don't stop until you've reached the green parking spaces." She repeated the instructions at least twenty times as she walked the length of the front end. Luca did the same, directing people to the two front exits.

She swept along grousing adults, clueless kids, and a few older customers who seemed much too entertained by this inconvenience.

Within ten minutes, they'd cleared the registers.

When Rebecca made it to the green-lined parking spaces, she looked for Luca. He arrived seconds later, shooing a half-dozen customers in front of him. Together, she and her fellow supervisor counted the cashiers and other front-end employees to make sure everyone was accounted for.

The walkie crackled indistinctly.

"Repeat that?" Rebecca said.

"Fire Department's on its way," said Nevaeh.

Rebecca rubbed cold hands together, wishing she'd grabbed her coat from the supervisor's station before leaving the store. There was no going back in until the fire department said they could. But she wasn't the only one less than thrilled to be in the cold. Most everyone huddled next to someone else or stuffed hands in pockets.

Good thing it wasn't snowing. That would have made the frenzy even worse.

Three assistant managers straggled outside, followed by the store manager. The man held up a bullhorn. "We apologize, folks. Looks like it's going to be an hour or two before we're clear to go back in. We appreciate your patience."

Unhappy murmurs and an imaginative array of curses rippled through the pre-Christmas crowd. Over half the shoppers immediately got into vehicles and left. The others took refuge in their cars too but stuck around.

Rebecca stepped onto a curb. "Cashiers, customer service, greeters, and cart pushers." She waved over everyone she was responsible for. Once her dozen charges were assembled, she said, "If your shift is over, let me or Luca know before you leave."

Four cashiers, including Natasha, headed toward Luca.

"If you go and you aren't supposed to, I will *personally* make sure you get double absence points," Rebecca added.

Three of the four cashiers stopped. The one who was actually supposed to be clocking out headed for Luca.

"Feel free to wait in your cars until we get notified to go back in." She stepped off the curb, buried frozen fingers in her vest pockets, and headed for her Prius.

A fire truck rolled into the parking lot and stopped in front of the store.

"Think it's serious?" Josiah appeared beside her.

Rebecca jumped but quickly hid how thoroughly he'd startled her. How did he keep doing that? "Nah. It's not like the building's engulfed or anything. Probably some idiot pulled a fire alarm or threw a cigarette in the bathroom trash can."

"It's the invisible problems that can end up being the most dangerous," he said, hands also in his pockets.

"What is it with people being stupid this week?" The remark escaped before she could cage it. "Sorry. It's been . . . crazy lately." Not that he hadn't had a time of it too.

"I thought I saw you at church Wednesday night."

Rebecca froze. She could deny it. Or just up her pace. He didn't seem the type to follow her to her car. But she *had* decided to keep visiting Oak Grove for the moment. That meant learning how to steer Josiah, and everyone else at the church, away from sensitive questions. Might as well give it a test run. "Yeah. That was me." Maybe she could deflect. "Those guys who came up after the service weren't too happy with you."

Josiah's head dipped just enough to send his eyes toward a line of parked cars instead of the front of the store. "No, not especially. Change can be . . . difficult for everyone. Especially when it means giving up something really important to you.”

Rebecca stopped her slow stroll toward her car. She was well-acquainted with loss. But that wasn’t his business. “I heard about the whole thing with Shaw wanting his son to move back to Burnsville.”

“That, and Brother Shaw’s wife passed recently too. So, aside from his sister, he doesn’t have family nearby.”

“That’s not an excuse to bully people.” Her fingers curled into the lint lining her vest pockets.

“No. It’s not. But being part of a family means looking past the angry words to the heart of the problem.” Josiah slipped both hands into his pants pockets. “And being a pastor means caring for the people in my church, helping them wherever God enables me to.”

“Even if the person causing trouble doesn’t want help?” Rebecca curbed the bitterness in her voice, but not enough to completely hide it.

“God changes hearts, and the Holy Spirit prepares us for those changes little by little. Sometimes steps toward change are painful and difficult. But if we’re willing to listen to God’s leading, incredible things happen.”

“It sounds like you’re defending those guys from last night.”

A second fire truck rolled up behind the first. Then, an ambulance came in through the entrance across the parking lot. All lights and sirens remained off.

“Just like this place”—he tossed a glance toward the store—“each body of believers is made up of flawed, opinionated, and even stubborn men and women. God works on all of us throughout our whole lives. Some just take longer than is wise to see what He's teaching them. And God can use the worst of circumstances—and the most selfish of people—for His glory."

"Even if those people don't want you there?" she fired back.

Without missing a beat, Josiah replied, "Sometimes God makes it clear we need to go somewhere specific. At times, He even uses the prejudice and poisoned words of others to help us see our time in one place has ended." He nudged a pebble away with one black Sketcher.

His unblinking eyes fixed on the pavement, as if remembering something. He smiled softly. "I've been thinking about that since Wednesday. But I believe God sends us where we need to go. Maybe Essie and I will be here for twenty years. Or maybe we'll have to move on after a few weeks. Either way, this is where God brought us, and I can't believe that's coincidence." He looked straight at her. "What brought *you* to Oak Grove?"

Rebecca pulled her hands out of her pockets and crossed her arms. This was the question she'd been dreading.

The whole story pooled in her throat, ready to pour out in one bitter recitation. For a few seconds, the urge rose to tell Josiah everything. Then that day at her former pastor's house and all the awful rumors he'd spread about her came back with such clarity her stomach turned. How could she explain being lied about? Being demeaned by people she'd grown up with and thought she knew? She'd left the church she'd spent her entire life in—the place her parents were buried—all so she could escape the comments, sideways glances, and fake smiles when they caught her looking. But she'd also left to escape a dictatorial "pastor" who thought legitimate questions were grounds for alienation.

She could spend the next month defending herself to this man she'd met a week ago, but what good would it do?

"It's . . . a long, complicated story," she said. Each memory of her old church deepened her frown and pushed buried emotions into her throat.

"There's a time to leave a congregation," Josiah said, tone firm but understanding. "Sin is deceptive, moving in when and where we least expect it, blinding us and making us think we're accomplishing God's will when the truth is, we're just doing what we want. Taking time to listen to what God has to say is the only cure for that. I don't know what happened to you, but when a church refuses to listen to God, separating from it is often necessary."

A third fire truck arrived and a few dozen more customers left. Fewer people to deal with when they were finally allowed back inside.

"God knows what we need and who can help us heal and grow." Josiah scanned the parking lot, his gaze finally stopping on her. "Maybe I'm here to help Lincoln Shaw. Maybe I'm not. All I know is, this is the place God's put me, so this is where I'm staying until He moves me somewhere else."

She'd spent too long under the auspices of fellow Christians who considered her less than nobody. The idea of staying in the same church as them, even for one more Sunday, lit a fire in her gut. If she were him, she'd leave as soon as possible. "I'm going to my car." She turned her back to Josiah and made the rest of the trek to her Prius in silence.

Chapter 12

It was two very boring hours before the fire department declared employees could go back into the store.

Rebecca met Luca at the curb she'd made announcements from earlier. Together, they corralled the front-end employees inside and over to Self-check.

Power was off and, judging by similar previous incidents, wouldn't be back on for at least another couple hours. And that was assuming this was a false alarm. Since management never told them anything right away, the soonest they'd get definitive answers would be this evening—or even tomorrow morning.

Unreasonably small emergency lights, mounted along the walls, glared at her. That, combined with the store's sparse skylight panels, provided just enough light to read product labels.

Abandoned carts littered the registers. No telling how many of them housed meat, milk, yogurt, ice cream, or—the one she hated most—tilapia. Not to mention a host of other cold food that would need to be thrown away. At least all she had to do was gather it. The scanning out and disposing weren't her responsibility.

"Everyone, start sorting these carts. Bring freezer food, dairy, and meat to Customer Service. Everything else goes back to the sales floor," Rebecca said.

Josiah headed for the service desk, and one greeter grabbed a cart. Everyone else kept staring at Rebecca.

"Go on." She shooed them all toward the waiting carts. "This mess isn't going to clean itself up."

Natasha started toward a sparsely filled shopping cart, glanced at Rebecca, then changed trajectory and headed for the women's room.

"If you're not back in fifteen minutes, I'm coming to get you," Rebecca called after her. "And I'd better not find you in Lawn and Garden again, unless you're restocking."

The girl shot her an exasperated look before ducking into the restroom.

Sometimes, getting Natasha to actually work reminded Rebecca of shoving pills down Chelsea's throat. Doable. But not without a lot of whining.

Once everyone was on task—including a grudging Natasha—Rebecca said to Luca, "If you've got this, I'm going to walkie management and then head to the service desk."

"Yeah. All good." Luca tossed a head of lettuce into a cart holding four dozen green bananas and an overripe tomato. He'd assign a cashier to run produce items back to the floor once everything had been sorted.

Rebecca pulled out the radio and pressed the talk button. "Any updates on the power situation?"

When none of the managers replied after a full five count, Rebecca repeated her inquiry.

This time, Nevaeh responded. "Electrical fire in the back offices. Store won't be open again until tomorrow." That was both a relief and a disaster. No customers for the rest of the day would let them put everything away. But it also meant tomorrow would be crazier than a circus tent full of three-year-olds.

Luca grabbed a tub of Yoplait and tossed it into a second cart. Apparently, he didn't notice it was partially open until a strawberry wave splashed across the nearest register. Luca exclaimed something uncomplimentary about the yogurt's mother. Spewing a few other choice words, he hunted for paper towels and cleaner.

This was going to be a long afternoon.

Chapter 13

At 3:22 Rebecca and Josiah stowed the last cartful of spoiled dairy products in the dark, already-warming milk cooler. It was almost time for Josiah to clock out, and Rebecca was nearly half an hour over schedule, but at least they'd made a lot of progress.

Unfortunately, the roll-down door had been up when the power went out, and there wasn't a way to pull it shut.

"I'll get the service desk straightened up and then head out," Josiah said as he pushed through the dozen clear plastic panels that hung from the top of the door frame and separated the cooler from the rest of the back room.

Several of the eight-inch-wide panels slapped Rebecca on her way out.

The overlapping plastic panels reached nearly to the floor and would keep in some cool air, but there was no saving anything inside the fridge area. The temperature had to be in the upper 40s by now—high enough to compromise pretty much everything in here. The whole dairy section was nothing more than a staging area for Claims now. Tomorrow, all the spoiled food would be scanned, then composted, poured out, or thrown in the compactor.

"See you Sunday?" said Josiah.

Rebecca side-stepped the question. "You off tomorrow?"

Josiah nodded. "Helping Essie get ready for Sunday night."

"Think that many people will show up at your house after an evening service?" She headed for the front of the store.

Josiah walked beside her. "Free food is a tried-and-true motivator."

"Can't argue with that." Would this guy ever stop with the misplaced optimism?

"Feel free to come by the meet-and-greet. Essie would love to talk with you again. She told me you sat with her during Sunday school last week. Said it was nice not to be both new and alone. Our friends are all back in Georgia, and it's been hard—for both of us, but especially for her. Having someone close by who wasn't firing a thousand questions helped her a lot."

"All I did was sit there for an hour."

"Well, she appreciated it."

As they passed the grocery section, three cashiers snaked through the aisles, putting back canned goods and other non-perishables—hopefully in the correct places. But stockers would definitely be fishing Vienna Sausages and Chef Boyardee out of the green beans until well after Christmas.

"Thanks for the invite." She wouldn't be there, but he didn't need to know that. Her Sunday night plans included a cup of peppermint cocoa, a blanket, and a Kleenex box while she sat on the couch with Chelsea and watched *Klaus* on Netflix. She wasn't ready to step foot inside a pastor's house again. "Have a good weekend."

"You too." Josiah peeled off toward the service desk just before they reached Self-check.

Had he considered what might happen if Shaw and his friend decided to show up Sunday night?

Chapter 14

Saturday passed in a blur. Too many customers, not enough cashiers, and far too many frayed nerves. It was the same story every Christmas season. And somehow, not having Josiah there made the day just a bit more hectic. This past week, she'd gotten used to him handling the vast majority of the customer service hiccups without her intervention.

Today had been a hurricane, earthquake, and multi-car pileup all rolled into one. She and Luca had constantly gone back and forth to the service desk and the regular registers.

Breaks were an hour or more late, multiple scheduled cashiers didn't show up, and they couldn't turn around without someone asking, "How much is this?" Plus, Natasha had disappeared for two hours again.

By the time Rebecca clocked out and got into her car, she barely had the energy to drive out of the parking lot.

Once home, she trudged upstairs, changed into her pajamas, and flopped face-down onto her bed.

Chelsea, who'd been following her since she'd walked in the door, settled beside Rebecca atop the comforter. Her damp nose nudged Rebecca's arm, and her tail thumped against the mattress.

"I'm happy to see you too," Rebecca said. But the comforter muffled it, so even if Chelsea understood English, her words wouldn't have made much sense with the fabric stifling them.

She blindly raised a hand and searched for the dog's head. When her fingers found soft fur, she ran a hand down

Chelsea's back. With a heavy sigh, she turned her face to the side and opened her eyes. "It's been a long day, girl." She scratched Chelsea's ears. "What do you say we just hang out again tonight?"

The dog nosed her cheek, leaving a patch of wet.

Rebecca swiped her face dry. "Yeah, I like you too."

Before she changed her mind, Rebecca rolled over with a groan and set both feet on the floor. Her toes curled at the cold. Quickly, she slipped into the fluffy purple slippers her aunt had sent her last Christmas. Warm feet made any winter day better.

Chelsea bounded down the stairs ahead of her, stopping only once to glance back at Rebecca before diving the rest of the way down the steps. She stood at the bottom of the stairs, waiting, tail wagging.

"Suppose I should get you dinner and let you out first."

At the word "dinner," Chelsea turned an excited circle.

Two minutes later, the golden had her face shoved into her newly-filled dog bowl.

Chelsea scarfed down her food with more enthusiasm than Rebecca had possessed in twenty years. Once Chelsea finished, Rebecca unlocked the doggy door leading to the back yard, so the dog could come inside when she finished fertilizing the lawn.

Rebecca headed to the couch and settled onto flower-print cushions in pastel pink and blue. She draped a light pink blanket over her legs. Just before she clicked the TV on, her father's Bible, still sitting on the coffee table three feet in front of the couch, caught her eye.

How long had it been since she'd opened her own Bible outside of church?

She reached for the old leather-bound book. Her fingers brushed a thin layer of dust from one corner of it.

Disturbing this book after half a year of leaving it alone seemed wrong. Not that her father would have wanted her to keep his Bible closed. Right now, leaving it where it was made it seem like he'd be back for it. One day, she would come downstairs to find him on the couch, or in his chair, reading.

She gripped the worn spine and pulled the Bible into her lap.

Her dad had never been much for leaving papers or bookmarks in his Bible. The only marker he'd ever used was the plain red ribbon sewn into the top of the binding.

She opened to the last place her dad had read from, the day before the ambulance had ferried him to the hospital for the last time.

Paul's first letter to the Corinthians. He'd been nearly finished reading it. She flipped to the beginning of the book and skimmed a few chapters.

This church had more problems than her old one and Oak Grove combined. So many petty disagreements, dysfunctional people, and serious shortcomings. But Paul hadn't given up on them. He'd taken the time to write at least twice. And these weren't short letters. A one-page handwritten note took her the better part of an afternoon. How much time must Paul—even with the help of a scribe—have invested in these many pages?

She didn't know if she would have the fortitude to care about a group of people who were as messed up as the ones in the Corinthian church.

When she reached chapter thirteen, she stopped. This section had prompted countless sermons. Everyone wanted to talk about how amazing and resilient love was. But no one mentioned how hard it was to actually love *other people*. Especially ones who seemed to be on a mission to ruin her life.

She closed her dad's Bible and set it back in its spot atop the coffee table.

The church was supposed to act as a unit, helping one another and showing the truth of Christ to others. But how could that happen when Christians were tearing each other apart?

Back from her romp around the yard, Chelsea hopped onto the couch beside Rebecca, her favorite toy—a worn red elephant whose squeaker had long since died—in her mouth. She laid the toy in Rebecca's lap. Chelsea had done this several times since Rebecca's abrupt exit from her old church. She wasn't sure if it was the dog's way of trying to help, or if she just really wanted Rebecca to hold onto the scruffy old elephant.

"Thanks, girl." She scratched the dog's head and wished her parents were still there. She missed talking with them, asking advice.

TV remote in hand, her thumb hovered over the power button.

Tomorrow night was the Christmas get-together at the Hugheses' house. She'd almost changed her mind about not going, but cocoa and a movie with Chelsea sounded a lot more pleasant than hanging around strangers at a pastor's house.

Still . . . would an angry Lincoln Shaw turn up at the Hugheses' doorstep. And if he did, what then?

Chapter 15

Sunday dawned drearily. No rain today, but it was windy and just a hair under freezing.

When Rebecca arrived at Oak Grove, the parking lot was full.

She got out of her Prius, tucked her Bible case under one arm, and hurried inside.

When she slipped into the foyer, the congregation was already singing.

"He took my sins and my sorrows; He made them His very own."

Everyone was still seated, so Rebecca waited. She'd sneak in during prayer or if the congregation stood for something.

The hymn ended with the last chorus, "How marvelous! How wonderful is my Savior's love for me."

At the front, Josiah took his place behind the podium. "Do we believe that?"

The congregation grew silent.

"Do we believe God's love is wonderful?" Josiah said. "He loved us so much He sent His Son to take our place—to shed His own innocent blood for our sins. If He could love us that much, why can't we show our fellow Christians a little understanding?"

This time, uncomfortable shuffling and the whisper of bulletin pages interspersed moments of quiet.

"Satan wants the church to rip itself to pieces because if we're focused on ourselves, we aren't helping one another grow in Christlikeness. We aren't seeking to reconcile with fellow believers. We aren't using the gifts He's given us to build the church and reach the lost. We aren't serving the One who suffered, bled, and died for us. When we stop doing those things, we turn away God's blessing."

Rebecca's chilled hand gripped her Bible case harder. The mountain of unkind—even hate-filled—words from those at her former church crashed over her. At Newton Hill, she had tried for so long to just keep pushing through—keep going. But no one was willing to listen to her. They all thought they knew what was true, and there was no convincing them otherwise. Leaving that place had been the right choice.

"The most difficult things in life can be God's means of helping us grow," Josiah continued. "Not that it's God's will for us to suffer the consequences of others' sin. But He can use even those awful things to direct us to Him."

A series of small, square windows sat three quarters of the way up the foyer door. They afforded Rebecca glimpses of Josiah as he gripped the edges of the pulpit. Hard to tell from here if he still had bags under his eyes.

"There is no secret cure-all to right every injustice—no magical solution to mend broken relationships," Josiah said. "But we serve the God who makes all things possible. Let's invite Him to work in our midst today." He bowed his head.

Rebecca cracked the door open as many in the congregation quieted and bowed for prayer. This could be her chance to slip in without interrupting anything or being noticed.

Just before she opened the door wide enough to step through, four people got up and headed for the door she stood behind. They would run straight into her in about five seconds.

The ladies' room was just across the foyer. She might make it in without being seen. Or she could pretend to have just arrived. But that might take too long.

She opted for the ladies' room.

With only an instant to spare, she pushed through the restroom door.

And ran straight into Essie Hughes.

Chapter 16

The restroom door clunked shut behind Rebecca.

Two steps away stood Essie, a crumpled paper towel jammed against her nose. Her minimal mascara had smeared, leaving false shadows under her eyes. The fluorescent lights highlighted the gray in her hair and wrinkles on her hands.

Essie started to hide her face, but when she met Rebecca's eyes, she stopped.

Rebecca knew that look. She'd seen it in the mirror every day for too long.

There was no point asking if the other woman was okay. Instead, she reached into her purse and pulled out a travel-pack of Kleenex. "Softer than paper towels." She added a wry snort to the end of the sentence.

Essie took them with a strangled "Thank you" and threw away the over-used brown paper towel she'd been holding.

Out in the foyer, the front door closed with a faint thunk, just audible from inside the ladies' room. Those disgruntled few had left the building. Unfortunately, Shaw and his friend weren't among them. When Essie left the restroom, she'd have to walk into the sanctuary under the glares of that bully and his balding minion.

Turning the other cheek was great and all, but there was a time to stand up for yourself. Heat rushed to Rebecca's face. She'd stood up for something once and look where it had gotten her. Maybe it was better if the Hugheses just left.

Essie swiped her face dry and rubbed away smeared makeup.

"Why are you staying at this church?" The words burst out before Rebecca could stop them.

Essie tossed her mangled tissue in the trash. "Because that's what God's asked of us, for now."

This again. Josiah had said almost the same thing.

"But there are people here who would rather key your car than talk to you." She wanted to shake the woman, tell her clearly that she and her husband needed to leave, find someplace they wouldn't be cornered and yelled at for pretend grievances. A place where no one was trying to run them off.

Essie pulled another tissue out of the travel pack and laughed a little. "Well, our car's nothing to look at, anyway." She dried a few more tears. "Other people's attitudes and actions are their choice."

"That doesn't make it any easier to deal with." Rebecca crossed her arms as memories of her former church shouted for attention. "I don't get why you're sticking around." That had sounded too much like Shaw, so she added, "It would be a lot easier to just go. Let these people draft somebody they'll *all* be happy about. Maybe even get that guy's son, like he wanted."

"Sometimes leaving a church is what God wants us to do," Essie said before shutting the Kleenex pack and returning it to Rebecca.

Almost exactly what Josiah had told her in the parking lot Friday.

Despite Essie's glassed eyes and the slight red shading around them, she mustered a smile that subtly sparked in her eyes. "And sometimes, God asks us to walk through a trial for someone else's sake."

That was something her dad would have said. In fact, she could almost hear him saying it. The way he would draw out the "o" in "God," or how the "ia" in trial would blend together. Mom had always been on him about his Southern accent and pronouncing things clearly.

"God has taken my hand and led both Josiah and me through too much for us to stop believing Him now. And if the people who don't want us here decide to behave uncharitably, that's their decision."

"But what if they don't quit? What if they just make your lives miserable?" Like everyone at her old church had done to her.

"Then they do." Essie's words hit hard. "These are our brothers and sisters in Christ, but they aren't perfect. Each one has their own struggles and weak points. If they wrong me, by God's grace, I'll forgive them and keep going. As part of the Body of Christ, we're called to love and help one another, even when that's difficult."

"But how do you . . ." The words stuck to Rebecca's tongue. "How do you forgive someone who's upended your entire life?" She almost wished she hadn't asked it, hadn't betrayed to the other woman hints of just how deeply the people at Newton Hill had hurt her.

Essie laid a hand on Rebecca's arm. "By looking to God for strength to hold everything with an open hand."

"That doesn't fix what they did." Her fingers curled tighter around her Bible case.

"No, it doesn't," Essie said, seeming to understand they weren't talking about Shaw anymore.

She wanted to keep her questions unspoken. But something about Essie pulled the words out of Rebecca. "Then how do I forgive something that hasn't been fixed? Someone who doesn't care what they've done?"

Essie leaned against one light blue wall. Periwinkle and purple hydrangea print paper cut across the middle of each one, as if whoever applied it hadn't been tall enough to put it in its proper place, near the ceiling. "Even when people don't seek God's forgiveness, He is ready and more than willing to give it. That is where we must live—in a place of willingness, with a heart open to forgiveness. Perhaps those who wrong us never acknowledge what they've done. However, we can choose not to let their sin poison us. We can look to the eternal hope of Christ and live in what is, not what might have been."

With a rumbling whir, the heat kicked on. Pleasant warmth filled the chilly restroom.

Essie checked the clock above the dual sink. "I'd better go in." She tossed the second mangled Kleenex.

That was it? Forgiveness?

"Sit with me during Sunday School again?"

"Yeah. Sure." Rebecca stepped aside to let the other woman pass.

When the restroom door opened, then the door to the sanctuary, the final strains of "Trust and Obey" momentarily filtered in.

Once silence returned, Rebecca stepped over to one sink. The mirror ran the length of the wall behind both faucets and ended about a foot from the ceiling.

Essie's words smashed together in her mind. How could she—or anyone, for that matter—forgive a hateful person? A hateful *Christian*? Sure, the Bible said to reconcile with others. But saying and doing were far different things. Certainly, God didn't expect the Hugheses to attempt to befriend Shaw and his puppet.

Didn't expect her to forgive her former pastor.

Plus, even if Josiah and Essie got past this whole debacle, nothing guaranteed those two angry old men wouldn't turn on the Hugheses again in the future.

She couldn't think about this right now.

Her haphazard bun had lost a handful of strands between home and here. Not that tucking them back into place would do much good. They'd just escape again.

She set her Bible and coffee beside the sink before pulling her hair clip free. A couple fluffs for volume, and walnut brown waves hid just enough of her rounded face to give the illusion of a jaw line.

The clock read fifteen after. If she didn't go in now, she'd miss the transition to Sunday School.

As Essie's words kept tumbling through her mind, she cracked open the restroom door.

Chapter 17

The rustle of people leaving pews and the opening bars of "Moment by Moment" mixed together.

Rebecca slipped into the foyer, then the sanctuary, without anyone accosting her. Thankfully, Josiah was nowhere in sight. Essie, however, still sat near the front. "You wanna head back?" Rebecca said when she reached Essie's pew.

A cluster of four women filed past, smiling pleasantly. Two waved at Essie and kept walking.

Jillian was on the other side of the room with her brother, Lincoln Shaw and the old man who'd fussed at Josiah the other night. Shaw and Jillian were deep in conversation.

"Just need my Bible." Essie picked up a bound, purple volume. It looked new. Brand new, in fact.

"Didn't you have a different one last time?"

Essie nodded as she walked with Rebecca out of the sanctuary, toward the ladies' Sunday School room. "I keep the old one at home on my nightstand for morning devotions now."

"Why the switch?" Rebecca said as they neared the classroom door.

"It was time for a fresh start."

That remained to be seen.

Once they'd claimed chairs in the back corner of the Sunday School room, a few other ladies sat near them. Some spoke to Essie; one even held a brief exchange with Rebecca.

Jillian hadn't come in yet.

When Sunday School finally started, the well-meaning chatter—thankfully—petered out.

"Ladies, please turn with me to Romans 12." The eighty-something woman at the front of the class—the same one who'd taught last week—flipped through a large-print Bible and peered over her glasses at the Scripture passage.

Rustling pages gradually replaced chatter before the woman teaching read several verses near the beginning of the chapter.

Rebecca stole a glance at Essie. Hopefully, today, there wouldn't be any surprises, like there'd been after Sunday School last week. Getting ambushed by an angry Lincoln Shaw wasn't an experience she'd wish on anybody—much less someone she sort of liked.

Chapter 18

Upon dismissal, most of the women flooded out, staying in groups. A few stragglers checked phones or rummaged through purses.

Jillian had never come to class. Maybe she and her brother were working things out. That could be good. Shaw might quit hassling the Hugheses.

Rebecca waited for Essie to get up before leaving her seat.

During the walk back to the auditorium, she kept expecting Shaw's angry bellow, or that other old guy—Bob something—to appear with a scowl and petty reprimand.

Essie seemed to expect a confrontation too. Her slightly pinched brows, eyes on the floor, and lips rolled inward just enough to create a straight line gave her away. Judging by the woman's deliberately measured breaths, she probably also had enough anxious butterflies to carry away a pickup truck.

The ladies ahead of Rebecca and Essie pushed through a set of swinging wooden doors and into the sanctuary. They followed a second or two behind.

Mostly women and kids stood around talking or sat in pews. A few of the younger children chased each other until someone scolded them for running in the sanctuary. Deterred, but not subdued, the kids crammed into one half of a pew and scrounged through a reusable shopping bag. They pulled out paper, colored pencils, and blunted crayons.

"My house is gonna be so big it has to go on *two* papers," a boy announced as he scrawled indecipherable lines and shapes.

"Well, mine's gonna need three," said a girl.

The boy—apparently not fond of being one-upped—stuck out his tongue at her. "Then I'm using four."

"Hey, I wanted the blue pencil!" A third kid broke in.

"You can use a crayon," said the boy, who now had his stated four pieces of paper laid out in the pew beside him.

"But I want the pencil!" Kid Three swiped for it, missing the pencil and smacking Kid One in the face.

A thirty-something woman swooped in. "Jesse, Peter, what have I told you about fighting in church?"

They needed to be more concerned about the *adults* fighting.

Rebecca and Essie made it past the squabbling kids and headed for Essie's preferred pew.

Jillian was still nowhere to be seen.

No pianist yet, either. Not even the song leader had made it back.

Six men—none of them Josiah—filtered into the auditorium.

"Will you sit with me during the service?" Essie gripped her Bible hard enough to dig her nails into the cover.

All too recently, Rebecca had needed a friend and not had one. "Sure."

She slipped into the pew right after Essie did, just as the pianist shuffled in. Without ceremony, he sat on the piano bench and opened the dark green hymnal. His fingers glided across worn keys in a show of admirable coordination.

"'Is Your All on the Altar?'" Essie named the song half an instant before Rebecca recognized it.

She expected the other woman to comment further, but Essie only smiled softly and kept her eyes focused on the pew in front of them.

More men arrived in ones and twos over the next few minutes. Most wore pensive expressions, and many tossed over-the-shoulder glances.

This was starting to look too much like last week. At least this time, if any disgruntled attendees decided to start something, Josiah would be the only immediate victim of their harassment.

Every time the swinging doors at the left front of the auditorium opened, Essie's gaze flickered that way.

"I'm sure everyone will be back in a minute," Rebecca said.

Essie nodded, but the subtle wrinkles between her eyebrows lingered.

The pianist had flipped several pages to "At the Cross," then "Will Jesus Find Us Watching," followed by "When I Can Read My Title Clear" by the time Quinton arrived.

Still no Josiah.

"Everyone, please find your seats and turn to four twenty-seven." Quinton grabbed a hymnal. "Four twenty-seven. 'I Know Whom I Have Believed.'" His voice carried over the shifting congregation.

Gaps between several seated family members meant people were still missing.

Rebecca opened a hymnal and held it up so Essie could share with her.

The first three verses passed quickly. When they started the fourth, the door to the Sunday School wing swung open, and Josiah stepped through. Alone.

Chapter 19

Rebecca absently sang the last chorus of the hymn as Josiah found a seat in the front row of the farthest section of pews.

"But 'I know whom I have believed,

And am persuaded that He is able

To keep that which I've committed

Unto Him against that day.'"

At least Josiah hadn't brought an angry mob with him. That would have been worst-case scenario. But his solitary entrance was impossible to interpret. Especially since multiple members of the congregation were still missing. Had several people taken Shaw's side and left? That didn't make sense if their families were still here.

The moment the song ended, Josiah stood and ascended the platform's four steps.

Quinton was checking a quarter sheet of paper—order of service, probably—and started when Josiah reached the pulpit.

The song leader cupped a hand over the microphone, but it didn't completely mask his next words. "I didn't know if you'd be back. After—"

So, something *had* happened during Sunday School. And by Quinton's tone, it hadn't been good.

The urge to reassure Essie piled in Rebecca's throat, but she kept her words caged behind clenched teeth. Not because she didn't want to comfort Essie. But because she didn't want to reveal any more of her own ordeal than she already had. The less she divulged, the better.

Josiah spoke more quietly than Quinton, which kept the mic from picking him up.

Quinton stepped aside, finger tucked between hymnal pages as Josiah replaced him at the pulpit.

"Minutes ago, just after the Sunday School hour ended, Brother Reinhart suffered a cardiac event."

That was Shaw's friend, the same guy who'd practically accosted Josiah on Wednesday.

A collective gasp filled the room.

Rebecca held in surprise too.

Josiah continued, cutting through a sea of murmurs. "We're very blessed to have two doctors and a paramedic in our congregation, and they're taking care of Bob until Emergency Services arrives."

She recognized the same even tone he'd used with upset customers several times these past two weeks. The calm voice, passive but clear sentences, and the unmistakeable sense that he actually cared infused every word.

If only her former pastor had possessed a tenth of Josiah's genuineness.

"There probably won't be sirens once they get past the intersection up the street," he continued, "but the dedicated EMTs of Burnsville will arrive any minute. Two deacons and Brother Shaw will be heading to the hospital to take care of whatever they can until family arrives." He bowed his head. "Lord, we bring to you our brother in Christ, Bob Reinhart."

How could he pray for that man's well-being? On top of that, how could he not be just the slightest bit relieved to be rid of his harassers for a while? If it were her former pastor they'd called EMS for, she'd have been sorely tempted to take satisfaction in the situation.

But Josiah's prayer never faltered. "You know his needs better than any of us. Guide his doctors and give peace to his family. It's in the name of Jesus we pray this. Amen."

Echoing Amens rippled through the congregation an instant before the wail of approaching sirens pierced the auditorium. Seconds later, they went silent.

Josiah left the pulpit and headed down the center aisle, straight toward the door to the foyer, passing Essie and Rebecca, without looking at them or anyone else. He grabbed doorstops and wedged them into place to keep both entryway doors open.

Rebecca leaned into the aisle. Two men were already holding open the wide glass doors leading outside.

Red lights flashed. The ambulance backed as close to the doors as possible. Two EMTs, both men, rolled in a gurney. Had they been called to churches often?

Hopefully the church members stayed where they were, out of the way.

Josiah led the EMTs out of the sanctuary and into the Sunday School wing.

Heavy silence filled the room. Even the kids fighting over colored pencils went quiet during the ninety seconds it took for the emergency responders to return, this time with an old man in tow. Even with an oxygen mask covering part of his face, Rebecca recognized the white hair and poorly executed combover—now out of place. Definitely Shaw's friend from the other night.

Served him right for his juvenile tirade.

The instant the thought flickered into being, she snuffed it. How could she even consider celebrating a heart attack?

Remorse pooled in Rebecca's gut.

Two more men, probably the aforementioned deacons, hurried after the emergency services guys. Lincoln Shaw followed them, face grim. Jillian trailed close behind. She must've been with her brother during Sunday School.

Once the paramedics, deacons, Shaw, and Jillian cleared the foyer, Josiah and the men holding the front doors shut the entrance and removed both doorstops.

The wail of sirens resumed but quickly faded as the ambulance left the parking lot.

With measured strides, Josiah crossed the distance from door to pulpit and addressed a still-stunned congregation. "Let's all keep Brother Reinhart in prayer, especially throughout the morning service."

Quinton, standing near the piano, hadn't budged an inch since the EMTs had arrived.

"We'll abbreviate singing, for the sake of time." Josiah nodded to Quinton, but the song leader didn't respond. "Ushers, if you'll come for the offering."

As the pianist began a shaky arrangement of "God's Refining Fire"—a song Rebecca loved but hadn't heard much in recent years—Josiah retreated from the pulpit and came alongside Quinton. He whispered inaudibly to the song leader before laying a firm, but not stern, hand on his shoulder and accompanying him to the edge of the platform.

In that moment, Josiah reminded Rebecca of her father. He'd been calm under stress too.

Quinton descended the four steps alone and made it back to his seat, still gripping the hymnal in one trembling hand. He spoke softly to his wife. His voice carried poorly, and the volume of the piano drowned even more of his words, but

Rebecca caught enough to understand. ". . . just never seen . . . before."

Maybe Oak Grove hadn't had an incident like this. At least, not recently. Not surprising. In her thirty-two years at her former church, she'd never seen a member rushed out on a gurney either. Not that the sight in general shocked her. At Durham's, EMS appearances occurred at least once a month. Multiple times during the summer, if they got too many tourists who didn't know how to stay hydrated.

When the ushers sat, the pianist headed for his pew, leaving the new pastor to fill the ensuing silence.

Chapter 20

Just after four o'clock Sunday afternoon, Rebecca sat on the couch with Chelsea. The dog's head draped over Rebecca's leg. Chelsea's eyes remained closed as Rebecca scratched the hard-to-reach ring of fur hiding under the golden's neon-pink collar.

Outside, it was warmer than Rebecca thought it would be. Sixty degrees, according to her phone.

Evening service at Oak Grove started at six. She hadn't planned to go tonight. But the forecast said temps wouldn't drop below fifty until almost eight. No snow or rain. A bit windy, but that wouldn't matter inside.

The box of Swiss Miss in the top kitchen cabinet called to her. It would be so nice to just stay in, watch her movie, chase marshmallows around a mug, and wear those idiotic Sasquatch slippers. Scuba gear was easier to walk in. But the slippers were so comfortable, Rebecca didn't care.

Her phone buzzed twice. An app notification. She dismissed it, and the time—4:05— hovered at the top of the screen. She'd need to start getting ready for the evening service soon. If she was going to attend.

The nearest blanket, crushed between Chelsea and the back of the couch, would be pleasantly warm by now. If she dug it out, she could spend the next few hours perfectly toasty. No wondering about other people's drama.

After the morning service, Essie had thanked Rebecca for sitting with her. Before Josiah headed her way though, Rebecca had made an excuse about having to get back home to feed the dog. Her social battery had died sometime Tuesday. Probably between listening to the guy with the goat and the woman who wouldn't stop asking her the aisle number for dryer sheets. But especially after this morning's incident, she had to know if Shaw would make an appearance at the Hugheses' tonight. And what he'd do if he *did* show.

Curiosity won, and with a sigh she patted Chelsea on the head. "Sorry girl. I've gotta get up."

Chelsea responded to "up" by hopping off the couch. Then, she trailed Rebecca upstairs and in and out of the bathroom for the next hour.

This would be Rebecca's first evening service at Oak Grove. It wasn't likely to be much different from the morning and mid-week services. They had their share of drama—more than Rebecca cared for—but that was it. Today's EMS-related incident and Shaw's antics aside, Oak Grove had proven fairly tame on the crazy scale, so far.

Rebecca finished blow drying damp curls. She attempted to put her hair up, but after twisting unruly ringlets four different ways, she left it down.

She unlocked the doggy-door so Chelsea could run around the fenced back yard for a few minutes before coming back in.

The clock said she had just enough time to make the service without being early or late. Perfect. Standing around talking was the last thing she wanted to do, anyway.

"Bye, girl." She gave Chelsea one last ear scratch. "Be back in a couple hours."

Bible in hand, light sweater on, and purse slung over one shoulder, she locked the front door.

Chapter 21

It was ten till when the service let out. Rebecca hadn't expected Josiah to cut it short, but she wouldn't complain. The last thing he'd said to the congregation was, "Our address is in the bulletin. We'll see all of you in a little while."

As people filed past her, she considered heading home. The last time she'd stepped foot inside a pastor's house had been uniquely disastrous. Just thinking about it made the back of her legs too tight and the overhead lights ten degrees warmer. The memory of her former pastor's enraged face loomed in her mind.

She couldn't do this. Not even out of curiosity. She headed for the foyer.

Ten feet from her goal, three men and two college guys flooded out of a nearby pew, clogging the center aisle.

Alternate routes to the door would take her past or through multiple other groups of strangers.

She'd never seen this many people at church on a Sunday night. Might be the Christmas-and-Easter people checking off their annual holiday attendance requirement a little early. Or, maybe Josiah's invitation to an after-church gathering had prompted more interest than anyone anticipated.

Whatever had brought them, they were dreadfully in the way. The filled aisle and populated pews reminded Rebecca too much of the mob who always waited until the morning of July Fourth to buy hotdog buns.

At least she didn't have to referee this particular crowd.

Rebecca faced the pulpit and squeezed past two women. There had to be other exits in this place. That was basic fire safety.

Several conversation snippets broke through the din as she headed for the door leading into the Sunday School wing.

". . . house is like?"

"Can you believe he said . . ."

". . . think happened . . . other church?"

"Hope they have Dr. Pepper."

Gossip and idle chatter. Two things she got more than enough of at Durham's.

Rebecca shouldered through the door leading to a classroom-filled hall. With sunset long gone, the overhead fluorescent lights cast the hall in a stark blue-white. They buzzed just loudly enough to survive the clamor of parents retrieving their kids from the nursery, half-way down the hall.

The bright red glow of an Exit sign a hundred feet ahead pulled her past the nursery just as a young couple stepped out, shepherding two identical little boys who couldn't have been older than three.

As she passed the ladies' Sunday School room, rustling pages and the creak of a folding chair stopped her. Except for the few who'd already made it to the parking lot, she'd thought everyone was either in the sanctuary or wrangling little kids.

Maybe it was the woman who taught the ladies' class getting in early lesson-prep before the week started.

But instead of the white-headed teacher, Essie sat at a tiny desk nestled into the far corner—probably borrowed from one of the other classrooms. With Bible open and head leaning on folded hands, Essie reminded Rebecca of a painting she'd seen once. Something about bread or being grateful.

The other woman leaned further over her open Bible.

Behind Rebecca, parents continued to pick up children. During the half-second lulls between screaming toddlers and wailing infants, the low, taut whisper of Essie's prayers bobbed across the vacant room.

Too many voices made it impossible to discern Essie's words, but by the woman's shaking shoulders and disregard for the cacophony in the hallway, whatever troubled her must be serious.

With quiet precision, Rebecca removed the wooden wedge holding the door open. She set it just inside the classroom and eased the door shut, blocking at least some of the noise and giving Essie more privacy.

Finally, she made it to the exit. She popped the door open. And nearly fell as she stepped down a full four inches to the sidewalk below. They really needed a Caution sign here. No wonder the paramedics hadn't used this entrance.

After regaining her footing, Rebecca ventured into the parking lot. Another group of four—two men and two women—talked a few feet away. But at least they weren't blocking her path.

"You're all welcome to come by tonight, along with everyone else."

The words stopped her just as the exit door thumped shut. Josiah was out here.

Now she wished she'd tried getting past the crowds inside. At least then she could have circled around the front of the building—stayed out of Josiah's line of sight. Avoided another invitation. There was no good way to explain that she'd intended to come, but when faced with actually doing it, she just couldn't.

A solid brick wall blocked her path to the left for at least a hundred feet. To the right, a patch of trees barred the way. Unless she wanted to wade through decomposing leaves or risk slipping on a mound of sweetgum balls, there wasn't another way out of this. Plus, heading back inside would look suspicious now. She had to move forward.

Best to keep walking and not draw attention to herself. Maybe, if she kept her head down and pace even, no one would see her. She'd successfully avoided customers that way for years.

Her Prius wasn't far. Maybe ten cars down the second parking row. She had a good chance of making it past Josiah's group undetected.

With silent steps, she started toward her car.

Chapter 22

Rebecca drew even with the man directly across from Josiah.

". . . doing all right, though," the man said. "Bob has always been stubborn about doctors."

They were talking about Shaw's friend—the guy who'd collapsed this morning. That was a conversation she'd much rather stay out of.

"Dad doesn't talk about his health either," said a woman—Bob's daughter, or maybe daughter-in-law. "We didn't know he was having trouble until you called us. I'm so sorry this happened. And on your second Sunday here, too."

Rebecca was nearly free. Only two dozen more steps, and obscurity would be hers. She could go home and watch her movie with Chelsea in peace. No belligerent church members. No memories she'd rather lock away. Just cocoa, a TV, and a sleepy golden retriever.

"It's all right," Josiah said. "I'm glad we were able to help him until EMS arrived."

"That must've been some way to start the morning service," said the man Rebecca didn't know.

This group didn't seem the type to yell across a parking lot. She just needed enough distance to make calling her back socially awkward. After that, if they saw her, it wouldn't matter.

"It's not the craziest thing I've dealt with," Josiah said.

He wasn't kidding. Flashbacks of last week's rubber chicken bandit came to mind. Some guy had wiped out

Durham's dog toy bin just after the store opened. That night, third shift had found all the missing toys—except the rubber chickens—jammed into the empty space behind six shelves of men's deodorant. They still didn't know if the chickens were hiding somewhere in the store, or if the guy had walked out with all thirty-six of them. Odds were, they'd never see those chickens again. The stashed dog toys had wound up at customer service, but not before being inexplicably coated in flour and more dust bunnies than any sane person would spend time counting.

"Rebecca can tell you more stories than I can. She's my supervisor at my day job."

All three people Josiah was talking with looked her way at the same time.

Rebecca's gut hit the pavement.

Her Prius's dented roof glinted beneath the streetlight less than thirty feet away. If she bolted now, she'd be safely inside in seconds. But the thought of strangers—or acquaintances, in Josiah's case—staring at her as she floored it out of the parking lot held her in place.

"Oh, hey." The woman who hadn't spoken yet waved. It was Jillian. "Nice to see you again. I didn't know you worked with Pastor Hughes." She kept a pleasant smile in place, but awkwardness tinged her words. After all, the last time they'd spoken, Jillian had been confessing her brother's personal problems. "This is Bob's daughter Linda and her husband Mark." She indicated the couple.

"So, what's it like being your pastor's boss?" said Mark.

The words, "He's not my pastor," tried to leap from her mouth. She twisted her tongue to hold them in and pasted on her customer service face. "He always does a good job."

"Where do you work?" Jillian said.

At least it wasn't a question about church.

"Durham's, out on 8th and Ridgecrest," supplied Josiah.

"The one that had the fire?" Linda's brows shot up until they disappeared beneath dark brown bangs.

Rebecca hoped her stomach would yoyo back to where it belonged instead of hanging out by her shoes. Not to mention her heart, which seemed to think she was on pace to win a hundred-yard dash. "It wasn't much of a fire," she said. "Old wires in a back office got to smoldering." At least, that's what management had told everyone yesterday. "It wasn't like the building went up in flames."

"Did you have to use a fire extinguisher?" Linda said—clearly having missed Rebecca's previous statement.

"No. Just made sure everyone in the checkout area got to the front door all right." Hopefully this wouldn't start a long line of ill-informed questions she'd have to answer straight-faced. At least no one seemed to notice the front of her coat vibrating with each slam of her pulse. This was the first time she'd been trapped in a conversation with church people since the incident at her old pastor's house. She could just leave. Walk away and let them wonder about her. But her shoes were glued to the pavement.

Thankfully, before Linda could ask anything else, her husband said, "Looks like you folks have quite the emergency crew in place. Two doctors—including Jill—a paramedic, a Durham's supervisor, and you." He nodded to Josiah, mercifully shifting some attention off Rebecca. "I'm glad my father-in-law was in such good hands today. If he'd been at home, there's no telling how long it would've taken for someone to find, much less help, him."

"There's something to be said for good old-fashioned grit, though," Josiah said. "When I got to the hospital around one, Brother Bob was already in a room, sitting up in bed."

With all eyes off her, Rebecca's stomach had made it up to her knees.

Why hadn't Josiah mentioned his run-in with Reinhart a few days ago? Was he really not going to bring up how awfully the man had treated him Wednesday night?

"Dad always was one to defy doctors' expectations. If he's not back in church next Sunday, I'll be shocked." For all Linda's talking about her father getting better, the shimmer of unshed tears in the woman's eyes said she was still worried. Probably always would be now—at least a little. Rebecca understood that. Heart-attacks changed everyone involved, not just the people who had them. Maybe Josiah hoped this would change Reinhart for the better.

Her stomach floated back into place. Finally. But the buttons on her coat still shook a tad more than normal.

If Bob's daughter and son-in-law were at Oak Grove tonight for the evening service, they must live within a couple hours of the church. Whether they'd head home tonight or stick around a few days was hard to say.

Rebecca eased toward her car, more than ready to slip away from this conversation.

"You're welcome to drop by along with everyone else tonight." Josiah nodded to Mark and Linda.

That was definitely her cue to get out of here.

"We'd love to talk with you more," said Mark. "With Dad Reinhart getting up there in years, and now . . . the heart attack . . . we're thinking about moving back to Burnsville. Which means we'll need a church home. Since Bob already goes here, that'll make things easier."

"I'd be happy to answer any questions, but depending on who shows up tonight, I might not be able to get to all of them," Josiah said. "Speaking of"—he checked his phone—"it's almost ten after. Essie and I need to get back to the house. See you there."

The group dispersed. Jillian glanced at Rebecca twice on her way to a black truck, but Mark and Linda never looked back.

Rebecca had just turned away from Josiah when he said, "You're more than welcome, too."

"I know." He'd only invited her three times. And he'd almost persuaded her. If only they'd had it at the church instead of their house. "Not really my thing."

Her heart was sprinting down a track again.

The face of her former pastor replaced carefully curated thoughts of marshmallows and fuzzy slippers. Last time she'd set foot in a pastor's house, she'd been called there under false pretenses. Expecting to discuss her father's upcoming funeral, she'd been shocked when the pastor had instead told her that disagreeing with him about matters of church hierarchy wasn't appropriate behavior for a member.

She remembered that moment with crystalline clarity. The way his mouth had pulled into a tight line. The red creeping up his neck and flushing his face. When she'd looked him in the eye instead of cowering, it had only made him angrier. She recalled the instant his hand had curled into a shaking fist, and he'd shoved a nearly overextended finger in her face. He'd told her never to contradict him again.

She'd left his house without saying a word about her dad's funeral. A headache had prompted nausea, and she'd had the deep desire to never see gray carpet—or the inside of a pastor's house—again.

That next Sunday was when the rumors had started. People saying she'd gone to the pastor's house for less-than-savory reasons. She knew who'd started it. The timing was too convenient to have been anyone except the pastor. And the speed at which it spread through the whole church had stunned her.

But that man was nothing like Josiah Hughes. At least, not the Josiah she'd seen so far. People tended to act differently in their own homes, though. What if tonight wasn't just her chance to see if Shaw showed out? What if it was also her opportunity to see if the Hugheses were as genuine as they seemed?

"But I guess I can swing by for a few minutes," Rebecca said, despite every muscle contracting as if she'd been sealed in a fully collapsed vacuum bag.

"Great." Josiah smiled. "Hopefully no one's already waiting at the house. I just need to find my wife, and we'll head home. Have you seen—"

"She's in the women's Sunday School room," Rebecca supplied.

"Thanks." Josiah excused himself and re-entered the building through the door she had used minutes ago. Unlike her though, the unmarked step didn't trip him.

Chapter 23

Rebecca was glad she'd tucked a bulletin into her Bible last week. Otherwise, she'd never have found the Hugheses' neighborhood. As it was, she'd wound up on a windy back road, circled the subdivision twice before finding an entrance, and had to wait for four college kids to carry a couch and two TVs across the narrow residential street a couple blocks over.

When she pulled up to the house, at least ten cars filled the driveway and parts of the front lawn. There could have been more around back, too.

She parked by the curb, far enough out of the way that she could leave easily whenever she liked.

The house was humbler than expected, a single-story home on a half-acre. No garage. Newly placed pave stones cut a curved path across short grass, browned by winter's fluctuating temperatures. Deep-green vinyl siding and white-trimmed windows gave the place a woodsy feel.

Two women—both at least ten years Rebecca's senior—stepped out of a silver Pontiac and approached the Hugheses' front door. Three knocks earned them immediate entrance.

If Essie was near the door, Rebecca didn't want the other woman to see her. Not that she minded talking with Essie, but tonight required invisibility—the kind she'd failed to employ earlier, while sneaking past Josiah, Jillian, and the other two.

She made it to the door—green with white trim, just like the house. A Christmas wreath with red and gold ornaments, and a cross situated in the center, hung above and to the left of the aged doorknob.

Under an old doorbell button hung a small but unmissable sign, "Please knock."

Entering someone's home without being let in sent a butterfly skittering up her throat. But there was no way she'd be knocking tonight. Not if she wanted to remain unseen.

As she stepped inside, she discovered, instead of carpet, hardwood floors. They made the entire house seem warmer.

The cramped entryway housed a pile of kid-sized shoes, two umbrellas, and a dozen light sweaters and jackets.

A short hall opened into a medium-sized living room, complete with couch, loveseat, fireplace, and an old wooden cabinet—closed—that could have been an entertainment center from thirty years ago.

Before anyone stopped her to talk, Rebecca slipped past a six-foot-something man. Arriving at the refreshment table, she flipped the tab on an insulated drink dispenser labeled "Hot Cocoa" and retreated to the room's farthest corner.

No one had even noticed her so far, and she'd like to keep it that way.

The Styrofoam cup warmed her hand without burning it as steam rose from her drink.

Five men wearing jeans and bright orange shirts sat in a half-circle of metal folding chairs, talking. A couple and three kids—presumably theirs—filled the couch, while a man large enough to be a professional linebacker occupied the loveseat.

Even with all these people, the room was neither stuffy nor drafty.

A well-decorated Christmas tree stood in the corner across from Rebecca. Red, blue, and gold lights made plain glass bulbs and silver tinsel glitter and shine. She hadn't put up a Christmas tree this year. After all, the only one to celebrate with was Chelsea, and as long as she got a rawhide chew, she'd be happy.

Instead of overhead lighting, four warm lamps scattered around the room and a row of recessed lights along the ceiling gave the place a pleasant, homey atmosphere.

The only thing better would have been a lit fireplace. Not that it was cold enough for that.

Between Rebecca and the couch, a group of kids—the owners of the shoes near the door, based on their socked feet—batted red and green balloons back and forth. Children's squeals of laughter and the plasticy *thwump* of swatted balloons punctuated adult conversations.

Shaw was nowhere in sight. Neither was Jillian. Maybe Shaw was still at the hospital with his friend, and Jillian had gone to support her brother.

Mark and Linda stood near the entrance to a second hallway, leading into the rest of the house. Josiah, as promised earlier, talked with them. As they conversed, Josiah's expression remained approachable and calm.

That accounted for him. But where was Essie?

Just in case Josiah glanced her way, Rebecca kept at least two guests between him and her as she scanned the room for their missing hostess.

The harsh, off-key notes of a dying doorbell pulled Essie through a door Rebecca hadn't even noticed. Painted to match the walls and situated just beside the refreshment table, it easily blended in. That had to be the kitchen entrance.

Jillian followed Essie out of the kitchen. Both women's eyes were damp, but neither had a firmly set mouth or fiery eyes. If anything, they seemed to harbor faint smiles.

Four dissonant bell rings later, Essie finally made it to the entryway. After dabbing her eyes with a tissue, she opened the front door.

Lincoln Shaw barreled through, jostling Essie to one side. The woman yelped in surprise, drawing Josiah's immediate attention. He excused himself from his conversation and headed for the front door, slipping through tangled knots of guests with an ease born of years working in customer-heavy retail stores.

And Josiah wasn't the only one to rush to the scene. Jillian hurried over too and raised a scolding finger to her brother. The woman's former calmness had vanished, replaced by a rigid mouth and unhappy eyes. "Can you not just leave these people alone?" Her angry voice carried, even over the din of gathered guests.

"I'm not leaving until I get an answer," Shaw shot back at Jillian.

Keeping a comfortable screen of church members between herself and the Hugheses, Rebecca crossed the room, stopping inches from the decorated Christmas tree. With a clear view of Essie, Josiah, Jillian, and Shaw, she quietly sipped her cooling cocoa. Maybe the warm drink would ease the tightness seeping into her neck and back.

Her cup shook slightly. Not enough to spill, but enough to betray her anxiety. She hated confrontations like this. Irate customers she could handle, but ever since what had happened at Newton Hill, dealing with angry people who claimed to be Christians made her nervous. Her free hand slipped into a coat pocket and gripped her cell. Just in case this slipped into dangerous territory.

Near the door, Shaw stared hard at Jillian, then Josiah.

Rebecca knew that look. Understood how it felt to have such animosity directed at her.

To hear better, she needed to get closer, but the tendons at the back of her knees pulled taut.

She pictured Chelsea racing around the backyard, that ridiculous elephant toy in her mouth.

Her knees unlocked enough to let her shuffle past a knot of church members, talking about plans for Christmas day.

Once she reached the closer end of the refreshment table, the voices of everyone in the entryway sharpened.

Shaw turned to Josiah as, behind him, Essie shut the wide-open front door. "Why won't you just go?" The already-large man seemed six inches taller now, with his neck craned to glare down at Josiah. "Get out of this church"—he pointed an animated finger at the now-closed door—"and let us all be."

"Lincoln Harold Shaw." Jillian approached her brother and tipped her head to look up at him. Compared to her brother, she seemed comically small. "These people have given up everything they know to come here and help us, and you've treated them *horribly*."

"You just can't agree with me about anything, can you?" he snapped at Jillian.

"Abigail would be ashamed," Jillian shot back. "She'd never have wanted you to run these people off."

The big man's shoulders slumped forward, and his jawline slacked.

People were most dangerous when angry or desperate, and Shaw had seemingly just jumped from one to the other.

She shouldn't have come tonight. What was she thinking? Stupid curiosity never did anyone any favors. Maybe there was a back door in the kitchen. She could slip out and leave before anything crazy happened.

But to get to the kitchen, she'd have to go around the refreshment table and walk almost directly behind Josiah.

The crowded living room suddenly seemed far too small.

Rebecca clamped her eyes shut and envisioned Chelsea holding her own leash and proudly walking herself around the front yard. She held onto that image until her breathing steadied, and the tension in her neck eased enough to allow her to turn her head.

At the door, Shaw's confrontation with the Hugheses continued.

"My wife's gone," Shaw said. "My son's on the other side of the continent. I have a grandson I've never met. Bob's in the hospital. Even our pastor's gone." He took three heavy steps toward Josiah and gripped him by the shoulders. "I can't deal with this anymore. My whole family's gone. Please, please, just go, so my son will come back."

Josiah didn't flinch at the bigger man's touch. "I'm sorry for everything you've been through. I know how hard it is to lose so many people you care about."

Shaw held Josiah's gaze, neither decrying his new pastor's assertion nor accepting it.

"When we left our church in Georgia, we had . . ." Josiah's voice cracked.

Essie, who had remained at the door until now, edged past Shaw, glassy eyes on her husband as she took her place beside him.

Josiah put an arm around Essie's waist and finished his sentence, ". . . we had just lost two very dear friends in a head-on collision." His voice strengthened with each word, as if

Essie's presence were shoring him up. "Last year, both my mother and my wife's sister passed. When we got the call that Oak Grove had accepted us, we weren't sure if it was God's calling, or us escaping grief. But over the past couple weeks, we've found a lot of others here who're hurting, just like us. You included, Brother Shaw."

The big man's hands slipped from Josiah's shoulders, and he wilted.

Rebecca's death grip on her pocketed cell eased, but she didn't completely let go of the phone. Shaw's moods had proven easily changeable. Better to be prepared, just in case.

"When God's people need healing, Jehovah Rapha is the only answer," Josiah said. "Often, He uses Christians—individual members of the Body of Christ—to help each other. But we have to be willing to become instruments of the Great Physician—the Lord our Healer. And we don't always do what God asks." He extended a hand to Shaw. "I'm sorry for all your losses—for everything you've endured. But I want you to know that my wife and I will be here for you, whenever you need someone to talk to. We're not trying to rip apart Oak Grove. We're here to help build it."

Shaw stared hard at Josiah's outstretched hand.

Rebecca paused, partially crushed cocoa cup halfway to her mouth.

Had the house been empty, silence would have stretched between the two men. Instead, rich laughter, children's happy squeals, and the hubbub of multiple conversations mixed together in the empty space separating Josiah Hughes and Lincoln Shaw.

Slowly—so slowly Rebecca almost missed it—Shaw reached for Josiah's hand.

The instant both men clasped hands, Jillian threw her arms around her much taller brother's chest. She squeezed him tightly.

Shaw's dour expression cracked, and though he didn't exactly smile, he didn't frown either. And instead of the stormy rage from last Sunday, his eyes were heavy. But gentle hints of hope flickered in them too.

Rebecca still clutched her mangled cocoa cup with shaking hands, but the tension behind her knees was mostly gone.

Essie turned around just enough to scan the room. She made eye contact before Rebecca looked away, and a smile, unlike anything Rebecca had ever seen from her, brightened the other woman's face. Essie exuded such relief and joy that one corner of Rebecca's mouth tipped upward—just a little— in response.

Chapter 24

Monday at Durham's was stupidly busy. With only nine days until Christmas, last-minute shoppers crammed aisles and crowded into checkout lanes. Self-check—Natasha specifically—had already called Rebecca five times for jammed receipt tape, and it was only 10 a. m.

Customer Service bustled with activity as Josiah fielded returns, money services, and probably too many off-the-wall questions to count.

Every time Rebecca chanced by the service desk, Josiah was helping someone. Despite the frenzied pace and abundance of absurd-looking shoppers, a steady smile remained on his face, and the shadows under his eyes were nearly gone.

Rebecca covered a yawn.

"Don't start that." Luca appeared beside her. "You'll have me doing it too, and I've still gotta hang around this place for another seven hours." His jaw stretched involuntarily. "See, there it is."

"Hey, you don't have to get up at five." Rebecca gave Luca an insincere side-eye before checking her handheld. "When did you send Natasha to break?"

"Just now, why?" Luca said.

"Lately, as soon as she's off a register or away from Self-check, she disappears. Just the other day, I found her hiding in Lawn and Garden, talking on the phone."

"I'll keep a watch on her," said Luca.

Just before Rebecca started toward the cash office to see if the recycler needed a coin refill, the shipping guy, Douglas, slipped through an unoccupied checkout lane, a small box in hand. "Got somethin' for you." He offered Rebecca the box. "Knew you were waitin' on it, so I ran it up here as soon as it came off the FedEx truck."

"Is this what I think it is?" She pried open the leafed-together box flaps.

"Yup. Brand new." Douglas grinned.

"Finally!" Rebecca wrangled an earpiece free of its plastic packaging, plugged it into her walkie, and looped it over one ear. To test it, she clicked the talk button three times.

"Who's doing that?" Nevaeh's irritated voice crackled through the earpiece.

Rebecca gave Douglas a grateful smile. "Thanks for walking this up here. You didn't have to."

"It's no trouble," Douglas replied. "Glad to help out someone who actually does their job." He headed for the back of the store, hands tucked into his pockets as he dodged customers and shopping carts.

"Now I don't have to guess what management's saying half the time," Rebecca said.

"Only took three months to get a replacement," Luca muttered.

"At least we have it now," Rebecca said.

The new earpiece crackled again. "Maintenance to Produce." Nevaeh was irritated, as always.

When no one responded, the assistant manager repeated, this time, more forcefully, "Maintenance to Produce. Right now!"

Who was supposed to be clocked in? Rebecca brought up the schedule on her handheld. The guy scheduled to be here at nine had called out, and the woman who'd come in at seven had taken an early lunch.

"Somebody, get over here," Nevaeh shouted into the walkie. A string of jumbled curses and more indistinct yelling prompted Rebecca to turn down the walkie volume.

The thunder of onions hitting the floor reached Rebecca moments before Nevaeh's angry shriek cut the air. "Get him away!"

"What the—" Luca's last words faded as he sprinted toward Produce.

Rebecca grabbed the broom from Self-check and hurried after Luca. She was nowhere near Nevaeh's biggest fan, but she was part of the Durham's crew, and Rebecca wouldn't stand for a customer harassing the other woman. Why hadn't Nevaeh called for the Asset Protection team? All Maintenance could do was smack the offender with a dust mop or maybe spray whoever it was with glass cleaner if the guy was attacking somebody.

They passed a display bin filled with Granny Smith apples.

Luca disappeared into a knot of customers blocking the vegetable coolers. Rebecca pushed through after him, broom ready.

Seconds later, she and Luca broke out of the gathered throng and found Nevaeh with one sparkling Jimmy Choo sneaker buried in a crate of cucumbers, and the other balanced precariously on the lip of the cooler. She held onto a hanging produce scale for balance as she screamed at a mid-sized raccoon.

Heedless of Nevaeh's screeching, the animal parked right beneath her and reached upward. The raccoon didn't seem off-balance and wasn't making strange noises or foaming at the mouth, so it was probably just curious, not rabid. With one paw, the creature touched Nevaeh's sparkly shoe.

Half an instant after the raccoon made contact with her sneaker, Nevaeh's blood-curdling shriek pulled another drove of customers and employees to Produce.

Just in time to witness the raccoon scamper away.

It dodged several dozen people and scurried straight out the front door.

"That filthy, grubby-handed little—" Nevaeh spouted a word she could have been fired for saying in front of customers. She glowered at the snickering crowd as she dragged one now damp and slightly green shoe out of the squashed cucumbers. "Clean this up," she ordered a nearby Produce worker who had clamped both hands over his mouth, probably to keep from laughing.

Rebecca turned her back to the scene and barely made it past three people before she burst into laughter. Luca hadn't even bothered to hide his reaction.

Nevaeh might not sink to outright verbal abuse, like Shaw had with Josiah, but her constant bad attitude made working with her tedious at best. Still, she was glad the woman's attacker had only been a curious animal.

Partway back to Self-check, the handheld buzzed. Josiah needed change.

She dropped off the broom she was still holding, grabbed quarters and dimes from the cash office, and headed for Customer Service. On the way there, she swiped away laughter-induced tears. Church gossip chains had nothing on the Durham's rumor mill. News of Nevaeh's run-in with a sparkle-loving raccoon would spread through the entire store before lunch.

When she reached the service desk, Josiah was waiting with an open till.

"Here ya go." Rebecca plunked both coin-filled plastic containers on the counter.

Josiah dumped the coins into his drawer and clicked it shut. He handed a fresh receipt, two quarters, and a dime to the lady he'd been helping. "Have a merry Christmas."

For the moment, there were no other customers in Josiah's line.

"Essie told me she saw you last night." He let the statement hang in the air as he straightened up the returns area. Shirts, socks, and a pink tutu ended up in a single pile, which he then deposited in a bin marked "Apparel."

No use denying it. "Yeah, I stopped by for a bit." She picked up a cheese grater and a muffin pan and headed for the Housewares bin.

"She also said you were by the door, listening to our conversation with Brother Shaw."

Rebecca fumbled the muffin pan and almost dropped the cheese grater.

"It's all right. Someone was bound to overhear, and it wasn't as if what's been happening was a secret." Josiah handed her a set of candy-cane print potholders to go with the pan and grater. "I'm thankful Essie and I can be here for Lincoln, Jillian, *and* Bob."

"You think Reinhart will quit with the scowls and finger shaking now that Shaw's cooled down?" Rebecca deposited her armload of items in the Housewares bin.

"He was pretty quiet when I visited him at Burnsville General yesterday afternoon. But whether he changes or not, I trust God's working on him in ways no human can. And he's my brother in Christ. Just like being part of the team at Durham's, putting up with a few things is part of being in a family."

Rebecca snorted. She could almost hear Nevaeh's unhappy voice screeching through the new earpiece and envision Natasha's scowl and rolling eyes. "A dysfunctional family, maybe."

Josiah's laugh startled her. It was deep, full, and bright, holding none of the heaviness he'd carried these past two weeks. "This side of Heaven, absolutely."

Epilogue

Services Wednesday night and yesterday had been shockingly pleasant. Shaw was quiet most of the time, and Jillian sat with him during all three services. The brother-sister pair had only separated during Sunday School, and neither had said a word about the past two weeks.

Now that Monday morning had arrived again, Rebecca was nearly ready to face another Christmas week. But just after her fourth cashier arrived, a horrendous crash cut across the front of the store. The sharp echo of far too much shattering glass and sloshing liquid pulled her toward Self-checkout.

The stench hit her before she made it halfway there. Thick, sour air wafted from the other end of the registers in waves.

Wine.

And Maintenance wouldn't be here for another two hours.

She went for the nearest janitor's closet, grabbed a squeegee, mop, and bucket, and quickly mixed hot water and cleaner. Just before leaving, she also grabbed a half-full tub of Spill Magic.

The distinct reek of fermentation permeated the whole front-end now, and multiple cashiers had sent assistance codes from their registers. She cleared the notifications out of the handheld's queue.

"It's just a wine spill at Self-check," she said to multiple cashiers on her way to the disaster zone. "Keep your line moving. If you need a mask, go get one at the supervisor station, then get right back to your register."

By the time she reached Self-checkout, her eyes watered from the concentrated odor wafting across the entire front-end.

A pile of glass and soaked cardboard mounded in the center of the Self-checkout area. Red wine spread in all directions. It had already taken over the majority of the thirty-by-thirty section and was trickling toward both Produce and the front door.

Four customers rolled carts through the mess. One stared at his phone as he walked. Two more chatted via Bluetooth headsets, and the fourth tried to keep her toddler from standing up in the shopping cart. Whoever had dropped the wine was long gone. The only evidence of their presence was an abandoned cart, holding another twelve loose bottles of cabernet—these still intact.

Natasha stood beside the sad pile, staring at the mess, eyes wide, hands clamped over her mouth. Reddish-purple splatters dotted her gray sneakers.

"Natasha, get everyone away from all this broken glass and into other lines," Rebecca directed.

The cashier didn't move.

"Natasha!" Rebecca repeated.

This time, the girl burst into action. She said nothing as glass crunched under her shoes. Natasha corralled the young mother and toddler first, then the other three who'd wandered into the spreading lake of red wine. She moved them out of the Self-check area and directed each customer to one of the three open registers. Her shoes creaked and squealed as the wine on both soles went from liquid to sticky residue.

"Go get the wet floor signs." Rebecca pointed to the janitor's closet when Natasha returned.

For once, the girl hurried to obey, eyes still round with shock.

Keeping a firm grip on the Spill Magic container's handle, Rebecca quickly spread a ring of white absorbent powder around the worst part of the oozing red lake. She didn't have enough of the stuff to absorb the entire spill, but at least she could keep it from spreading.

Her shoes squeaked as she stepped carefully through the mess. The shallower puddles near the edge of the creeping pond were already drying.

Natasha arrived with the signs and, without being told, parked one yellow sign at both the entrance and exit to Self-check.

"Grab whoever you can find in Produce and get them over here to watch this a minute," Rebecca said as she used a squeegee to tighten the Spill Magic circle. Each time she pushed another section of the white powder further into the spilled wine, more liquid seeped into the absorbent, turning it a deep maroon.

Within minutes, Natasha returned, this time with a twenty-something guy.

"I was almost done restocking potatoes. Couldn't you have grabbed somebody else?" the produce guy whined. His name tag would have read Jamarcus, but half the *S* was missing.

Natasha said nothing, just pointed at Rebecca.

To keep the squeegee from falling into the mess, Rebecca propped it against the nearest candy display. "You'll only be here long enough for me to get Natasha a till and open another checkout line. After that, you can go back to your potatoes. I promise. In the meantime, make sure no one comes through here."

Jamarcus crossed his arms and leaned against an upright cooler filled with Monster energy drinks.

Before leaving Self-check, Rebecca swiped the bottom of her shoes with damp paper towels. Dirt and sticky wine came off in black and red smears. Here she was, dealing with other people's messes, just like Josiah.

Lines were already backing up. No time for a second round of paper towels.

She ushered Natasha into the cash office.

The instant the door shut, Natasha leaned against it and burst into tears. "I'm sorry."

Usually Natasha's responses involved either exasperation or annoyance. But this time, anxiety radiated from the girl.

"It's okay." Rebecca grabbed an open Kleenex box and offered it to Natasha. "Accidents are part of life." Natasha needed to know this could have happened to anybody, needed to understand everything would be okay. "Customers pick up stuff they shouldn't all the time." Attempting to lighten the mood, she added, "I'm not even sure where they got a wine bottle box to begin with. Those aren't supposed to be on the shelves."

"It wasn't the customer's fault." Natasha swiped wet eyes with a tissue. "They asked for h-help scanning their stuff. Th-the bottles were in that big box, and I didn't know they were the same as the ones in the cart. The b-barcode was in a w-weird place, so I picked up the box and balanced it on the edge of the shopping cart." She sucked in an unsteady breath. "When I couldn't find the right thing to scan, I took out one of the bottles and l-lost my grip. The whole box just—" A scared sob racked Natasha. "The red just kept spreading! And there was so much glass!"

Josiah's exchange with Shaw a little over a week ago came to mind. Shaw's anger had run much deeper than mere dislike for the Hugheses.

Natasha's tears today weren't about broken wine bottles. Something else was going on, and she'd been too distracted by the girl's immature antics to notice.

Regret lassoed her stomach and pulled.

Rebecca set down the empty till she'd just fished from a shelf and put her arm around the cashier. "It's okay," she said, voice much softer than it usually was when Natasha was involved.

"My—my brother, he . . ." Natasha covered her face with another tissue. "This past summer, we drove to the store, and—and a guy—he hit us when we were pulling out of the parking lot. Tyler cut his head, and it just kept bleeding." She sobbed into the quickly withering Kleenex. "The glass. It was everywhere. I was so scared!" The last word came out half-wail, half-sob.

"I'm sorry you went through that. It's hard to have something frightening happen to us. It's even worse when someone we care about is involved. We've all had stuff rattle us."

"E-even you?" Natasha's voice squeaked, making her sound like a surprised mouse. "*Nothing* fazes you. Not even those crazy people who scream when you won't give them a refund."

Rebecca could almost hear the clandestine murmurs at her old church as she walked past people before services started. But hadn't she also been afraid to trust the Hugheses? Afraid to be ostracized by even more fellow Christians? Her fears might seem quieter than Natasha's, but she understood what it meant to be ruled by them. "Yeah. Even me."

"How—how'd you get over it?" Natasha dared to peek out from behind her tissue.

As the cashier's breathing evened out, Rebecca let her go, picked up the empty register till, and set it atop the cash recycler. On the big machine's monitor, she selected the option to dispense the correct amount of bills and coins. The whir of paper and clink of metal filled the room for a handful of seconds.

She recalled the first time she'd stepped into Oak Grove Baptist Church. The anxiety that had hit her then. But now, when she thought back on that moment, the fear that had gripped her then no longer stung as much. Because she knew that—even though they were far from perfect—the people there cared about each other—cared about *her*.

Once Rebecca had placed everything in its proper till slot, she said, "I think God heals us slowly, one moment at a time."

When she'd seen Josiah standing behind the pulpit, her first instinct had been to hide, protect herself from the inevitable hurt he would cause her. But at some point, watching Josiah and Essie treat everyone around them, even the people who wronged them, with love and understanding had set her at ease in a way she'd never experienced.

"And He often uses people to do it."

Natasha sniffed one last time before wiping away partially dried tears. "I'm not really religious, or anything," she said quietly. "But I kinda get what you're saying."

"I know we can't really talk on the clock, but if you ever want to hear more about God . . ." The words hung heavy on her tongue. When was the last time she'd actually discussed her faith with someone else? "Just let me know."

"O-okay." Natasha wiped the last traces of tears from her eyes and cheeks. Dark mascara and light brown foundation smeared the Kleenex.

"We'd better let Jamarcus get back to his potatoes." Rebecca offered Natasha an encouraging pat on the shoulder as she handed the girl her new till. "I'll walk you to register twelve."

Within three minutes, Natasha had five shopping carts lined up at her register.

"You good?" Rebecca said.

Natasha nodded. "I'll be okay." The girl's voice was a bit less flimsy than it had been a minute ago.

"All right. You know where I'll be." She tipped her head toward Self-check and the waiting mess.

The moment she turned her back to the newly opened register, Rebecca caught Josiah looking her way from Customer Service. As if he knew exactly what had transpired during the past ten minutes, he offered her a smile and nod.

Before heading back to Self-check, she returned his nod. As she returned to the waiting pile of Spill Magic and cabernet, one corner of her mouth and then the other tugged upward.

"What're you so happy about?" Jamarcus said as Rebecca approached.

"Huh?"

"You're grinning like some stupid little kid."

"Get back to Produce." She shooed him away.

While Jamarcus returned to stocking russets and Idaho Golds, Rebecca dunked her mop into now-lukewarm water.

She sopped up the sticky purple sheen covering the floor outside the Spill Magic circle.

Tomorrow was Christmas Eve.

This year, she was looking forward to the candlelight service at her new church with all of its imperfect, mistake-making, blood-bought people.

Acknowledgements

I did not intend to write this novella. But when the opportunity rose to collaborate with eight other Brave Authors, I decided to jump in. Having experienced my share of church hurt, these hundred pages were a battle—one I couldn't have won if not for the Saviour who loves me and helped me walk through each word and sentence with Him.

Thank you to everyone who was excited for the release of this story. Your enthusiasm was an incredible encouragement to me.

Thank you to Sarah H. and Nicole. Your comments helped me understand how to convey the heart of this story.

Thank you, Sarah E. for your thorough proofreading. As you may have noticed, hyphenated words are not my forte.

And thank you, readers, for spending your time with this novella and both others in the *Every Voice Heard* collection. I hope *Rapha* has been just a brief glimpse at how God can heal slowly, quietly, and beautifully.

For the Love of Truth

Sarah Hanks

Chapter 1

Candi shifted in her rolling office chair as she fumbled for an answer to the staff members' questions. As Richard's personal assistant, she should be able to field anything they threw at her, but Richard hadn't coached her through this one. Maybe he'd thought no one would notice the absence of a couple of families in a church that boasted a thousand attendees each service.

She tapped her toes, her navy-blue pumps clicking against the linoleum. How should she answer? By far the youngest person in the room at twenty, she pulled at her blue turtleneck. Air. She needed air.

Mark, still standing around the oval conference table, asked his question again. "Why'd they leave? The Bringer and Reynold families have been here for over a decade. There must be a reason they left so abruptly."

She'd opened her mouth to say, *"I don't know,"* when Pastor Richard breezed into the room, saving her. He flashed his 1,000-kilowatt smile at her, then at the fifteen other staff members seated at the table. "Mind if I take this one, Candi?"

A slow breath slipped past her lips. With an easy flick of her fingers, she motioned for him to go on. "By all means."

He took the empty seat beside her, pointing a finger at Mark. "Great question. Thanks for asking." Tenting his fingertips on the polished oak table, his expression melted into one of regret and concern. The gray at his temples glinted in the overhead lighting.

"Scripture says in 1 John 2:19, 'They went out from us, but they were not of us; for if they had been of us, they would have continued with us. But they went out, that it might become plain that they are not of us.' That's the simple, yet painful truth of the matter. The Bringer and Reynold families left because they were never truly one of us."

Mark's forehead dimpled and his eyes widened. "I don't understand. John Bringer was an usher. Their family led a small group. The Reynolds were in children's ministry." He sounded aghast at such a possibility.

Richard's eyes misted with unshed tears. "I know. It grieves me deeply. But the Bible warns us of wolves who come in sheep's clothing. It tells us that not everyone who says, 'Lord, Lord,' will enter the Kingdom of heaven. There will be many we assume are strong believers who the Lord will say, 'Depart from Me. I never knew you.'"

"The great falling away," Mark whispered, shaking his head. He slunk into his chair.

Richard had just preached about this hard truth last Sunday. Candi's heart twisted at the hurt etched on his face. How it must grieve him to learn that two families he'd trusted turned out to be pretenders, out to harm the body of Christ instead of building it up. A glance around showed a room of downcast faces.

Somehow, Richard managed to smile. "But it will be okay. We'll get through this together. We're a church family, and as true followers of Christ, we'll always be there for each other."

Candi took a deep breath. Gratitude warmed her chest as she met Richard's encouraging gaze. How thankful she was to be part of the Impact Church family. Her mother and father may have forsaken her, but Richard had taken her under his wing. Spoke life into her. Made her believe she could rise above the tough circumstances of her childhood. Here, she'd found purpose, a sense of belonging, and lifelong friends. There wasn't a day that went by that she didn't thank God for this church. And for Richard stepping in as her spiritual father.

"Let's move on to better news, shall we?" Richard angled toward her. "Candi, please give us the ministry update."

All eyes focused on her. She smoothed back a strand of hair that had fallen from her ponytail, grabbed the packet in front of her, and rattled off the statistics. Attendance had grown fifteen percent over the past month. Thirty-two people had given their lives to Christ. Twenty were baptized. Fifty-two completed the membership class. All good news. No doubt Impact Church lived up to its name.

"Excellent." Richard grinned as he led the room in applause. "Thank you, Candi."

Bob gave the financial report, utilizing the giant dry erase board mounted to the wall. More good news. Then Abby relayed how the children's ministry was thriving. Mark gave an update on three of the dozens of missions Impact Church funded.

Candi's heart swelled with pride. What an amazing group of people. Superstars for the Kingdom, every one of them.

Richard rubbed his hands together. "Now, let's talk about some exciting new opportunities we'll be taking advantage of moving forward."

Candi straightened in her chair. New opportunities? Richard had never mentioned as much to her, and if anyone should have had a heads-up, it was her.

"Church TV approached me and asked that I do a weekly show, teaching from the gospels. I would have never sought the spotlight in this way, but the Lord has made it clear that this is of Him. Think of all the people we'll be able to impact worldwide."

Delighted comments peppered the room as the staff praised the Lord for an open door.

Once again, Richard turned toward her, hands in a prayer gesture. "Candi, you know I hate to add to your workload, as you already do so much for our church. This new opportunity will demand more sacrifices for all of us, but for you and me specifically. I'll need you to attend all the filming and prepare a summary of each week's lesson to send to the station. Transcribe my notes. That kind of thing. There's also some paperwork that needs to be taken care of."

"No problem." The answer effortlessly glided from her lips. "Anything to further the gospel."

"That's my girl." He returned his magnetic gaze to the rest of the room. "That's why I call her Can*do*. You can do anything, right, dear?"

She repeated the verse he'd ingrained in her over the two years she'd worked for him. The first verse she'd ever memorized. "I can do all things through Christ who gives me strength."

"Absolutely. Isn't she amazing?"

Another round of applause broke out. Warmth flooded her cheeks. She waved them off then pointed upward. "It's all God."

He was the One who enabled her to give of herself day after day. She did it all for Him. She'd be nothing without Jesus' grace and strength. More than anything, she yearned to be in the Lord's inner circle, like Peter, James, and John were while He walked the earth. *Many are called, but few are chosen.* Oh, to be a chosen one. One God delighted to draw near to. One He could trust with His heart. Richard had taught her that she could be among the honored elect, if only she continued offering herself daily as a living sacrifice.

When the meeting ended and Richard wrapped her in a side hug, her soul soared. Even if her parents never understood her choice to follow Christ a few years ago, even if they never accepted her, she had found a place of love and belonging. She mattered here, and no one could take that away from her.

*****

Justice pulled into one of the few remaining parking spaces in front of Impact Church ten minutes before the scheduled service. Time for a new beginning. As sorry as he was to see his home church dissolve after three years, excitement brewed within him at the thought of connecting with a new community. A church this size must have a plethora of outreach opportunities. Plenty of chances to serve. And probably even a small group for people his age, mid-twenties.

Yeah, this change might be just the thing he needed. He'd asked around about churches in his area and many had recommended Impact, claiming the teaching was outstanding and the worship experience meaningful. Now, here he was, eager to see if the place lived up to all the hype.

He approached the front door only to have a teenager open it for him, sporting a warm smile. "Welcome to Impact Church. We're happy you came."

He clasped the teen's outstretched hand. "Thanks."

Four additional greeters met him on his way in, each brimming with enthusiasm. He passed a welcome desk on the right. Depending on how the service went, he'd check that out later. He'd feel the place out first before looking for ways to connect and before giving them his contact information.

Upbeat music emanated from the sanctuary, drawing him in. Several other volunteers greeted him and shook his hand as he made his way to a seat in the middle near the back. A perfect spot to observe. Man, everyone looked thrilled to be here. If anyone had peeled themselves from bed this morning and dragged themselves here, he would never be able to tell. The enthusiasm was contagious. Groups of people of all ages milled around, chatting and laughing. Several guys in the front right section appeared to be around his age. He liked this place already.

Within minutes, worship began with the strum of a guitar and trill of keys. He stood to his feet. Some songs were familiar, others not. It moved him deeply until he lost all sense of time and place. As if it were just him and the Lord. He hadn't experienced such powerful worship in years. Did it have to do with the undeniable talent of the worship team, or was God's presence truly inhabiting this place in a special way?

After worship came a video with announcements. The skit about an upcoming series proved creative and humorous. He found himself chuckling along with the people around him at the actors with eighties' hairdos. The striking blonde in the next video highlighted several intriguing opportunities. Something about a men's breakfast, small-group sign-ups, and an upcoming worship night. The details of when and where those events would take place fell out of his mind like sand through someone's fingers as he stared at the blonde with the most vibrant eyes he'd ever seen. He shook himself from that distraction. He'd come hunting for a new church, not a girlfriend. If he happened to find a girlfriend at his new church, that would be delightfully unexpected. He turned to prayer to refocus.

Is this where you want me to plant myself, Lord?

No clear answer, but he settled in to enjoy the sermon. The man who strode to the stage and introduced himself as Pastor Richard Blake radiated warmth. Perhaps in his late forties, early fifties, the faint lines around his eyes and mouth spoke of laughter and joy, while the slight graying at his temples hinted at wisdom. His outfit of jeans and a t-shirt with a sports coat made him seem approachable, yet like he took his job seriously. And then he spoke.

After opening with a joke that caused the congregation to erupt in laughter, he transitioned to preaching on the Sermon on the Mount. A few minutes in and Justice snatched a pen and a welcome card from the seat back in front of him and jotted notes in the empty spaces.

"Humility isn't thinking less of yourself. It's thinking of yourself less."

Justice *amened* with the rest of the congregation. He renewed his inner pledge to go low and consider other people's needs as more important than his own. After all, Jesus came down from heaven to serve.

No wonder this church came so highly recommended. Pastor Richard was charismatic, engaging, and insightful. He held his congregation in rapt attention all the way until the final prayer. No nodding off in this church.

Thank You, Lord, for leading me here. No doubt this would be his new church home.

After the service, he made a beeline to the welcome desk, eager to discover how to get connected. An older woman stood behind the counter ready to greet him, but before he reached her, a young blonde approached her and started a conversation. He drew near to wait. The blonde turned to him, meeting his gaze with her brilliant blue eyes. His heart rate accelerated at the recognition. The woman from the announcement video.

"Sorry to squeeze in." The corners of her eyes crinkled as she smiled at him. "Marge is a busy lady."

Huh? Oh, the attendant's name tag proclaimed her to be Marge. "N-no problem." He stuck out his hand. "I'm Justice. It's my first time here."

The blonde shook his hand. Such a delicate touch. Smooth skin. "I'm Candi. Nice to meet you." She tilted her head toward the older woman next to her. "This is Marge. She should be able to answer any questions you might have."

He shook Marge's hand as well.

Candi took a step away from the Welcome Desk.

Justice clamped his mouth shut to keep from calling, *Wait! Don't go.* If only he could keep her talking, but she sauntered away.

Marge gave him a knowing smile. "Candi's a doll. Such a sweetheart. She's teaching the intro meeting next Saturday." Her voice crinkled like wrapping paper. "It's a one-hour class meant to show newcomers what Impact Church is all about and how to get connected."

He cast another glance in the direction Candi had gone. "Sounds perfect."

"Uh huh. Thought so." She wrote the class's date and time on a brochure and handed it to him. "I hope to see you again, Justice."

He stuck the brochure into his back pocket. "I'm sure you will."

Chapter 2

Candi stood at the front of the meeting room, a spiral-bound welcome guide in hand. Guests nearly filled the eight long plastic tables to capacity. She had to fight to make eye contact with each interested person and not allow Justice to monopolize her attention. Because he pulled at her like the moon drew the tide.

"I'm so glad to see all of you here. What a great turnout. Our purpose this morning is to explore Impact Church's mission, vision, and values, as well as showcase the many opportunities for you to get involved." There went her gaze again. Straight to the handsome man front and center. His lips quirked up in a smile. She returned it, then forced herself to look away.

"The welcome guides in front of you are yours to keep. I won't read from them word for word, and there's a lot we won't have time to cover. Feel free to read through it at your own pace, and of course, we're here to answer any questions you may have."

With that, she began the introductory video, then stood back to watch the story she'd heard hundreds of times. A slightly younger version of Richard filled the screen, explaining how the church had started and how it'd grown over the years. From a small storefront in a strip mall, to a building that seated six hundred, to their current building with an occupancy limit of fifteen hundred.

Then Richard spoke of his powerful salvation experience when he was nineteen. This part always brought her to the verge of tears. God took a lost, drug-addicted youth and radically transformed him into the powerful minister he was today, impacting millions across the globe. Was there anything God couldn't do?

When the video ended, Candi returned to her place up front. "If Pastor Richard looks familiar, it's probably because you've seen him on the 700 Club or on the cover of one of a dozen magazines. Impact Church is truly impacting many lives all over the world. Our services are live streamed and reach thousands each week."

Several people nodded.

"If you attended service this past weekend, you heard about one of our core values. Humility." She reiterated several aspects of humility that Richard had instilled in her. "Pastor Richard has created a culture of humility here. This community truly seeks to honor one another, and our members are some of the most gracious and forgiving people you will ever meet." Oh, how she loved the community here. They'd wrapped her in grace and love. She'd made lifelong friends, and in Pastor Richard and his wife Natalie, she'd found spiritual parents and mentors.

"Another important value we have is generosity. Pastor Richard leads the way with this value. He lives simply and sacrificially, so he can give money and other resources to the poor and lost." It was one of the things she admired most about him. "Impact Church supports over a dozen missions, partnering to combat poverty, illiteracy, and human trafficking."

"Amazing," the woman in the front row murmured.

"We've helped build wells all over Africa and have provided medical care to many in third-world countries. When you give to Impact, those finances are going to Kingdom work here and abroad. A full list of missions we support is on page ten."

The rustle of turning pages filled the room. She paused to allow them to peruse the list before continuing. "Our third and most important core value is devotion. Pastor Richard encourages everyone in wholehearted devotion to the Kingdom of God. Like Mary of Bethany with the perfume, we pour ourselves out at the feet of Jesus, giving him everything. This is not a church that tickles the ears once a week to make you comfortable in a lukewarm lifestyle."

A few people said, "Amen." One of them might have been Justice.

She transitioned to another short video about some of the small groups Impact offered and their value. When it ended, Justice's hand popped up.

"Yes?"

"Do you have a group for young adults? Or perhaps a singles group?" His face reddened.

Did that mean he was single? No ring, but that didn't guarantee anything. How could she find out? She schooled her expression.

"We have both a young marrieds group and a young singles group." She bit the inside of her cheek, then asked, "Might you be interested in either of those?"

"I might be." His smile sent a tingle up her spine.

Gracious, was he flirting? Was she? Now *her* cheeks warmed. Time to change the subject. Refocus.

"Another great way to get connected and form relationships is to serve." Her voice tripped over the word *relationships* and then cracked. Sheesh. She was making a fool of herself. "We have many volunteer opportunities, including greeting, working in children's ministry, manning the café, directing traffic in the parking lot, and groundskeeping." She wouldn't let herself look in Justice's direction. "A full list of opportunities is on page 22." More page shuffling.

Someone cleared their throat. She looked toward the sound. Justice had raised his hand again. Her stomach wobbled as she nodded to him to speak.

"What's the next step if you'd like to become a member?"

Membership? Man, he was all in. Was that good news or bad news? Good, of course. Plugging into this church was the best decision she'd ever made, apart from salvation. But her nerves might not be able to handle seeing him here regularly. There was something about him that grabbed at her. An enthusiasm. A zest for life. This guy was a go getter. Exactly the kind of person they needed at Impact Church.

She couldn't hold back her smile. "We have a membership class the second Sunday of every month, after the second service. We'd love to see you there."

*****

Justice walked through the front doors of Impact Church twenty minutes before the start of first service. That would give him time to grab a coffee from their café. And if he was fortunate enough, maybe he'd run into Candi.

Everything about her intrigued him, from the way she glided instead of simply walked, to the slight gap in her two front teeth. Adorable. He could liken her voice to caffeine the way it stirred him and made his heart beat a little faster. And her eyes. Heavens, he'd never seen eyes that pure blue.

Oh, brother. He needed to stop thinking about her. People buzzed around him, the chatter of happy voices falling like early morning mist. He'd come for church, not for a date. One of this church's core values was devotion to God. He needed to focus on the Almighty.

He strode up to the barista, ordered a double cappuccino, and stuck a five-dollar bill in the tip jar. Core value number two. Generosity. Financially frugal, he hadn't always been the most generous person. Though he'd always tithed, he was far more likely to save a chunk of money than donate it. But maybe that was changing. Impact church was living up to its name.

Once he had the cappuccino in hand, he opted to mill about, studying the pictures on the wall. There was one of what looked to be a groundbreaking ceremony for the current church building. Others sported Pastor Richard in what seemed like foreign countries with groups of missionaries. There were a few powerful photos of corporate praise. His gaze zeroed in on one woman in particular. One hand covering her heart, while the other was raised in worship. Candi. His chest warmed. What more could he want than a woman who loved Jesus with all her heart, mind, soul, and strength. He couldn't be one hundred percent certain, but Candi sure seemed to fit that description. He savored a sip of coffee.

"Justice, welcome back."

He turned to find the woman he'd just been thinking about. His drink went down the wrong pipe. He coughed and sputtered, banging his chest with his fist. Real smooth.

Her eyes widened. "You okay?"

He nodded, then squeaked out, "Hi, Candi." The urge to cough finally lessened, but by now his face was as hot as a campfire. "I'm fine." Only about to die of embarrassment.

"Okay, well …" She shifted her weight and glanced down the hall. "I have to go. Just wanted to say hi."

He waved. "Hi."

She waved back. "Hi." She bit the corner of her lip. "Anyway." She pointed down the hall.

He couldn't just let her walk away. "So, what's your role here? Are you—"

"Pastor Richard's personal assistant."

Oh. He'd been about to guess the head of hospitality. "You're staff then?"

"Yep. Full time."

What must it be like to work closely with such a gifted speaker? The Lord's hand was clearly all over Pastor Richard. "Cool."

She beamed. "I love my job. Love this church." She shifted her weight again. "But I really gotta run."

"Of course. Sorry to keep you." A lie. If only he could keep her talking for longer. But of course, she had important duties here. He needed to put the core value of humility into practice and not dominate her time.

She waved off his apology. "Maybe I'll see you after service."

She'd taken three steps down the hall when he called after her. "Or what about dinner Tuesday evening?"

His stomach dropped. Had he just blurted that out? What had gotten into him? He braced himself for a humiliating rejection that would certainly make the rest of his time here awkward.

She played with a strand of hair. "I have Bible study Tuesday night."

Of course she did. Or else that was a sweet church girl's way of letting him down easy. He forced an insincere smile and started to nod.

"What about Wednesday?"

His breath stuttered. "Wednesday? Yeah, that works."

Her eyes sparkled. "Text me the details. My number is in the back of that welcome packet."

"S-sure."

With one last wave, she spun around and sauntered away. He could pinch—or slap—himself for how ridiculous he'd acted around her. Like he was some prepubescent boy with his first crush. How had she managed to unravel him? How in the world could he pay attention to the sermon now?

But he did. Worship time this week was just as powerful as the last. The songs took his mind off everything else but the Lord and his gratitude for what God had done for him. The announcement video didn't feature Candi. He couldn't deny the sliver of disappointment that snaked through him, but it was better this way. Less distracting.

Richard preached about meekness and how it differed from weakness. Strength under restraint, he called it, and it saturated the entire Sermon on the Mount. *Blessed are the meek, for they will inherit the earth.* God sure placed high value on this character trait. He left resolving to study meekness throughout the week during his personal time with the Lord.

He made it halfway to his car before he remembered he had a date with a beautiful, God-fearing woman. Yet another reason to thank God for leading him to Impact Church.

Chapter 3

Candi settled next to her friend Rachel on the green sofa adorning Richard's living room. She cradled a plate of chips and salsa in her lap. Other friends filled the space, some on couches and recliners, others on the plush floral rug. A fire crackled in the fireplace, creating a cozy ambiance. Tuesday night Bible study was by far her favorite time of the week.

Impact Church boasted many small groups, but the one held at Richard's house every Tuesday at six p.m. wasn't listed on the website or welcome packet. It was an invitation only gathering. Richard said he prayed about who to invite, and the Lord highlighted a dozen people who were pure of heart and ready to seek the deep things of God. Though he added members to the group from time to time, it still felt small and intimate. The twenty people—all female—who were here now had become her closest friends. No, more than that. They'd become family.

Richard and his wife Natalie sat on the love seat across from her. Natalie welcomed the group, then pulled her guitar to her lap and began to play. Worship time here was far different than at the weekend services. Simple strings swirled with a mixture of pure voices, raised in, not contemporary worship songs, but hymns. There was a soulfulness about it all. A tenderness. And Candi relished every minute, snack temporarily forgotten.

When the music ended, Natalie led them in prayer, and peace permeated Candi's body. It was as if she'd soaked in a long bubble bath. *Thank You, Lord. You're working all things out for my good and Your glory. You are here, and You're at work in me.*

After the prayer, Richard leaned forward, elbows on his knees, and worn Bible in his hands. "Please open your Bibles to Matthew 7:13."

Candi grabbed her Bible from the coffee table and flipped to the passage. The only sounds in the room were pages turning and the hiss and pop from the fireplace. Soon, all eyes locked onto Richard.

"Scripture says, 'Enter by the narrow gate; for wide is the gate and broad is the way that leads to destruction, and there are many who go in by it. Because narrow is the gate and difficult is the way which leads to life, and there are few who find it.'

"The words *narrow*, *difficult*, and *few* stand out to me here. We live in a culture where most everyone thinks they're saved. They think they're going to Heaven. They imagine they know God *enough* to coast through this life and end up on the good side of eternity. But many are wrong. Narrow. Difficult. Few. I don't know about you, but I want to be one of those few."

So did she. If only a small percentage of those who called themselves Christian were indeed true believers, she needed to be one of the few who weren't deceiving themselves.

"If we jump down to verse 21, we'll see Jesus continues in a similar vein. 'Not everyone who says to Me, "Lord, Lord," shall enter the kingdom of heaven, but he who does the will of My Father in heaven. Many will say to Me in that day, "Lord, Lord, have we not prophesied in Your name, cast out demons in Your name, and done many wonders in Your name?" And then I will declare to them, "I never knew you; depart from Me, you who practice lawlessness!"'"

Candi shuddered. A glance around showed solemn expressions. This was scary stuff.

"We can look at this passage like a sandwich. One slice of bread being narrow, difficult, and few. The other slice of bread being 'Not everyone who says to Me, "Lord, Lord", shall enter the kingdom of heaven.' At Impact Church, I teach how to be one of those few whom the Father will not deny. Our values of humility, generosity, and devotion ensure that we're on the right track to seeking God with all of our hearts and being one of the elite, fully entering into God's Kingdom."

Candi took a deep breath, filling her lungs with lavender-scented air. Her future was secure because she was in the right place. This group of deeply devoted followers of Jesus were no doubt the cream of the Christian crop. All sought the Lord passionately. They wouldn't be left behind.

"In light of these verses, I'm calling this group specifically to fast for two days a week, in addition to the monthly fast we do as a church. You've heard me preach on the value of fasting, so I don't need to go over the reasons why we engage in this spiritual discipline. I've chosen each of you to be in this group because I believe the Lord highlighted you. You're special. You serve the Lord with utmost devotion. Fasting two days a week will help you draw even closer to God's heart and will heighten your love for Him."

Candi couldn't help but squirm. Two days a week, in addition to the three-day monthly fast? That was a lot. She dared to meet Rachel's eyes, which mirrored her uncertainty. No one spoke. Were the rest of them thinking the same thing? If only someone would ask him if this was truly necessary.

Couldn't they at least start with fewer fast days and work up to more? But, of course, no one would dare challenge Richard on this. If they did, it would prove they weren't as devoted as he'd thought.

"I know what you're thinking." Richard offered a warm smile. "Your flesh is resisting right now. It's whining and complaining, saying 'This is too hard.' I encourage you to silence your flesh by repeating, 'narrow, difficult, and few.'"

Of course. The discomfort that spread through her wasn't of God. It was her wicked flesh. She had to master it, wrestle it into submission. She could do this, and she would. So help her God.

"Now, if those two verses are the bread of this passage, let's look at the meat. We find it in verse 15. 'Beware of false prophets, who come to you in sheep's clothing, but inwardly they are ravenous wolves.'"

The skin on Candi's neck prickled. She set her plate on the coffee table, brought her knees to her chest, and wrapped her arms around them.

"The reason few will be proven true believers is because of the wolves. You must watch out for the wolves." He studied each person there, his gaze filled with fatherly concern. "These wolves will appear to be Christians. They'll come to our services, join our church, attend small groups, worship with uplifted hands. But they're liars and pretenders. Their true aim is to weaken your devotion to Christ. They're out to bring you down. You must not let them."

Wolves among them. Who might they be? Clearly, she couldn't trust everyone who walked through the doors of Impact Church. What if … her heart thudded against her rib cage. No, not Justice. Certainly not. Surely he had a genuine relationship with the Lord. But, how could she really tell? She lifted a shaky hand.

Richard gestured toward her. "Yes, Can*do*?"

"How do we know who the wolves are?"

His smile broadened. "Great question. The answer lies in the next verse. It says, 'You will know them by their fruits.' Are they willing to die to their flesh and live a consecrated lifestyle? If they say they're believers, but shirk from walking the narrow, difficult road, you can know they're hypocrites. Wolves."

She swallowed. That made sense. She'd need to get to know Justice more and see how serious he was about wholeheartedly following Jesus. Maybe she could invite him to fast with her. His response would prove his devotion. Their date would be a test to ensure he was a true sheep.

*****

Justice had been agonizing over what to plan for his date with Candi ever since she'd agreed to go out with him. Dinner certainly wasn't enough. Not for someone as special as her. A movie sounded lame, but without knowing more about her hobbies and interests, he was at a loss. Until he spotted a billboard for the botanical garden's glow walk. In preparation for the upcoming Christmas season, they'd decked the garden with lights of all sizes and colors. It sounded like something a woman would find magical and romantic. Perfect. They'd go to dinner first, then have a memorable stroll.

He punched her address into his phone and discovered she lived less than a block from the church. Interesting. And convenient, since she worked at Impact. He pulled up to her apartment complex and stepped out, intending to walk the flight of steps and pick her up at her door, but she was nearly to his car by the time he shut the driver's side door.

"Hi." Her smile stretched wide, her voice breathy. She wore jeans, tennis shoes, and a puffy pink coat. Perfect. He'd told her to dress warm.

"Hey." He rushed to the passenger's side and opened her door.

"Thank you." She ducked inside, setting her small purple purse on her lap.

"Of course."

Once behind the wheel, his mind tripped over what to say. How should he start a conversation when he wanted to know literally everything about her?

"So, where are we going?" She moistened her lips, her smile barely suppressed.

That would be a good place to start. "DeAngelo's first, then to the botanical garden."

She clapped. "The garden glow?"

"Exactly." A thrill shot through him. He'd chosen well.

"I've always wanted to go."

"Then tonight's your night."

Country music played quietly in the background. The heater whispered warm air. Thankfully, the weather was cooperating. Chilly, but clear. Tonight was his night, too.

"DeAngelo's is a bit pricy though, isn't it? I don't need anything that fancy. McDonalds would be fine."

He spit out a laugh. "There's no way I'm taking you to McDonalds."

She chuckled. "I'm just saying."

"Let me do this for you. Please?"

Her cheeks matched her coat.

"Okay." A beat of silence, and she continued. "Tell me about your relationship with the Lord. What church did you go to before coming to Impact? When were you saved? What's your testimony."

And to think he'd been afraid of pelting *her* with questions. Jesus was clearly her top priority. Amazing. "Before Impact, I attended a home church that came out of The Way Community Church. The Way's attendance dwindled, and the congregation disbanded into several home churches, but after a few years, my home church kinda died too. Not enough young blood, I guess."

"That's sad."

"It was, but 'for everything there is a season', right? Apparently, it was the Lord's timing for us to move on. It's encouraging to see how vibrant Impact is. It doesn't seem like I'll have the same problem there."

"Definitely not. Our attendance keeps growing. We're going to have to add another service before too long. Pastor Richard always says healthy things grow."

He tilted his head. That was probably true. Healthy things did expand. But didn't some unhealthy things spread as well? Just that morning the news proclaimed that flu cases were rising at an alarming rate.

"To answer your other questions, I found Jesus—or rather He found me—when I was sixteen. I grew up in a stable family who said they believed in God, but we didn't attend church or read our Bibles or anything. A friend on my high school basketball team kept inviting me to church. Eventually, I gave in. Jesus met me there."

She gave a contented-sounding sigh.

"What about you?"

She took a minute to answer. "I … grew up in foster care." Her voice came much quieter now. "Five different families, so, not as bad as a lot of kids I knew. One family, the Roberts, took us to church. It was nice, but all too soon, it was over. The Roberts moved to be closer to family and my caseworker shuffled me to a different home."

His heart ached for her. His fingers uncurled from the steering wheel and moved toward her shoulder. But no. Too forward. Not the right time. He let his hand fall to the center console. "I'm sorry to hear that."

"When I turned eighteen, I finally reunited with my birthparents. It seemed like we were starting to build a relationship. But when I started going to Impact, they pulled away. They don't like Richard for some reason and certainly didn't want me to work for the church. We barely talk now. It's like they abandoned me all over again."

What a gut punch. At least he could be thankful she hadn't shared this story over dinner. He might have lost his appetite. "You seem remarkably well adjusted in light of … everything."

"Thanks to Impact. They became my family." A smile lilted through her words.

Family. "Just what you needed."

They arrived at the restaurant and Justice took her arm, escorting her inside. Once seated, he said, "Don't even think of ordering the cheapest thing on the menu."

She scrunched her nose. Adorable. "How'd you know?"

"I can tell what section of the menu you're browsing." He pointed to a selection of entrees. "Try here."

"You're sure?"

"Completely."

Her eyes sparked as she redirected her attention to the delicious selections. Did she realize she was licking her lips? Cute. If only he could switch to her side of the booth and wrap her in his arms.

"The sirloin?" She sounded afraid to ask.

"It's amazing. You should definitely order it if steak is your thing."

She chuckled. "I wouldn't know. It's been so long since I've had it."

"That settles it." He pushed his menu to the side. "We can both get the sirloin."

Her mouth parted, but he beat her to it. "Yes, I'm sure."

She placed her menu on top of his. "What do you do for a living?" He got the gist of what she wasn't saying. *How can you afford this meal?*

"I work at a call center. Collections."

She winced.

"Yeah, I know. Not glamorous, but it pays the bills, and I get a hefty commission. My expenses are low, so I can afford to splurge every now and then." He nearly told her about his podcast, a hobby that took a considerable chunk of his time, but he bit back the words. Did his hesitation stem from a check in his spirit or fear she'd look down on him for it? Whatever the reason, now wasn't the time to share.

Time to redirect. "What would you be eating right now if you were at home?"

She laughed without humor. "Raman. Or boxed mac 'n cheese."

"Seriously?" He tried not to cringe. Were they paying her so little she couldn't afford a decent meal?

She answered his question as if he'd asked it out loud. "I don't get much of a salary, but Richard pays for my apartment, so my bills are minimal."

Oddly worded. "Richard pays?"

She nodded, then sipped her water. "He covers it personally. He practices what he preaches about generosity."

"Hmm." That seemed strange.

"I'm happy with the arrangement. I wouldn't want to take finances away from the missions organizations Impact supports. I'm not doing it for the money. I wanted a job that would make a difference." She smiled brightly. "And I have it."

She gushed about how much she loved Impact until the waitress brought their entrees. He reached for her hands across the table and prayed for their meal. If only he didn't have to let go.

He watched her dig into her steak. She closed her eyes. "Oh my goodness. This is amazing."

How great would it be to treat her to decadent meals every week? Spoiling her would be fun.

"Tell me about your Tuesday night Bible study." He forked a bite of still-glistening steak into his mouth. She hadn't lied. Delicious.

"Richard hosts and leads it, along with his wife, Natalie. It's a wonderful group of women who want to go deep into the Word."

His fork paused. "Only women?" He'd relish the opportunity to attend a Bible study with Candi. It'd be a great way to get to know her more.

She pursed her lips. "I think that's just coincidence. He never said it was women only." Her face lit up. "Would you like to come? I can ask Richard."

"I'd love to."

The night only got better once they reached the botanical gardens. Candi's wide-eyed wonder at each display left him almost giddy. And when he gathered the courage to take her gloved hand in his and she didn't pull away, he could easily claim this as one of the best nights of his life.

Chapter 4

Candi nearly floated into the office the next day. Her date with Justice had been magical. After he'd shared his testimony so sincerely, there'd been no need to ask him to fast with her to prove his devotion. No way he could be a wolf. He was a godly man through and through, and he certainly seemed interested in her.

No kiss at the door when dropping her off. A good sign the man didn't kiss on a first date. It proved he was out for more than just the physical and signaled he'd be careful with her heart. She could wait for the right moment. God's timing.

After setting her purse on her desk, she breezed into Richard's office. He sat bent over his Bible, notebook and pen at the ready.

She knocked on the door frame. "Is there anything you need from me before I assemble volunteer packets?"

When he looked up at her, he lacked his usual smile. "You were busy last night?"

She hadn't told him she had a date. Why would she? He didn't need to know every aspect of her life. "Yeah." Why did guilt prick her under his perusal? She couldn't make eye contact. Instead, her gaze lingered on a potted fern in the corner. The edges of its leaves were brown.

"It took you two hours to return my text. That's unlike you. Are you okay?" His voice oozed concern.

Her cheeks heated. "Yes, I'm fine. I was out with a friend." Not a lie, but for some reason she hesitated to tell him the full truth.

He sat back and folded his hands across his middle. "Oh? What friend?" Was he interrogating her or simply making pleasant conversation? It had to be the latter. She rarely held anything back from him. No need to start now.

"Justice." Her stomach wobbled at the mention of his name. "He's new to Impact. Came from a home church. Solid faith." The inexplicable urge to defend him rose inside her.

He frowned. "You were on a date?"

No use denying it. Besides, Justice was someone she could be proud to know. "Yes. A date."

Richard stood so abruptly, she startled. A couple pieces of paper fluttered from his desk onto the floor. He paced from one side of the office to the other. "Why didn't you tell me you were going on a date? You consider me your spiritual father, and you didn't think to bring up something like this? I would have wanted to meet him first."

Oh. She hadn't thought of that. "I-I'm sorry." She toed the carpet, gaze fixed on her black heels.

When he sighed deeply, she chanced looking at him. He ran a hand through his hair and leaned against the front of his desk. "I forgive you, Candi. Everyone makes mistakes. Every human stumbles. Christ will forgive your sin and cast it into the depths of the sea. Let me pray for you."

Her insides tangled into knots. What stung more? His disappointment or the fact that he hadn't used his nickname for her? She choked out a, "Thank you," and bowed her head.

His voice rang with authority and commanded her attention. "Heavenly Father, I come before you on behalf of my spiritual daughter. Your Word says to honor your father and mother, and yet Candi has not honored me. She confesses this sin to You now and asks that You make her clean." He paused, and an awkward silence snaked between them. "Go ahead. Confess to him."

Oh, it was her turn to pray. "Jesus, I—"

"Heavenly Father."

Right. How could she forget the way Richard had taught her to pray correctly. "Heavenly Father, I confess my sin of … of …" What had she done wrong again? She certainly hadn't meant any harm.

"Not honoring me."

"Not honoring Pastor Richard, my spiritual father."

"And hiding things from me."

She looked up. "I didn't mean to—"

"Direct your prayer to the Lord, Candi." He gestured for her to continue.

"And hiding things from him." She took a deep breath, then continued, "You said that if we confess our sin, You are faithful and just to forgive us and cleanse us of all unrighteousness. I ask that You do so for me. Amen."

"Amen." He patted her on the back. "I trust that you'll be more considerate in the future."

She nodded, even though confusion swirled. She'd never intended to do anything wrong. It hadn't even occurred to her that she'd dishonored Richard until he brought it up. How could she avoid future mistakes when she'd been so ignorant about this one?

Richard rounded his desk and reclaimed his chair. "So, tell me about Justice."

She sat on the edge of the chair across from him, her nerves popping like firecrackers. "Like I said, he's new to Impact." Her voice shook. She willed it to steady. "He attended the informational class Saturday and seems excited to get involved.”

Richard frowned at her. How could she make him see what a wonderful man Justice was?

“He shared his testimony with me and—”

Richard waved her off. “That’s talk. Anyone can talk. What about fruit?”

She bit her lip. What did that even mean? “He … he’s very kind.”

Richard scoffed. “Of course he is. He’s trying to impress you.” He shook his head, as if disappointed in her naïveté. “It’s hard to believe that just one day after I talked about wolves, you go on a date with one.”

“He’s not a wolf. I promise you.”

“How can you truly know, Candi? Your eyes are blinded.”

No. He didn’t know what he was saying. “I’ll introduce you to him on Sunday. I’m sure you’ll like him once you meet him. You can see for yourself, he’s no wolf.”

His smile seemed forced. “Be sure to do that. I’d like to meet him.” He shuffled some papers on his desk. “Now, if you’ll excuse me, I have a sermon to prepare.”

She nearly jumped to her feet. “Of course. I’ll leave you to it.”

“I’ll pray about your young man. See if the Lord reveals anything to me.”

She left Richard’s office in a daze. How could he be so wrong about Justice? Or … was she?

That night she’d just started to boil water for mac n’ cheese when her doorbell rang. A DoorDash delivery sat outside her apartment door. A surprise from Justice? She brought it inside. Fettuccine Alfredo from her favorite Italian restaurant. How did Justice know?

Her phone dinged with a text. Richard. "Enjoy your meal. A gesture of good faith to show all is forgiven."

Some of the excitement drained. This wasn't from Justice at all. But at least she was back on good terms with Richard. She should be thankful to have a spiritual leader who cared so much about her. He was only looking out for her. She had to show him Justice wasn't a threat.

*****

Justice had just finished brushing his teeth when his phone buzzed with a text. Candi checking in? He dashed to his bedside table and snatched up his phone. Bummer. Not Candi. Why was he so disappointed? He needed to tamp his expectations. They'd only been on one date.

With a sigh, he opened his friend Brian's text.

Brian: What's the name of the church you started going to?

Did Brian want to come too? That'd be fun.

Justice: Impact Church. Sunday services at 9 and 11. Want to join me?

Brian: That's what I thought. You're going to want to hear what Sammie has to say. I'm sending her your info.

And no, not interested in going. You'll see why when you hear from Sammie.

Sammie who? Brian wasn't making any sense. Unless …

Justice: Is this about my podcast?

Brian: Yeah.

And your wellbeing.

What did that mean? Uneasiness slithered through him. It'd never been his dream to start a podcast highlighting church abuse. In his ideal world, there wouldn't be a need, and if there was, he'd stay far away from the topic. But when his friend Matthias had spilled his story, righteous indignation had flamed within. He'd needed to do something, and punching the pastor who'd sexually assaulted Matthias's wife hadn't been a viable option. So, the For the Love of Truth podcast was born.

He'd interviewed Matthias for the first episode, then followed a sickening trail from one victim to another in that dysfunctional church. That one pastor had provided six months of material. By allowing the victims to share their stories, Justice had hopefully made the world a safer place for well-meaning Christians. That pastor was now behind bars.

After that, he'd assumed his work was done, and he could go back to relaxing on his time off. He'd been wrong. Others came forward, each with a painful story of suffering at the hands of spiritual leaders who were supposed to protect them. The podcast had been going strong for two years. How unfortunate. He prayed daily that soon there'd be no stories to spotlight.

But what did that have to do with Impact? He'd certainly not detected anything off with that church. It was thriving. The members nearly glowed with joy. If there was anything amiss, wouldn't Candi be one of the first to know? She was the pastor's right-hand woman. She wouldn't gush about the church if Richard or any of the other leaders were abusive. There had to be some kind of misunderstanding. Was there another Impact Church? Or a different church with a similar name? Maybe Brian had misheard.

The possibilities bothered him all day. He didn't usually have problems focusing at work. He'd become one of the top collectors due to his ability to avoid distractions and get the job done. But not today. He kept checking his email and text messages for something from Brian or Sammie. The answer didn't appear in his inbox until after dinner.

Subject: Spiritual Abuse at Impact Church

Justice,

Your friend Brian gave me your contact information after hearing my story. He told me about your podcast and how you want to shine a light on spiritual abuse in the church. I'm terrified to speak out. I don't know what kind of retaliation I'll face. But if I can save one other woman from going through what I did, it'll be worth it.

Pastor Richard Blake is not what he seems. I'm willing to tell you what happened to me at Impact, as long as you don't make my name public. I can even speak on the podcast if you disguise my voice and don't show my face.

If you're interested in hearing more, please let me know, and we can arrange to meet.

Thanks,

S.S.

Justice's stomach dropped as he reread the email, then read it again. Now he couldn't deny that she was talking about *his* Impact Church. Richard wasn't what he seemed? Did Candi know? *Please, God, don't let her be complicit.*

What if she didn't have a clue? What if she wasn't safe?

His heart thrummed in his ears as he replied to the email.

Let's talk. Name a time and place. I'll be there.

Chapter 5

Candi tossed and turned all night, finally giving up around three a.m. Might as well wake up and get a head start on today's workload. The television network wanted a summary of all the messages Richard planned to share for the first two months. It was up to her to somehow put together Richard's scrambled notes and compose cohesive summaries from them. Good thing she had plenty of experience deciphering his handwriting.

After a hot shower and a breakfast of oatmeal and strong coffee, she headed to the office. How strange to enter the empty building alone. She ought to get a lot of work done in such a quiet environment. No distractions. Instead, eeriness put her on edge. Every noise, from the heater kicking on to a nearby tree branch scratching a window, made her jump.

When her phone lit up with a text, she yelped, hand over her heart. How ridiculous. It was only Justice.

Justice: I need to talk to you when you wake up.

Richard's warning reverberated in the back of her mind. But he was wrong, wasn't he? Justice was a good guy. Definitely not a threat. Still, she probably shouldn't agree to meet him again without Richard's permission.

Candi: What about?

She waited as three dots appeared. And waited. How long of a message was he typing?

Justice: Too much to explain over text. Can I call now?

Candi scanned the empty office. No better time. Was it about their relationship? Or was he in some kind of trouble?

She wouldn't be able to get any work done without knowing what was so important.

Candi: Sure.

She hugged herself as she waited for his call. How would Richard feel if he knew she was talking to Justice at four-thirty in the morning? There were no security cameras, right? He wouldn't find out. She could slap herself. Why did it matter if she had a phone call with a guy? She wasn't doing anything wrong. So why did it feel like she was?

Her phone rang. She answered with a shaky, "Hello?"

"Candi, hi. I didn't think you'd be up this early. I didn't wake you, did I? You said you slept with your phone's volume off."

"I usually do. I couldn't sleep."

"Me either. Listen, I have something important to ask you. Will you promise to be honest with me?"

What could this possibly be about? Her fingers trembled. "Yes."

"Do you feel safe at Impact? With Richard, I mean."

She huffed. What kind of question was that? "Of course. Why?" Why wouldn't she feel safe around the godly man who'd taken her under his wing?

"You're sure?"

"Justice, what's this about?"

He sighed. "A friend of a friend emailed me last night, a former member of your church. She said Richard spiritually abused her at Impact."

"That's crazy." Candi stood and began to pace. "Who was it? Krista? Irene?"

A beat of silence. "I'm not at liberty to say."

Anger burned through her as her heels clacked against the hardwood floor. "It's got to be one of them. They left the church, and now they're out to tarnish Richard's reputation. The snakes." No, not snakes. Wolves.

"Woah. Don't you think you should hear her story before jumping to that conclusion?"

"Jumping to—are you out of your mind? I see Richard every single day. I work with him more closely than anyone. Don't you think I'd know if he was anything other than the godly, selfless leader everyone knows him to be?"

"That's what I was thinking too. I figured if anyone would know if these claims were valid, it should be you."

"You're darn right."

"But then I got worried for you. If her claims *are* true, you'd be in danger of abuse as well."

Her fury cooled a smidge. He had pure intentions, however misguided. He cared about her enough to ask a hard question. It wasn't his fault he'd gotten false information.

"I promise, I'm fine. Richard's integrity is spotless."

"Okay. I just wanted to check." He didn't sound convinced, but maybe he'd drop the subject now.

"Go back to bed." Poor guy had lost sleep over her.

"I don't think that's happening, but I'll go to bed early tonight if it'd make you feel better."

She found a smile. "It would."

"Okay, then. Have a good day."

"You too."

She sat in silence, thinking. How dare that woman lie about Richard. Why would she try to take Richard down? If the mystery woman was Valerie or Anaka, this betrayal would sting. Hard. Candi had befriended both women, and though they'd never been best friends, she couldn't fathom them slinging such horrible lies. "You think you know a person," she mumbled to the empty room.

But what if …

No. Ridiculous to entertain the idea for even a second. Richard would never do something like that.

Maybe if she searched his office, she'd feel better. Once she saw there was no condemning evidence there, she'd breathe easier. She could be sure he wasn't hiding anything. She eyed his office door.

What was she thinking? If dating Justice without asking Richard's permission dishonored him, how much more would snooping around his office. If he ever found out, the shame would weigh her down. No, she couldn't violate his privacy, not even to prove him innocent.

Best to get to work.

She dove into Richard's notes. His first televised program would be about the accuser of the brethren. Goosebumps peppered her arms as she continued to read and compile. *In the last days believers will turn on one another and fling accusations. When you accuse a believer, you're partnering with Satan's agenda. The Lord wants us to believe the best about other people. Love believes all things, hopes all things.*

It was as if Richard knew someone would fling crazy allegations at him. As if the Lord had shown him what would take place. That woman, whoever she might be, was partnering with Satan as an accuser. Did that mean Justice was too? No. He'd only asked a question about what he'd heard. He'd never said he agreed with it.

It was as if this was a game of tug of war, and she was a rope. Justice pulled one end, Richard the other—both men probably wary of each other and wanting to protect her. How could she help them reconcile with each other?

*****

Uneasiness cloaked Justice in a fog as he walked into Impact Church on Sunday morning. Tomorrow, he'd meet with Sammie. Today, he'd scope out the church he'd been so close to joining. Maybe he still would. If he listened and watched and nothing appeared amiss, he might still attend the membership class. If internal warning bells blared, however, he'd need to convince Candi to jump ship. Would she listen?

She was so invested in Impact. So sure Richard was a righteous man. Was she deceived? Or was Sammie out to discredit a man of God? His stomach wobbled.

As usual, several people in blue Impact Church shirts greeted him warmly. Keeping an eye out for Candi, he grabbed a coffee and took a seat at a small table in the café. He'd people watch for now. See if anything seemed off.

"Can I sit here?" A young woman with curly brown hair stood by his table. She held a scone-laden paper plate and a coffee.

"Of course." He motioned to the seat across from him. "I'm Justice."

"Angela. Nice to meet you." She sat and studied him with a wry smile. "Sorry to disturb you. You look deep in thought."

He shrugged. "Not really. Just observing."

"You're new here." It wasn't a question.

"Yeah. How long have you been coming?"

She blew a raspberry. "Four years? Maybe five."

"And you like it?" Dumb question. If she didn't, she wouldn't be here.

257

"Love it." She closed her eyes briefly as she bit into her scone's flaky crust.

"What do you love about it?" He sipped his coffee. Maybe he should buy a pastry too.

"What's not to love? Everyone here is so friendly. I've made a ton of great friends." She sipped her coffee. "Worship is excellent, and Pastor Richard's sermons are deep and insightful."

"Do you know Pastor Richard personally?" Maybe she could shed some light on the man's true nature.

"Oh yeah. I'm part of his VIP Tuesday night Bible study."

"The one Candi attends?"

A smirk lifted one corner of her mouth. "You know Candi?"

How much should he reveal? Best not to claim he was dating her. It might shut down the conversation. "Yeah." He'd keep it simple.

"She's Pastor's favorite. He showers her with gifts and attention, put her up in that apartment, has her number on speed dial." She leaned forward and lowered her voice. "Rumor is, Candi is number two on his speed dial and his wife is number three."

He studied her. Was she jealous of Candi's relationship with Richard? Or was it something more? "Are you implying something …" He paused, searching for the right word. "Inappropriate?"

She sat back and shook her head. "No. I mean there are rumors, but I don't believe them. Candi's as straight and narrow as they come."

"And Richard?"

"Oh, he obviously loves his wife. And the Lord. No question."

If there was no question, why had Angela brought it up? Jealousy probably played a factor. "Does he treat her like a favorite daughter?"

She gave a decisive nod. "Yeah. That's it. Everyone would love to be the center of his attention, but that spot is reserved for Candi."

A small cough caused him to look up. "Candi." She wore black slacks and a top that matched her blue eyes perfectly. And heels. She always wore heels. "Hi."

"Sorry to interrupt your … conversation, but can I grab you for a minute? Pastor Richard wants to meet you."

He pointed to himself. "Me?"

"Yeah." She bit her lip. Nervous? That did little to put him at ease. Why did the pastor want to meet him? Maybe he introduced himself to all new attendees. It could be a thing.

"Sure." He drained the rest of his coffee and stood. "Nice to meet you, Angela."

"Same."

"See ya, Angie," Candi said before turning to walk toward the sanctuary. When they were out of Angela's earshot, Candi cast him a side-eyed glance. "I heard my name. You were talking about me?"

Yikes. How much had she heard? "Nothing bad. Angela was saying how Richard really seems to like you."

She raised a brow as if she didn't believe him.

"What?"

"Nothing." She walked at a fast clip. "Richard has a second little office backstage. Follow me."

He had to work to keep up. "Why does he want to meet me?"

Her eyes focused straight ahead as they passed the front few rows and ascended the stage's steps. "I told him about you. He's protective of me, I guess. Wants to vet you."

He stopped. "He wants to vet me?"

She paused and met his eyes. "Yeah. See if you're worthy of me or something."

Like what a father would do. "Okay." He resumed following her. He'd met a few fathers before when he'd dated in the past. They normally liked him. Nothing to fear. And this would give him a chance to see the man up close, without his stage persona.

Candi led him backstage to a small office area. Richard sat behind a desk, Bible open before him. She knocked on the open door. "Pastor? Here's Justice."

Richard stood, breaking into a wide smile. He stepped forward and shook Justice's hand eagerly. "Well, hello, young man. So great to meet you."

Any tension Justice had been carrying immediately melted away. What had he been nervous about? "An honor to meet you, sir."

Richard blew out a breath. "Oh, don't sir me. I'm just a man, like you." He sat on the edge of his desk. "I hear you're interested in my Candi."

He fought the urge to squirm at his possessive use of *my*. "Yes, sir. Uh, Pastor."

Richard chuckled. "Well, I don't blame you. She's quite a special girl. She's been an asset to me and my ministry."

"I can imagine."

"How are you enjoying Impact so far?"

Justice hesitated a beat. He'd been loving the church until he heard from Sammie. But, although he was leery, he hadn't observed anything especially concerning. "I like everything I've seen."

"Good. Good." Richard patted him on the back, then put a protective arm around Candi's shoulders.

Her tight smile betrayed her discomfort. But why wouldn't she be? It was always awkward introducing a significant other to authority figures.

After a squeeze to her shoulder, Richard dropped his arm and returned to his side of the desk. "Well, I don't want to keep you. Just wanted to meet the man my Candi has taken an interest in. Enjoy the service."

"I'm sure I will." Justice moved toward the door, Candi on his heels.

"Candi, dear," Richard called out after she'd crossed the threshold. "I need you for a minute."

"Sure thing." She tossed Justice a sympathetic smile. "Can you find your way out of here?"

"No problem. See you later?"

"For sure." She retreated into the office, closing the door behind her.

Chapter 6

When the last congregants filed out of the building, Candi approached Richard. She waited while he talked with Matt, the sound guy. As soon as he finished the conversation, she pounced. After Justice had left earlier, Richard had detained her to ask her opinion on the new chairs the church administrator was ordering for the sanctuary. No chance to ask what he thought of Justice before the service began. She couldn't wait another minute to hear his opinion.

"So, what did you think?" He'd been congenial when meeting Justice. Surely, he now approved.

The smile he'd spouted with Matt fell away. He put a hand on her shoulder. "You're a grown woman. I can't tell you what to do."

What? His friendly demeanor during their brief meeting couldn't have been an act. "I don't understand. You seemed to like him."

His hand dropped. "I only warn you to be careful. Not everyone is who they seem."

Confusion swirled. "But you're not forbidding me to date him?"

He shook his head. "I don't have the authority to do that."

Then why had he made such a big deal about their first date? None of this made sense. His reluctant permission left her insides slimy. These two men were important to her. Why couldn't they like each other? She wrapped her arms around her middle. "Okay." She walked away in a daze.

When Justice texted a few hours later, asking if he could take her out the next night, she hesitated. Her thumbs hovered over her phone as she slipped off her shoes and settled on her couch. Richard didn't forbid her dating. His warning to be careful reverberated in her mind. He had it all wrong. Even pastors made mistakes. He had only spoken with Justice for a couple of minutes. So few words. How could she expect him to form an accurate opinion in such a short amount of time? Once Richard got to know Justice more, he'd see.

She replied with a yes, then asked when and where.

Justice: 5 p.m. and it's a surprise.

A thrill climbed her spine. Then her stomach sank. She was fasting tomorrow and Tuesday, per Richard's instructions, though she planned to still have liquids. She wouldn't be able to enjoy another indulgent meal. Bummer.

But at least she'd get to spend time with Justice. What did he have planned this time? No way he could top their last date, but he might match it. She could hardly sleep that night, her mind whirling with possibilities.

*****

She arrived at the office Monday morning with a mug full of coffee. Was coffee okay during a fast? Anything liquid was fair game, right? But the pointed look and frown Richard tossed her as she walked into the morning meeting made guilt pool in her gut. He was probably doing a water fast. Or maybe fasting both food and water. If only she could live up to his high standards.

"Good morning, team." Richard's smile fell back in place as he greeted the fifteen staff members in attendance. "I'm

263

excited to hear the progress you've made on preparing for our Christmas service later this month."

One by one, Richard called on each department head to give an update. Normally, he called on her first, but now he didn't even look at her. He aimed his enthusiasm and praise at each spokesman. Why did she feel like a puppy begging for scraps? Had she fallen out of his good graces? And if so, why? It could be her coffee mug, or maybe it was Justice.

"All right, team." He clapped his hands. "This all sounds great. As you know, our Christmas services are the second most highly attended. Many unbelievers will walk through our doors, and it's important they feel welcome and appreciated. We'll touch base again next week."

Wait, he was dismissing the meeting? She hadn't shared about the invitation cards she'd created for members to hand out to their friends, or the special Christmas bulletin. No one seemed to notice the absence of her voice as they filed from the room. When Richard stood, she spoke.

"Did you want to hear my updates?" How pitiful her question sounded. As if she were once again a little girl yearning for a foster parent's attention.

He barely glanced at her. "No, it's fine."

Fine. In other words, it didn't matter if she contributed or not. Her heart was like a bird flapping its wings, desperate to fly but going nowhere. Too immature to take to the skies. "Did I do something wrong?" Her voice trembled.

He met her eyes, face lined with weariness. "I just expected more from you. That's all." And then he walked away.

She stood rooted in place. Stunned. He expected more … more what? More devotion to Jesus? More dedication to the church? How could she correct her trajectory if she didn't know what she'd done wrong? How could she find a way back into his favor? She was his Can*do*. Surely she could do it. The itch to set things right clawed at her.

Perhaps he'd found out about her second date with Justice. Only she hadn't told anyone. That couldn't be it. But if he *did* find out, she'd be in an even worse position. He expected her to choose wisely, and dating Justice couldn't fit that expectation in his eyes. Should she cancel?

Her phone buzzed in her pocket. A text from Justice.

Looking forward to tonight.

Insides in knots, she glanced out the meeting room door and texted back a lie.

Me too.

*****

Would Justice's nerves always jitter when he knocked on Candi's door? Maybe someday they'd become so familiar with each other, it'd be like visiting his mom. Yikes. Bad comparison.

Candi answered the door with a rosy-cheeked smile, her hair in some kind of updo with small tendrils framing her face. His breath caught. How could she be this beautiful? It should be illegal.

"Wow," he said, then his gaze took in the rest of her. Her open coat revealed a soft mint-green sweater, modest, yet complimenting her curves. A dainty golden heart necklace. And a black skirt with leggings underneath. Boots with fuzzy tops adorned her feet. "You look…" What was the word? "Wow."

She giggled. "Should I change? If we're walking outside again, these leggings won't be warm enough."

"No need." He pivoted and stuck out his arm.

She pulled her purse over her shoulder, then hooked her arm around his, closing the door behind her. "You going to tell me where we're going?"

"Not yet." Hopefully she'd like his surprise. Find it charming instead of lame. He'd taken a gamble with this one, but if his instincts were correct, she'd find it delightful.

Her eyes sparkled. "Mysterious."

"You know me." He winked.

She didn't really know him. Not yet. But if he had his way, they'd be spending a lot more time together.

It took him until they were nearly to the restaurant to notice something was different with her. She said the right things in a pleasant tone, but something was off. When he parked and took her in, it hit him. Her eyes. Throughout the short drive, he'd studied her face at every stoplight. Though those mesmerizing blue eyes contained pieces of life, they had dulled. A clear indication that something was bugging her.

After parking, he reached over the center console and put a hand on her arm. "Is anything wrong?"

Her smile faltered. "Not really."

That had to mean there was something wrong, but she didn't trust him enough to share. Okay, then. He could wait for her to open up.

He rushed around to open her door for her, but she beat him to it. He offered his arm and escorted her into Belle's Restaurant. The scent of freshly baked bread and herbs wafted as they entered.

"I've never been here before." A pained look crossed her face.

Had he chosen the wrong restaurant? She didn't seem pleased. Maybe her mind was just on other things.

When they sat, she ordered water, then chicken soup. No steak? He opted for a club sandwich. It wouldn't do for him to eat steak in front of her.

When the waitress left, he set a hand on hers. "Are you sure you only want soup? You can get whatever you'd like. I can wave down the waitress if you want to change your order."

She shook her head. Bit her lip. "I'm …" Red tinged her cheeks. "I'm fasting. Liquids only for me."

He sat back. "Really? I wish you had said something. We didn't have to go to dinner."

She traced her finger in the condensation on her glass. "It's fine. I'll drink the broth. It'll be the best thing I've had all day." Her laugh fell flat.

"Do you fast often?"

She tilted her head. "We normally fast the first through the third of each month, but Rich … Pastor Richard—" Her lips twisted as if she were trying to find the right word. "Challenged us to fast every Monday and Tuesday."

His mouth dropped open. "Two days every week?"

She nodded, her expression somber.

"That's a lot." An understatement.

"Yeah, I know." She sighed. "But fasting is a great way to grow closer to the Lord. The Bible says *when* you fast, not *if* you fast. It's supposed to be a regular part of a Christian's lifestyle." The spouted line sounded rehearsed.

A twinge in his gut sent a warning to proceed with caution. "So, you felt the Lord stirring you to fast more?"

Her gaze dropped to her hands in her lap. "Not exactly. Pastor Richard encouraged us—"

"Who's us?" The pastor hadn't said anything from the pulpit on Sunday.

"The Tuesday night Bible study group."

Ahh. The one she'd wanted him to join.

He hesitated. She'd grown so angry when he'd suggested Richard might have abused someone. Would she get just as defensive if he spoke up now? Sammie's warning from her email echoed in his mind. He had nothing against fasting, as long as the Lord led one to do so. But if she was only fasting because her pastor pressured her to, it wasn't right. How could he not say anything?

"You're right. Scripture talks about fasting like it's a normal part of the Christian lifestyle. The early church seemed to fast often. The modern church has fallen out of practice."

Her shoulders rolled forward. "Exactly."

"But I believe the Holy Spirit is the one who leads us to fast. When He calls us to something, He provides grace for it. If we try to do it in our own strength, we'll only grow frustrated." He took her hand again, giving it a squeeze. "Has the Holy Spirit inspired you to participate in this fast?"

Her grunt spoke frustration. "The Bible says to submit to spiritual authority. Pastor Richard is in authority over me, and I'm submitting to him with this fast. It's Biblical."

"Which passage are you referring to?" He kept his tone light. Non-confrontational.

She groaned. "I don't know the precise verse. Just that it's in there."

"Hmm." He drew a soft circle on the back of her hand with his finger. "If you're talking about 1 Peter 2, it talks about submitting to human institutions, like the emperor or governors. I don't believe it's referring to pastors. Somewhere in Hebrews it says to obey those who rule over us, but again, I don't think it means pastors."

She withdrew her hand and unrolled her silverware. "I told you, I'm not good with where verses are in the Bible. But I'm confident submitting to spiritual authority is Biblical."

"Maybe." He'd have to study it more. What did Scripture truly say about following pastors' directions? Of course, they had spiritual authority, but did that mean they were supposed to dictate everything, including their congregation's diet? It sounded like a slippery slope. Would Candi do anything Richard told her to? Where would she draw the line?

"Can we drop this subject?" She shot him a pleading gaze.

"Absolutely." He hadn't meant to ruin their second date by pressing the issue. If only he could be confident of Richard's motives. Confident Candi was safe under his care. He might never have questioned it if he hadn't heard from Sammie. He forced a half smile. "Did Pastor Richard say anything about me after we met?"

She paled. "Let's talk about something other than church stuff."

So, Richard *had* mentioned him. Apparently, not in a positive light. Odd, since he'd seemed delighted in their brief meeting. Did the pastor know about Justice's podcast? Did he think it "divisive"? It wouldn't be the first time someone had held that opinion. "Sorry." What was he apologizing for? Certainly not for existing, and not for desiring a relationship with Candi. Maybe only for causing her stress or pain in any way.

She waved him off. "It's fine. The good news is he said it was okay to date you."

Wait, what? "You asked his permission?"

There went those cheeks again. Red as roses.

"Well, yeah. He's like my spiritual father. If I had a good relationship with my dad, I'd ask him for permission to date a guy. That's normal, isn't it?"

Her tone held uncertainty. She'd asked him to change the subject, and it was best if he didn't follow this tangent now. Maybe later, they could explore it together. For now … "So, do you like kids?"

"What?" She pressed her hands to her cheeks.

Oh, great. Did she think he was asking if she wanted to have kids with him? That hadn't been where he was going. Not yet, anyway.

"Where we're going next has kids. A bunch of them. I wanted to make sure that's okay?" His voice lilted up as if that were a question. Way to project confidence.

"Oh." Her smile seemed genuine. "Yes, I love kids."

Their meals arrived. Guilt swirled in him as he bit into his sandwich while she sipped broth with a spoon. If only she'd mentioned she would be fasting.

"So, we're going somewhere with a lot of children. The zoo? No, that's closed by now. A park?"

He chuckled. "Not in this weather." With the temperature hovering near two degrees, the parks would be deserted.

"Then I have no idea."

After dinner, he drove them to a nearby elementary school.

The side of her mouth quirked up. "What's this?"

"Welcome to my niece's Christmas concert. She's in the choir."

"Oh!" She clapped. "I love Christmas music."

He walked around and opened the passenger door for her. "Hopefully, you'll love fifth graders singing Christmas music." He scrunched his nose. "I hope this isn't too corny."

"Not at all. Children's voices are so pure. This is perfect."

As they sat next to each other on the hard wooden bleachers in the smelly gym, he had to admit she was right. Her wonder and delight made the night perfect. He could easily imagine the two of them married and viewing their own child's concert someday. Way to get ahead of himself. If only questions didn't linger between them. If Candi had to choose between him and Richard, which would she pick?

Chapter 7

Candi's limbs shook as Richard called her into his office the next morning. Had he found out about her second date with Justice? But he'd told her she could date him if she wanted, even if he'd made it clear he wasn't happy about it. Was this about her lukewarm fasting? Or something else? His somber tone and the grim set of his jaw proved this wasn't a fun catch-up meeting.

She stepped through the doorway and perched on the cushioned chair across from his desk, pressing her knees together to hide their trembling. Maybe her shakiness was due to fasting. Physically weak and mentally foggy, she was certainly not at her best. Richard shut the door behind her.

She swallowed hard.

Was that a half-eaten muffin on his desk? Couldn't be. He was fasting, too. It must have been from a few days ago, or perhaps someone else had left it there.

"Candi, I'm starting to think this position is too much for you." His frown deepened.

"W-what do you mean?" Too much for her? Was she in danger of him firing her?

"Something's changed within the past couple of weeks. You used to do your work with excellence and diligence. I had complete confidence you were all in. That you believed in the mission here at Impact and wanted to touch lives for the Kingdom."

"I do." She stood, her fingers fidgeting at her middle.

He shook his head. "You've been distracted lately and have let your work slip."

Distracted, yes. Thoughts of Justice occupied her mind most days. But she hadn't allowed it to affect her work, had she? She'd turned in everything Richard had asked for, even if she'd stayed up till midnight to finish it. "What work hasn't met your standards?" Her lip wobbled. Tears stung the back of her eyelids.

"Most everything."

Everything? Her thoughts stumbled over themselves as she recalled tasks she'd done the past two weeks. Transcribing his notes. Invite cards. Announcement prep and videos. Paperwork for the station. Volunteer schedules. Where had she dropped the ball? She rubbed her temples.

"If this position is too much for you, I know of several other young ladies who would be happy to take it off your hands. Of course, as the apartment comes with the job—"

"No. I can do it." Her breath came in hot, short bursts. "I can do better. I know I can."

His classic smile slipped into place. "If you're sure …"

"I am. I won't let you down again." An impossible promise to keep when she couldn't figure out what she'd done wrong. But somehow, she *would* keep it. She couldn't lose her job or her apartment. Couldn't lose Richard's favor.

"Maybe you've just been stressed." He stepped behind her and kneaded her tight shoulder muscles. A massage. That was normal for a father to do for his daughter, wasn't it? But her stomach churned as his breath hit her neck.

When she took a step forward, he did too. Another step and he followed. Now her knees pressed up against his desk and his chest pushed against her back. This was normal, right?

If she'd had a caring father, he would have likely done the same when she was anxious. Justice's warning swirled inside her, a breeze pushing leaves in circles.

"I believe in you, Can*do*. You've been a delight to me for two full years. I would hate to lose you now." His lips brushed her hair. A fatherly kiss?

Her feet itched to move. She needed space. How could she extricate herself gracefully? She reached up and patted his hand, firm on her shoulder. He took it and squeezed. This … this didn't feel right. A tingle crept up her spine. She had to get away.

Taking a sidestep, she tripped over Richard's shoe and tumbled forward. Her head collided with the edge of his desk, then smacked into the floor. Pain shot through her temple, zigzagging throughout every nerve in her body. Her vision darkened, awareness fading like a sunset.

*****

She awoke with a headache, florescent lights stabbing her eyes. Where was she? Lying on the couch in the break room. Her arms and side ached. What had happened? Fog clouded her mind.

Richard strode in, a gentle smile lifting when his eyes met hers. "Oh good. You're awake."

She attempted to sit up, but a wave of dizziness crashed into her. Time to put her head back down. "What happened?" Her voice came out a hoarse croak, her throat parched.

He studied her. "You don't remember?"

She shook her head, then winced. Best not to move.

"You brought me the transcribed notes for Saturday, then tripped and fell. Your head smacked against my desk."

274

That explained the piercing pain.

"Here, have some water." He pulled a bottle from the fridge and handed it to her. "Do you need help drinking?"

"I don't think so." Uneasiness niggled her gut. Something didn't sit right. Was there more to the story of how she'd gotten injured? If only concentrating didn't hurt so much.

It took effort, but she managed to untwist the bottle top and tip the water to her lips. Some dribbled down her chin. She swiped it away with the back of her hand.

"How long was I out?"

"Nearly an hour."

She gasped. That long? "You didn't take me to a hospital?"

A sudden fury flickered in his gaze. She blinked and it was gone, replaced by his usual kind demeanor. It must have been the headache, tricking her mind. This was Richard. One of the godliest men she'd ever known. Her mentor. Her friend.

"I gathered the leadership team to come pray for you. No need for a hospital. Scripture says the prayer of faith shall save the sick."

The whole team had prayed for her? She must have been really out of it not to wake up during that commotion. "Thank you."

"Of course. You're my girl."

My girl. A fatherly term of endearment. So why did it make her insides squirm?

*****

Justice walked into the Mexican restaurant and scanned booths—most empty—until his eyes rested on a woman in a black baseball cap. He approached with slow steps. Yep. She wore a Nike sweatshirt. Right person.

"Sammie?"

Her head jerked up. "Justice?"

"That's me." He slid into the booth across from her. No wonder she wanted to meet here. The place was as empty as she'd predicted it would be. Her words from their earlier phone conversation rose to the top of his memory. *Most of the waiters speak limited English. Less chance someone will snoop.*

"I nearly walked out." She set her hands on the colorfully patterned table and picked at her cuticle, already red and raw.

"I'm glad you didn't."

"You can't use my name on the podcast." Her whispered tone spoke of panic.

He kept his voice gentle, lest she spook. "I won't. I promise."

When she lifted her head slightly, he took in her features. She looked to be in her thirties, a bit older than Candi. Though she'd pulled her ponytail through her ball cap, wisps of brown hair framed her worried face, her lips pressed into a straight line.

"I want to hear your story, but anything you don't want me to share, just let me know. As you requested, I'm not recording this or taking notes. Right now, I'm here to listen. If, after we're finished, you'd like to share on my podcast, you're welcome to." He folded his hands on the table. *Please Lord, let her be willing.* "If not, I'll relay as much of your story as you want."

She tucked her thumbnail in between her teeth. "Yeah, okay. I think I can do this."

A waiter brought chips and salsa, then took their drink and food orders. At least that interruption was over.

"Do you mind starting with how you became acquainted with Impact Church and Pastor Richard?"

"Sure." She took a deep breath and closed her eyes briefly as she blew it out. "I started going to Impact eight years ago, when I was twenty."

He nodded for her to go on.

"Richard was—is—a dynamic person. Magnetic almost. His smile and friendly personality drew me in immediately. When he came up to me during the membership class and asked if I'd like to be his personal assistant, I jumped at the chance. Though it paid less than my current job as a barista, it came with free housing, so it was a step up for me. I was still living at home and was excited to move out on my own." She sipped her water, gaze aimed to the left of Justice's shoulder as if watching a movie of past events.

"At the time, I was taking night classes at the community college."

"What were you majoring in?"

"Computer science. I planned to get my associate's degree there, then transfer to a four-year university. I told Richard as much, and he said it was fine. The job as his assistant wouldn't get in the way of my studies or plans."

"So, you became his personal assistant?" His gut churned at this common thread tying her to Candi. He nibbled a chip to settle his stomach.

"Yes. I joined the staff, and for a while, things were fine. Great, even."

"How long did things go well?"

"A year or two. It was a heavy workload, and Richard kept adding to it. At first, I didn't mind. I believed in what I was doing and felt my job was important. Richard always talked about how the Christian life was about sacrifice and dying to your flesh, so whenever I had a reservation, I figured it was only my flesh putting up a fight against the Holy Spirit's work. If I gave in to it, I was being selfish, but if I pushed through …" She shrugged. "I don't know. I guess I thought Jesus would be proud of me. Richard certainly applauded every sacrifice I made. He poured on the praise."

"What was that like?"

Her mouth twitched like she was about to smile, but then it fell again. "It was like sunshine on my face. Like my heart grew wings. Being in the center of his approval became like a drug. I always wanted a fix. His smile. His praise. I came to live for it." She dropped her head. "It's pathetic, isn't it?"

"Not pathetic. Understandable."

She twisted a chain-link bracelet around her wrist. "Anyway, it grew harder and harder to keep up with my classes as my workload increased. I started to get the feeling that he didn't *need* me to stay late going over the next Sunday's sermon. He *wanted* me there." Red mottled her neck. "Like he wanted to spend time with me, I guess. Which was weird, but also … I don't know. Nice? To be wanted."

She gripped the edge of the table. "I don't know if I can do this." She glanced toward the door.

"You're doing great." He held himself back from begging her to continue. He couldn't scare her away with pressure.

She released a slow breath. "He said—" She swigged down a gulp of water. "He said college was distracting me from the more important work of the Kingdom. That it was a worldly pursuit that amounted to wood, hay, and stubble in the eyes of God. He told me if I wanted to love the Lord with all my heart, I'd give up college and be all in at Impact."

Justice's chest burned. The nerve of that guy. "So, you quit?"

"Yeah." Her eyes watered. "It was around then that things changed."

His stomach sank. "How so?"

"He became more … affectionate." She shuddered. "He used to give these side hugs, but then he started hugging me from the front. Lingering. He'd play with my hair. Kiss me on the cheek."

Justice pictured Richard making the same moves on Candi and nearly gagged. He needed to focus. "Did that make you uncomfortable?"

"Not at first." She bit her other thumbnail as she stared into space for a minute before continuing. "I thought about how my grandpa would hug me and kiss the top of my head and figured Richard was doing the same. Some people are more touchy-feely, right? When I finally mentioned to another staff member how he pecked me on the cheek, she said that's just the way he was. I didn't question it further. Not until …"

He leaned forward, elbows on the table. "Until what?"

She glanced at the door again. "We'd been fasting for four days, and he told me when fasting, mints were fair game. He asked if I wanted one. When I said I did, he—" her hand went to her throat. "He kissed me and pushed a mint from his mouth into mine."

Justice's jaw unhinged. He clenched his hands, his fingernails biting into his palms. "What did you do?"

"I was so shocked. I choked on the mint. It literally lodged in my throat. Richard slapped my back. Hard. When it finally went down, he gave me a bottle of water and pretended nothing had happened."

"How so?"

"When I calmed down, he said 'Where were we,' then went back to discussing the upcoming women's event as if he hadn't done a thing."

"What did you do?"

"I thought I was crazy. That I'd imagined the whole thing." She shook her head. "You must think I'm an idiot."

He opened his mouth to tell her he wasn't thinking that, but she rushed on.

"But he was my *pastor*. Not only that but my mentor. My spiritual hero. He'd become a father figure to me. And everybody loves the guy. Ask just about anyone at the church and they'll gush about him as if he were the most pious man who ever lived." A tear trickled down her cheek. "There's just something about him that draws you in, you know?"

"Yes. I do." He'd experienced as much.

The waiter brought their food and refilled their glasses. Too bad he wasn't hungry anymore. Apparently, Sammie wasn't either. Though she picked up her fork, she only pushed rice around her plate.

"How'd you get away?"

Sammie's gaze fixed on her uneaten meal. "I met Troy, my husband. When we started dating, Richard backed off. He got pretty irritable about my relationship with Troy, but by then, I didn't care as much about his approval and attention. When Richard told me it was probably time he find a new personal assistant, I was relieved. I began attending Troy's church. We were married there, and we go there to this day."

"This happened, what, seven years ago? Why do you want to tell your story now?" Hopefully, that came across in the spirit he intended. Not accusatory, but curious.

She let out a humorless laugh. "Fair question. A friend who remained at Impact until recently told me Richard has a new personal assistant, and that they seem rather friendly." She bit her lip. "All this time I thought I was the only one, but if there's a chance he's doing this to someone else …"

Oh, Lord. Not Candi.

"Looking back, I can see a slew of things that weren't right. He completely isolated me from my family, my friends, my school. He monopolized my time. I used to love how he'd shower me with gifts. It made me feel special. Now, I look back and wonder how I ever considered that normal. What pastor buys his assistant a diamond necklace?"

"And the apartment?"

"Oh, he had a key. Sometimes he would let himself in when I was in the other room. I'd come into the living room to find him lounging on my couch. It scared me to death the first time. Then I came to expect it. After all, he was paying for it." She palmed her forehead. "I was so stupid."

"You were young. He clearly groomed you over time so that you became desensitized. It's a common tactic of predators." He picked up a chip, only to put it back down on his plate. Definitely not hungry. "Did he go any further than that kiss?"

She shook her head. "I don't think so. Thankfully, I met Troy soon after."

"You don't think so?"

She wrapped her hands around her glass. "I know this sounds ridiculous, but I didn't remember that kiss until recently. I pushed a lot of things out of my mind. There could be more, but … that's all I remember."

He nodded. The similarities between Sammie and Candi were undeniable. Both young and beautiful. Both isolated. The fasting, long hours, seclusion. Might Richard have already crossed the line with Candi? Or was every one of his moves strategic to get her to that place? He had to warn her. Again.

"Do you see why I can't go public? At least not with my name, face, or voice? People will tear me apart. They'll say I was complicit, or that I'm trying to bring down Richard's ministry. Everyone will side with him. Everyone. It's his word against mine."

If only he could promise her worst fears wouldn't become reality. But he'd seen people tear victims to shreds time and time again. Every time someone spoke out on his podcast, that person suffered backlash. "I believe you." It was all he could offer. "If you come on the podcast and tell your story, you never know who might find freedom. There could be other victims who are just as afraid to speak out. You could give them courage."

"Do you think my friend was right? Is there a current girl going through what I did?"

His throat burned. *Lord, please let him not have touched Candi.* "There very well might be. He has a young female personal assistant right now. I don't know her full story." He had to find out. Had to help her see Richard's true character. His eyes stung. *Candi.*

She clamped her hands together on the table. Her jaw firmed. "Okay, I'll do it. I'll talk on your podcast."

Chapter 8

Candi ambled into Tuesday night Bible study the next week to find a group of five girls huddled in the corner, talking in hushed tones. After nodding a greeting to Richard, wrapping Natalie in a hug, then depositing her purse and coat into the guest bedroom, she intruded into the whispering circle. The Blakes no longer served food at these meetings, since everyone was supposed to be fasting. More time to chat. Or count down the hours until they could eat again. As soon as Candi stepped close to her friends, the chatter quieted.

She eyed the group. "What's going on? What were you talking about?"

The girls exchanged uneasy glances. "Nothing," Rachel said.

She planted her right hand on her hip. "Don't give me that. Something's going on and I want to know what it is."

Every one of them looked over their shoulders, scanning the room. What were they searching for? One by one, their gazes fell on Richard, leaning against the kitchen counter talking with Melody.

"Go ahead." Linda nudged Rachel. "Tell her."

Rachel leaned in closer. "A podcast aired about Pastor Richard a couple of days ago."

"Okay. So?" Richard was always being featured on podcasts, TV, blogs, and vlogs. Nothing unusual about that.

Rachel shook her head. "A woman said …" She lowered her voice even more. "Richard assaulted her. Sexually."

Candi took a step back, shaking her head. "No way. He wouldn't do that. She must have some hidden agenda."

Rachel shifted her weight. "She used to be his personal assistant."

With that proclamation, everyone in the group stared at her.

She scoffed. "He's certainly never done anything to me, if that's what you're wondering."

What was that look in Linda's eyes? Relief, maybe. But Rachel frowned, doubt written on her face.

The words she'd transcribed for Richard about accusers floated to the top of her mind. Of course, that was it. Whoever this woman was, she was partnering with Satan as an accuser of the brethren. Trying to either bring Impact Church down or else attempting to extort money from Richard. Despicable. Spiritual warfare at its worst.

"Who was this woman? And how'd you find out about it anyway?" Richard encouraged the Tuesday night group to refrain from TV, worldly movies, and secular radio. The only thing most of them listened to was worship music put out by Impact's team. Apparently, Rachel wasn't as wholehearted as Candi had thought.

"My mom heard the episode and forwarded it to me. She was concerned." Rachel's eyes widened as she looked over Candi's shoulder.

A glance behind her showed Richard was making his way to the living room. "You can tell her she has nothing to worry about." Candi's voice came out like a hiss.

"I don't know. You should listen to it."

With Richard's approach, the group dispersed and settled into their places on couches, armchairs, and the floor. Though worship time was beautiful, Candi couldn't concentrate. Her hand absentmindedly trailed the embossed lettering on her Bible. *Cando.* A gift from Richard.

Was it a strange coincidence that Justice had mentioned spiritual abuse, and then Rachel brought up this podcast? The woman Justice had talked to must have been the same woman. The same Jezebel who sought to bring division. An accuser. A wolf.

Candi had assumed this woman was one of the people to recently leave the church, but neither of them had ever been Richard's personal assistant. It had to be unrelated. Would more people leave Impact if they heard the podcast? It would be harder to recruit volunteers, and with fewer tithes and offerings coming in, they might not be able to continue supporting all their missionaries. Did this woman realize she was basically taking food away from starving children by stirring up strife? How self-centered.

Worship finished, Natalie led the group in prayer, and then Richard opened his Bible. The bent and worn pages and highlighted passages proved this man couldn't be evil. He loved the Word. Loved God. Loved the flock. Every week, he encouraged them with Scripture. *"You shall know them by their fruit,"* Right? Well, Impact Church was growing. Thriving. That had to mean Richard was a good tree planted in good soil.

Richard welcomed everyone with a gentle smile, but stern lines transformed his expression as soon as he began to read from the Word. "Scripture says in 1 John 2:18, 'Little children, it is the last hour; and as you have heard that the Antichrist is coming, even now many antichrists have come, by which we know that it is the last hour.'"

Candi flipped to the passage. They'd been going through the gospels, but for the last few weeks, Richard had jumped around, led by the Holy Spirit to address other things.

"When you hear the word antichrist, you likely think of the man who will be revealed in the End Times. But in this passage, we see that there are many antichrists who have come and will come before the main Antichrist. These are people who oppose God's purposes on the earth. They are anti-Christian."

Could that be the case with the woman on the podcast? Candi's insides quivered. Calling someone she didn't know an antichrist seemed wrong. Antichrist. Accuser. Wolf. Without knowing the whole story, all three labels suddenly didn't sit right. Her foggy brain grasped to recall if Richard had ever mentioned his previous assistants. Who might the woman be? What motive did she have for flinging dirt on an upstanding pastor?

Her stomach growled, and she put a hand on it. As if that could quell the hunger gnawing inside. If she'd been honest with Justice, she'd have confessed how much she detested fasting. Especially when it felt forced. Only, she didn't *have* to agree with Richard's recommendation of this new fasting schedule. How might he have reacted if she'd refused?

She'd have to be half backslidden to refuse the godly discipline of fasting. No, this was right and good. The flesh would always resist, but she needed to master it.

"Let my accusers be clothed with shame, and let them cover themselves with their own disgrace as with a mantle."

Richard's booming voice startled her from her mental wanderings. How much had she missed? She peeked over Rachel's shoulder to see what passage they were on. Psalm

109. As discreetly as she could, she flipped to the correct page and read. And squirmed in her seat.

> For the mouth of the wicked and the mouth of the deceitful Have opened against me; They have spoken against me with a lying tongue. They have also surrounded me with words of hatred And fought against me without a cause.
> In return for my love they are my accusers…

It was almost like Richard knew of the woman's accusations. Had he heard about the podcast? Was he empathizing with David's plight or using scripture to declare himself not guilty? She studied him as he finished the psalm. His shirt sported wrinkled sleeves. So unlike perfectly polished Richard. How had she not noticed earlier?

"We must heed the warning to beware of antichrists. Beware of accusers."

Some of the girls nodded their agreement, while others, like Rachel, stared at their laps.

"To sever ourselves from an antichrist influence, I highly encourage all of you to abstain from media for a season. Most of you have already given up television. Your sacrifice is a sweet-smelling aroma to the Lord. I urge you to also fast from social media, radio, and online articles. The antichrist spirit thrives in journalism, and most journalists are possessed with it."

Possessed with an antichrist spirit? She could see how that might be the case, but the word *most* gave her pause. It seemed like a sweeping generalization. Surely there were many noble journalists who sought only justice.

Justice. What would he think of all of this?

After Richard closed the study in prayer, Candi grabbed her coat from the guest bedroom. She needed time to think. No mingling tonight. Rachel came into the room and gently took hold of her arm. "I'll send you the link to that podcast. Listen to it. Please."

Candi shrugged her off. "But Richard called us to a media fast."

"Why do you think he did that? He doesn't want us to find out."

Candi stared at her friend. Could that be true? No, Richard wouldn't do that. He'd always beckoned them into lives of more extravagant devotion. He wanted them all to be as close to Jesus as possible. How could someone who fasted, studied Scripture, and prayed have such a manipulative intention? Richard preached the Word with power every Sunday. He spoke of the Lord in nearly every sentence.

Maybe Rachel had already been infected with an antichrist virus. Perhaps *she* was the one Candi needed to steer clear of.

"Please, Candi. Just listen to it."

Candi zipped her coat with trembling fingers. "I'm not making any promises."

*****

Wrecked. That was the only word to describe Justice's emotional state after Sammie's interview a couple of days ago. It'd taken her such courage to share, such boldness. And every word of her testimony brought his thoughts to Candi. How eerily similar their stories were. He could only pray Candi would get out before Richard had a chance to reel her in completely.

Since the podcast had aired, two other women had contacted him offering to share their own stories of Richard's abuse. He'd meet with them next week. How could he have been so duped? Of course, he wasn't the only one. The growing congregation proved the charismatic pastor had fooled many others. Little comfort that brought. Sweet Candi. If Richard had put a hand on her, it would take everything in Justice not to punch the guy.

He used his fifteen-minute break at work to sift through the emails that had flooded his inbox over the past couple of days. He'd about given up on the social media comments. Many of those had sickened him. No wonder victims had such fear of speaking out. The public crucified them.

She sure doesn't seem like a victim to me.

If her story is true, why didn't she come forward sooner?

Sounds like she's out to defame another man of God.

And, of course, all the comments that ridiculed her for not having the guts to show her face and use her real name.

What's she hiding?

Why can't she be transparent?

People who tell the truth don't have to hide.

A pang sliced his heart as he read the first email. Another woman coming forward. Four victims total. Would Candi be the fifth?

Not if he could help it.

For the fourth time in twenty-four hours, he dialed Candi's number. It went to voicemail, just like the other times he'd called. She could be extremely busy with the upcoming Christmas services on the horizon. Or she could be avoiding him. What were the chances she'd listened to the podcast? From what she'd told him during one of their many late night phone conversations, she had a personal conviction against watching television or listening to radio. She didn't even have a social media account. Doubtful she would have heard it, unless someone else had steered her in that direction. Had Richard heard and spoken out against the podcast?

Wait … It likely wasn't a personal conviction that drove Candi to avoid the outside world. Richard's fingerprints were all over that. Control. The weasel was all about control. He had to dictate what his victims watched, listened to, even ate.

Justice palmed his forehead. Why hadn't he seen it earlier? He should have said something. Though, Richard had spent years gaining her trust. What chance did he have against such strategic manipulation?

He started a text.

Hi, Candi. Just wondering why you're avoiding me.

No, too accusatory. He had no evidence she was avoiding him. Delete.

Hi, Candi. Just wanted you to know Richard is a snake and an abuser. Get out while you can.

Delete. No way he should have that conversation over text.

Hi, Candi. Just wondering how you are. Miss you.

Better, and honest, except for the "just." He had many more questions to ask her.

Lord, open her eyes. Please don't let her shut me out. Protect her, Father.

All day, he sneaked glances at his phone, internally begging her to reply.

No answer.

Chapter 9

Finally finished with her fast, Candi stress-ate all day. Donut holes. Chips. Even animal crackers from the children's ministry closet. She nearly deleted Rachel's text without clicking the link. Why give credence to someone intent on sowing discord and creating division in the body of Christ? Better to ignore it and press on, doing Kingdom work for eternal reward. But her fingers froze, refusing to delete the text.

All night long, she tossed and turned, falling into a fitful sleep only to wake in a cold sweat and the nagging feeling something was wrong.

Around two in the morning, she shot up in bed, a nightmare vivid in her memory. She'd dreamt Richard had trapped her against his desk, kissing her hair, his hands on her shoulders. "Get behind me, Satan." Her command came in a whispered, shaky voice, not one with authority. The devil was sowing doubt in her mind. Surely, that had to be it. Richard had never acted inappropriately with her. Had he? She flipped through her memories.

Side hugs. Friendly pats to her back. Kind smiles. Nothing that raised red flags. Proof she needed to delete that text. She picked up her phone, finger hovering again.

Maybe she needed to see what lies Richard was up against. If she listened to the podcast armed with the truth of his innocence, she could better combat any falsehoods. Scripture warned God's people not to be ignorant of the devil's devices. She winced as she tapped the text and opened the link.

Her blood chilled at the name proclaimed at the top. Justice Howard. *No. Please, God. No.*

Justice ran a podcast? He'd never mentioned a thing … which meant he was clearly hiding it for a reason.

Richard had been right to warn her about him. Had Justice been using her to get dirt on Richard, fodder for his agenda to drag Impact into the dirt? All their interactions, all those questions … he'd been exploiting her the whole time. Tears pricked her eyes. His kind smile and gentle manner? What a scam. He was nothing but a wolf dressed in sheep's clothing, just like Richard had cautioned them about.

These wolves will appear to be Christians. They'll join our church, attend small groups, worship with uplifted hands. But they're liars and pretenders. Their true aim is to weaken your devotion to Christ. They're out to bring you down. You must not let them.

She'd been deceived, even with all the warnings. How could she have been so naive? Justice had never cared for her. He'd been on a mission, and she was left to pick up the pieces after his betrayal.

How could she listen to this podcast without getting sick? But she needed to hear the specifics of his duplicity. Even if doing so smashed her insides to pieces.

She pressed play. At the sound of Justice's voice, the tears flowed. This man had listened to her. Seemed to truly care for her. Had snuck his way into her heart, wrapping it in hope and promise. Fake. All of it was fake. *Oh, God, how can I bear it?* But even Jesus had been betrayed by a friend. He knew her pain. She could take comfort in that.

Sitting in bed, she hugged a pillow to her chest, tissues in hand, and listened to the whole thing. The woman's claims were ridiculous. Laughable. As if Richard would ever kiss a staff member. She'd seen how he acted with Natalie. He loved his wife. Doted on her. Respected her. How ludicrous to think he'd cheat on her.

Had Justice fed the woman information from his and Candi's conversations? He probably told her to say Richard paid for her apartment because Candi had told him he'd paid for hers. Their stories were too similar to be a coincidence. This woman and Justice must have conspired together, using the intel Candi had unknowingly fed him. Their crafted narrative would seem compelling to anyone who didn't know Richard personally. Anyone who *did* know the humble, generous man wouldn't dare believe it.

But Rachel seemed so shaken. Surely, she could see it was all an elaborate lie, intended to bring Richard down. Then again, her friend didn't know about Candi's relationship with Justice. She couldn't see how he'd twisted Candi's experiences to create this fabrication.

Candi wiped her nose with a tissue. At least she could thank God she'd discovered Justice's true character sooner rather than later. She'd fallen for him so quickly. If she hadn't heeded Rachel's insistence to listen to the podcast, she could have wasted months more with the fraud. It was God's grace that He'd opened her eyes now. As painful as it would be to cut Justice out of her life, it would have been far more torturous to do so after more magical dates and grand gestures.

No wonder he hadn't kissed her. He'd wined and dined her, spoiling her with steak to get her to open up. She'd considered him a gentleman. But he wasn't attracted to her and was far from falling in love.

She bunched her pillow and screamed into it. Even after all the rejection she'd experienced throughout foster care, and then from her parents, this hurt the worst. Or maybe it only seemed like it now. With time, she might gain perspective. But right now, her heart lay in pieces at her feet.

*****

Justice wavered, hand on the key in his car's ignition. His insides squirmed at the thought of walking through the doors of Impact Church again. He'd prefer to stay as far from that no-good pastor as possible. How could he stand to listen to the man preach the Word, knowing his life didn't align with the words spewing from his mouth? Attending service seemed like stamping the evil man with his approval. But he had to see Candi.

For days, he'd called and texted with no response. Clearly, she was avoiding him. She must've heard the podcast and didn't believe Sammie's testimony. Would she change her mind when she heard more stories from women who were victimized? What would it take for her to break free from Richard's brainwashing?

She might not give him the chance to speak, but he had to try. He shuddered at the thought of her trapped by Richard's manipulation.

He exited his car and headed for the doors. How many people here had heard the podcast? Would any of them associate him with the host? Too bad he didn't have a more common name. John or Chris. He'd be able to remain inconspicuous. But the name *Justice* stood out.

The volunteers at the door greeted him with the same enthusiasm. They must not know. Coffee sounded good, but he couldn't justify giving even a minimal amount of money to this place. He'd have to skip the cappuccino. Instead, he'd wander the lobby and keep an eye out for Candi.

There she was, nearly sprinting down the hall. Frantically busy? Or had she spotted him and been desperate to get away?

He rushed after her. "Candi," he called.

She turned, face void of surprise. "Oh, hi, Justice." She must have seen him before dashing away. "I have some things to do before service. Maybe I'll catch you later."

A brush off if he'd ever heard one. "Wait. It'll only take a minute."

She tapped her foot as she waited, casting glances down the empty hall. "I really don't have time."

"You've been avoiding me." He crossed his arms over his chest then dropped them to his sides. Better to not seem defensive. "You heard?" Best not to spell out what she'd likely heard in case he was wrong.

"Heard the podcast, you mean?" Her jaw tightened. "Yes, I heard you and that woman spew lies. You obviously put all the information I unknowingly fed you to good use."

"What?" The information she'd fed him? What was she talking about?

"It was interesting how her situation was so similar to mine. Almost like you used everything I told you to concoct a whopper of a story."

His chest clenched. She thought he'd used her. "I did nothing of the sort. Candi, can't you see? Your situations are similar because Richard has an M.O. He's grooming you, just like he did Sammie."

"Sammie?"

He winced. Shoot. He'd said her name and broken confidentiality. Stupid mistake.

She rolled her eyes. "I don't have time to stand here and listen to your lies. I have Kingdom work to do." She spun around and rushed away.

His shoulders drooped. How could she have it so wrong? Richard had her solidly in his clutches. She'd been so manipulated she couldn't see the truth right in front of her. It was only a matter of time before Richard took full advantage.

Oh, Lord. Help! He could find no other words. Desperation clawed at him. What else could he do to convince her? He had no way to get through to her. Nothing but prayer could help her see.

In the sanctuary, he slumped into his seat. Even worship felt tainted. Almost like if he joined in, it would contaminate him. He couldn't wrap his brain around it. This church attracted excellent people. Thousands of congregants lifted up praise every weekend. People were getting saved. The announcements proclaimed an upcoming baptism service. Impact supported a plethora of good causes. Was there good happening in this place, even amongst the evil?

The parable of the wheat and the tares came to mind. In that story, Jesus sowed good seed, but the enemy came and sowed bad seed in the field. When the wheat sprouted, the tares, or weeds, sprouted as well. Good and evil together. The enemy was responsible for the tares, but the owner didn't want his servants to pull them up prematurely, lest they destroy the good wheat. At harvest time, He'd gather the wheat into bundles and burn the tares.

That proved there could be good in a place like this, didn't it? That "Kingdom work", as Candi had called it, could happen alongside despicable practices. Was it harvest time for Impact Church? Was it God's timing to expose the weeds?

Chapter 10

Candi turned her phone off and shoved it in her pocket. Justice had better stop calling her before she answered and told him off. She returned her attention to Richard. He sat with his feet propped on his desk, leaning back with his hands behind his head. As if he didn't have a care in the world. As if Sammie's allegations didn't affect him in the least. Whatever unrest she'd glimpsed in his wrinkled shirt sleeves at Tuesday night's Bible study had fizzled into languid peace.

"Don't worry, Can*do*. These false allegations won't stand. Give it time, and everything will blow over."

She tapped her pen against her notepad. "Okay, but what do I say when reporters and podcasters call asking for a statement?" It had already happened twice, and she'd floundered, finally spouting, "No comment." Did that make him look more guilty?

"Tell them the truth. That I'm the godliest man you've ever known. "

"Okay." But her stomach rocked like a rowboat in a gale. It *was* the truth, wasn't it? She could think of no mere human more holy. At one time, Justice might have battled for that title, but not anymore.

Richard swung his feet down and folded his hands on his desk. "I've got another meeting, so I'm going to let you lead the team briefing on this matter."

Her hand rose to the base of her throat. "M-me?"

"Of course. No one I trust more." His charming smile backed his words.

"I don't feel qualified. Wouldn't it be better coming from you?"

"Remember, Can*do*, you can do ..."

"All things through Christ who strengthens me. Yes, I know."

He stacked papers. Her cue to leave. She capped her pen and stood, notepad in hand. "I'll just relay everything you told me, then?" She should have taken more detailed notes.

He pointed at her. "Remember to emphasize how Sammie didn't use the Matthew 18 process. She operated outside of Biblical procedures and was therefore out of godly alignment. She should have come directly to me."

"Got it." She made for the door. Wait. How had he learned the anonymous person's name?

"Also relay how it's been almost a decade since the alleged incident. If there were legitimate concerns, she would have come forward much sooner."

"Yes. Of course."

"Oh, one more thing."

She turned and studied him as his smile twisted into something that nearly looked sinister. "Her husband was recently fired from his corporate job. Something regarding fraud, I believe. The timing is certainly convenient, isn't it? She's out for money. I'm sure of it."

He had information about her family? "How do you know this?" The question escaped before she had a chance to censor it. Hopefully her question rang of curiosity and not challenge.

He shrugged, face impassive. "People talk."

With a nod, she walked from his office into the meeting room. There, she paced. *Oh, Lord, I can do anything through You. Why does this feel so daunting?* She merely had to relay to the team all the holes in Sammie's claims. Tell the group how to respond to inquiries about the matter. But it felt like something a lawyer should do, not Richard's assistant. He had chosen her to play the part of his defender.

Which she could do, of course. She believed in his innocence and had more contact with the man than anyone else on staff. If he were a predator, she'd know. Why, then, did her nerves feel like they'd been zapped with electricity? Why was her stomach in knots?

People filed in for the meeting, each one asking where Richard was. Frowns marred their faces when she told them he wouldn't be coming and that she would lead the meeting. "He had somewhere else to be." But where? There hadn't been any appointments on his shared calendar.

When everyone arrived and sat, she began, "I'm sure you're aware of why we're here."

Solemn nods all around the room.

"Some serious but illegitimate accusations have been leveled against Pastor Richard. They're circulating around social media."

"And local media. The paper had an article about it today," Mark said.

Oh great. She hadn't seen that one. She couldn't let her confident tone falter. No matter who said what, the truth was clear to anyone who knew Richard. The allegations were ludicrous.

Weren't they? An image from her reoccurring nightmare surfaced in her mind. Richard trapping her against his desk. She shook it off. She needed to focus.

"The allegations hold no weight, of course. There is no evidence to back them up. It's her word against Pastor Richard's, and she's been known to not be credible."

Mark spoke up again. "How so?"

The pulse thrumming her neck intensified. How so? Richard hadn't specified. Why hadn't she thought to ask? The answer was obvious. She hadn't wanted to challenge him or appear to question him in any way. How should she answer?

"Her husband was recently fired for fraudulent practices. She wants a settlement, and the timing isn't coincidental."

More nods. Unlike her, they apparently were going to accept this without question. What else was she supposed to say?

"She is clearly out of biblical alignment because she didn't follow the Matthew 18 process of going straight to Richard to work out her dispute. Instead, she went on a podcast. Clearly, this is out of God's will and akin to gossip. Plus, if her allegations were valid, she wouldn't have waited nearly a decade to bring them up." Why was her voice trembling? She had to speak with confidence. Assure everyone there was nothing to these claims.

"Richard asks that we not get defensive on his behalf. He's certain the Lord will defend him."

"What should we say when someone brings it up?" Abby asked.

Candi pasted on a smile and repeated the script Richard had given her. "The truth. That he's the godliest man you've ever known."

After fielding a few more questions, she dismissed the meeting and everyone except Mark returned to their desks. He lingered at the door, running his hand up and down the frame.

"Hey, did you ever find out why the Bringer and Reynold families left the church? Their reasoning, I mean."

Candi shook her head. She hadn't given it a second thought. Had simply accepted what Richard had said about them not being true sheep of God's flock. But wasn't that a bit of a leap? Couldn't someone leave a church without disowning the faith? She forced a swallow down her tight throat. "I can ask."

Fear chased her statement. What would Richard think? Would he see it as a betrayal? She'd have to make sure he didn't find out.

*****

Justice sent Candi a text, then pocketed his phone. Six weeks of not hearing from her had caused weight to settle on his shoulders. She was in danger. Warning sirens blared deep inside him. But how could he rescue someone who didn't see their need for it?

Father, protect her. Open her eyes to see the truth. Lift the fog Richard has placed her under. Bring freedom.

Right after the podcast, he'd called and texted her multiple times per day. After their confrontation at church, he'd dropped down to once a day. Worry had gotten the best of him. After her silence made it clear she wanted nothing to do with him, his attempts to reach out had dwindled to two or three times a week. It was important for her to know he was still here for her. When realization of Richard's manipulation did dawn on her, she'd need a safe place to turn. His texts were a reminder that he'd be that place when she was ready. Today's text simply said, I'm here if you want to talk.

If only he could take her far away from Impact. Together they'd discover what healthy Christian community and leadership looked like. But that wasn't the way freedom worked. He'd once been trapped in his sin, blind to the bondage it held him in. Jesus hadn't forced him to choose Him. Hadn't forced the truth on him. He'd wooed Justice's heart until he chose the One who'd first chosen him. Free will was the only way for true love to bloom. Now, Candi had to choose freedom and truth.

Might he be a conduit of Jesus' patient, faithful love to her? He'd continue to pursue her gently for as long as the Lord led him to do so.

He stepped out of his car and braced himself against the biting wind. Another woman wanted to speak to him about her experience with Richard. Like the others, she didn't want to use her name, and didn't want bystanders to overhear. He wouldn't allow himself slip up this time. He'd keep her identity a secret. They'd agreed to meet at a pavilion in a local park. Of course, when they'd made plans, the weather had been a bit more agreeable. Now … well, hopefully she could get her point across before he froze into an icicle. At least this plan assured no one would eavesdrop on their conversation.

Pulling his knit cap lower onto his forehead, he trudged toward a woman in a fluffy navy-blue coat. She sat on a pavilion bench, a travel mug cupped in her hands, steam wafting into her face. Smart woman. She'd brought liquid reinforcement.

He neared and lifted a friendly smile. "Anne?"

She nodded. "You must be Justice."

"That's me. Did you want to sit here or …"

"Why don't we walk. Keep our limbs moving."

"Good idea." He sidled up beside her as she started down a walking path.

"I guess I'll get right to it. It's too cold to waste time and words."

He pressed his lips together. Agreeing might make it seem like he didn't want to hear everything she had to say. He didn't come for a cliff notes version. But she was right. Best to dive in.

She sighed and began her story. "I was an assistant children's ministry director at Impact for three years. Technically part-time staff, even if my hours edged closer and closer to full-time status. Richard seemed to take a special interest in me. He always greeted me with a huge grin and a, 'How's my girl?' He bought me presents. Little trinkets here and there. I love chickens, and he'd bring me different chicken figurines. Said he saw them and thought of me. I thought it was sweet. But then it got weird."

"How so?"

"He brought a gift bag to the office and told me not to open it in front of anyone. When I opened it later, I found a tight ribbed, low-cut tee that said *Hot Chick* on it. Later, Richard walked by my desk and asked me if I liked it. He winked at me, and it felt … slimy."

"What did you think about that gift?"

"That it was weird, and probably inappropriate, but that surely he didn't mean it that way."

Justice's hands clenched in his pockets. "What other way would he mean it?"

She shrugged. "I guess I figured he was an old man who didn't understand the implications of such a gift. But then there was the knee thing."

"What knee thing?" He ground out the words through clenched teeth, then relaxed. "I'm not mad at you." Based on a couple of other testimonies, he had a pretty good idea where this story was going.

"I understand." Her mouth twitched up in a sympathetic half-smile which fell away as she continued. "At first, he would pat my knee under the table. Sometimes during a meeting, or sometimes when the team would go out for a meal. It started out as a friendly pat."

He forced a hard swallow. Yep. This sounded familiar. "And then?"

"His pats got longer and rose up my leg. Gradually, mind you. A little more each time. Until …" She turned her head away from him, staring into the distance. "Until he was rubbing my thigh under my skirt."

He could strangle the man. How dare anyone treat God's children like that. What if Candi … No, he couldn't go there. "How did you respond?"

"I was shocked. I didn't know what to do. He smiled and his tone remained friendly as he talked about whatever the subject was. No one else knew what he'd done under the table, and he continued on as if nothing had happened. I thought maybe I was going crazy. Maybe nothing *did* happen. I wondered if I'd imagined the whole thing." Tears choked her words. "But I started making excuses not to sit next to him. He'd fight me on it. Say, 'Anne, my girl, take a seat right here.' He'd point to a chair next to him. I was terrified he'd do it again, and I'd say, 'I need to tell Polly something' or the like in order to sit at the other end of the table."

"How'd you get out." His number one question, as Candi once again entered his mind.

"I eventually told a friend, and she talked some sense into me. She helped me get a job at a preschool. I'd never been so relieved as I was when I gave him my two-week's notice."

"How did he take it?"

She laughed without humor. "He accused me of selling out. Of abandoning 'Kingdom work' to rub shoulders with the world." Her mouth twisted. "Thankfully, I had my friend's support to lean upon."

"Thank God." His breath puffed out, creating a little cloud that floated into the air. Their path circled back, and they neared the pavilion. Time to find out where to go from here. "Are you willing to share on 'For the Love of Truth'?"

She sipped from her mug, then nodded. "If there's a chance it will help someone else, I'll share."

"Thank you." These women were so brave. They risked much by coming forward. Public ridicule. Slanderous accusations. Outright hate. Several had stated fear of Richard's retaliation. Though no one could quite pinpoint what that would look like, they couldn't imagine him not reacting in anger. "You have no idea the impact your testimony might have." He stopped short of telling her there was someone currently in danger of Richard's abuse. He shouldn't spread rumors when he didn't have proof Richard had targeted Candi.

Four women had come forward now. How many others were there? What would it take to stop this man?

Chapter 11

Candi stepped out of the shower and wrapped herself in a towel. Exhaustion weighed down her limbs as she applied moisturizer to her face. It had to be after eleven. She'd put off calling the Bringer and Reynolds families again, and now it was far too late at night. She needed to knuckle down and do it. It's not like she was afraid of what she'd find out. Was she? No. Her lack of sleep had been getting to her, that's all.

A full night's sleep would do her good—if she could banish the nightmares. Or rather, *nightmare*. Always the same one where Richard trapped her against his desk. Would she ever be free of it?

She relished the cool blast of air as she stepped out of the bathroom, heading to her bedroom. Something caught her attention from the corner of her eye. A figure on her sofa? She screamed.

"Candi, it's just me." Richard stood and smiled at her.

She stepped back, clutching her towel. "W-what are you doing here?"

"Just came for a visit." His words slurred together. He almost sounded … drunk. Impossible. Richard didn't drink.

Images from her nightmare flashed through her mind, along with Sammie's words. Pulse thudding, she inched toward her bedroom door. "It's late." Her voice squeaked.

"Not too late."

Too late for what? She sucked in a breath. *Oh, Lord, what do I do?*

"How'd you get in?" The answer was obvious. It was no secret he had a key, though he'd never used it before. It was supposed to be for emergencies. In case she lost hers or got locked out.

He dangled the key in his hand. "Why would you give this to me if you didn't want me to use it?" He stumbled forward and bumped into a side table. The stench of alcohol wafted on his breath. "After all you've done to protect me, I know you want this."

The edges of her vision blurred as her breathing came faster and faster. Another step toward her bedroom. "You should leave."

He tossed her a sloppy grin and fiddled with his shirt's top button.

"Natalie is probably wondering where you are."

He threw back his head and laughed. "She knows. She doesn't care."

Oh, God! Help!

With a burst of adrenaline, she dashed into her room, shutting and locking the door. A crash sounded. Broken glass? Probably the lamp. Frantically, she looked around. She needed something to barricade herself in the room. She wedged her desk chair under the doorknob. Now what?

She should get dressed. If he broke in, she wouldn't make things easy for him. She stumbled into her pajamas while scanning the space for her phone. Where had she left it?

Shoot. In the kitchen. No way she was going out there. A glance out the window showed no safe way to climb down. Maybe breaking her neck would be worth it if he found a way in.

She strained to listen over the erratic pulsing in her ears. Was he coming closer? Trying to get in? Another crash. Bumping. Clanging. Had he stumbled into her other table, knocking her mug and books to the floor?

He banged on her door. "Let me in, Can*do*. You know you want to."

She held her breath. Let him think she escaped out the window. Maybe then he'd leave.

Several minutes of pounding, another bang from farther away, then silence. Had he gone, or was it a trap? She wouldn't risk it. After what had to be at least ten minutes of listening to nothing, she huddled on the floor under her window. Another span of time and she grabbed the pillow from her bed. Eventually, she drifted to sleep on the floor only to wake up with her pulse racing. No sounds from the other room. Thank God.

She moved to her bed in the middle of the night, tossing and turning, but it wasn't until dawn stretched through her window that she dared open her door and cautiously peek out. No Richard. He must have left, locking the door behind him. She raced over and secured the deadbolt.

Now she could grab her phone. A low battery warning blinked at her. Great. She shot Justice a quick text.

Call me, please.

Funny how he was the first person to come to mind. Should she call the police? They'd never believe her. Not about charming Pastor Richard. He was basically a local celebrity. Besides, it wasn't like he'd broken in. He had a key. No, she'd wait to hear from Justice. Surely he'd have solid advice.

While she waited, she searched through her contacts. No more putting it off. Time for her to call the Bringer and Reynolds families to see why they'd left Impact Church.

She called Krista Reynolds and left a message before her phone died.

*****

Justice's phone alarm blared, and he swiped blindly to silence it. Five more minutes, and he'd get up. But when the annoying beeping persisted, he squinted open bleary eyes to shut it off. As soon as he did, Candi's text stared back at him.

Suddenly, he was wide awake. He catapulted up in bed and dialed her number. Straight to voicemail. Had she finally seen the danger she was in? Or was there another reason she'd contacted him after over a month of silence? He had to find out.

After rushing through his morning routine, he dashed out the front door. She could be in trouble. In fact, the sinking in his gut told him that was the case. He texted a quick On my way over, then shot his car into drive.

As he drove, he prayed. *Lord, protect her. Be her defender. Let truth and peace rein in her right now. Don't let her cower to fear.* He neared Impact Church. Should he look for her in the offices or at her apartment? The conversation they needed to have wasn't one for coworkers to overhear. He'd try her apartment first.

He took the steps two at a time and knocked on her door with more force than necessary.

A startled cry leaked through. Something was definitely wrong.

310

"Candi? It's me, Justice. Can I come in?" He pressed his ear to the door.

"Justice?"

"Yeah. It's me. I got your text." He stepped back so she could see him through the peep hole.

A lock clicked, and she creaked the door open an inch, peeking through the slit. A relieved sigh escaped her lips. She let him in.

The woman staring back at him was an altered version of the one he'd spent time with a month and a half ago. She'd lost weight, and dark bags marred her pale face. He wouldn't call her gaunt, but she was trending in that direction. Her red-rimmed eyes filled with tears as she took him in. She closed and locked the door behind him, then fell into his arms.

He held her tight against his chest. "What is it? What happened?"

Her shoulders shook with sobs. "You were right."

Oh, how his heart cracked with those words. *No. Not Candi.* He pulled back and rested his hands on her shoulders. "What did he do to you?"

She opened her mouth but shut it again as a new flow of tears coursed down her cheeks.

"Candi, you're scaring me. Did Richard take advantage of you?" His mind begged her to say no, to deny this had anything to do with the scandal surrounding Impact's pastor.

She froze. Neither a definitive yes, nor a solid no. If only he could coax an answer out of her, but he stilled his body. She'd tell him when she was ready. He'd waited this long. He could wait a little longer.

She headed to the couch and perched on the edge. After several deep breaths, she spoke. "I called Krista Reynolds.

She's from one of the families who left the church right before you came. I'd been meaning to call her for weeks. I just… couldn't bring myself to do it."

He sat next to her on the couch, nodding for her to continue.

She wiped at her wet cheeks with the back of her hand. "She left because she saw Richard run his hand up someone's leg."

"Anne's?"

Her forehead bunched. "How'd you know?"

"I talked with Anne last week. She told me her story."

Candi shuddered. "Krista knew it wasn't appropriate but didn't want to make waves, so she left. Her husband confronted Richard about it, but Richard denied everything."

"Of course."

She braced her hands on her knees. "Last night, he came here."

The back of Justice's neck pricked. "Richard did?"

"Yes." She seemed to choke on the word, leaning forward and coughing.

He almost asked her if she was okay but stopped himself. Of course, she wasn't okay. Anyone could see her distress. He waited for her to continue.

"He was drunk. I came out of the shower to find him there." She pointed to the spot Justice inhabited.

As if the area were contaminated, he scooted over. "How did he get in?"

"He has a key." Her hands shook, and she clasped them in her lap.

He clamped down on the *Why* that attempted to leap out. It would sound accusatory toward her, and that's not what she needed. Besides, she'd told him Richard paid for her apartment. The creep might have insisted on keeping a key. A dozen other questions swirled in his mind, but he clamped his mouth shut and waited for her to further confide in him.

"He said Natalie knew and didn't care. When he came toward me …" She squeezed her eyes shut and shook her head.

"Please tell me you got away in time." He held his breath.

Her lip wobbled. "I did. Locked myself in my room and barricaded the door, but I was so scared."

Moving toward her might frighten her, so he opened his arms, an invitation to take refuge within. She scooted close and buried herself in his embrace. "Oh, sweet Candi. I'm so sorry."

She pulled back and searched his eyes with her dewy ones. "You tried to warn me."

Yes, but, "It's hard to wrangle free when you're in the middle of the web."

"Nearly impossible alone."

He took her hand. "You're not alone."

Her phone rang from where it was plugged in on the kitchen island. She jumped up to answer it. "Hello?" She covered the mouthpiece and whispered, "It's Irene Reynolds, from the other family who left Impact." She stepped closer to him. The conversation would be easy for him to decipher from that distance. "Hi, Irene. I called because I have a question for you."

"Yes?"

"Why did you leave Impact Church?"

Silence.

"Irene?"

A small cough. "I'd rather not say."

Justice closed his eyes and once again prayed for God to expose evil and reveal truth.

"Have you heard about the recent allegations against Pastor Richard?"

A cautious, "Yes."

"I'm asking because …" Candi's voice was so fragile a feather might break it. "I have reason to believe the allegations are true. I'm wondering if you might have your own reasons."

"Are you asking as Richard's assistant?"

"No. I'm asking as a woman searching for the truth."

Though hesitant, the story slowly unfurled. Irene had a funny feeling about Richard from the beginning, an instinct that something wasn't right, but she pushed it down because no one else seemed to have any reservations. "I witnessed Richard being extra friendly with someone. A young mom. He played with her hair. Kissed her cheek. Ogled her as she walked away." Irene sighed. "I had no proof anything more than that was happening. Seemed like gossip to say anything. So, I didn't." Instead she'd started looking for a new church.

"Thank you for sharing." Candi sounded like sandpaper had lodged in her throat.

"Sure thing. Be careful."

"I will."

Candi ended the call and stared at Justice. "How many women has Richard acted inappropriately towards?"

"Counting the young mom Irene spoke of, that would make at least six."

"What can we do?" She sat on the couch again, fiddling with the phone in her hand.

"Step one is getting you out of this apartment and away from Richard."

"How? I have nowhere else to live. I don't have money for a downpayment on another apartment." Her chin quivered. "How can I get an apartment if I don't have a job?"

"What about your parents?"

She shook her head. "They barely talk to me."

"That might change once they hear what's happened."

"Doubtful." Her face drooped with a frown and haunted eyes.

Best not to argue. Things might change with her parents, but it would likely take time. Time she didn't have.

"Any friends?"

She bit her lip. "All my friends are at Impact. If I leave, Richard will poison them against me, just like he did with the others. No one will believe me."

If only he could say that wasn't true, but it very well might be. He had room for her to move into his place, but he wouldn't offer. People would certainly talk, and her reputation would take another hit. There had to be another way.

"I'll find a place for you to live." It was a pledge he was clueless as to how to keep, but he'd come through for her. Someone needed to. "Until I can work out something more permanent, I'll pay for a room at an extended stay hotel." It was the least he could do.

"I couldn't ask you to do that."

"You're not. I'm offering." Though the similarity to Richard's *gift* of an apartment soured his stomach. To think of resembling that man in the slightest sent bile rising in his throat. "You can pay me back if you want to. No pressure though."

She firmed her jaw. "As soon as I can get a different job, I will."

"I know." Doubtless it was true. Candi had gumption and grit. She'd emerge from this mess in spectacular fashion.

Her phone chirped. She frowned as she read the text notification. "It's Richard. He's wondering why I'm running late." She looked at him with wide eyes. "What should I say?"

He leaned forward, resting his elbows on his knees and tenting his hands. "Call his bluff. If I were you, I'd say something like *I think you know why*."

Her nod was hesitant.

"You can't ignore what happened and slink away, Candi. Someone's got to confront him." *Please God, give her the courage to do so.*

"Okay. I'll do it." Her fingers typed out the message. She winced as she sent it. "Now what?"

"Now, you pack."

Chapter 12

A loneliness she'd never experienced circled her like a pack of wolves. Justice had just left her alone in her hotel room. She stared at the suitcase and four boxes she'd frantically packed before escaping. What would she do now? Like broken glass, her life lay shattered around her feet.

Her entire world had revolved around Impact. Not only her income and housing, but the people she'd considered family. Every friendly face, every listening ear was tied up in that place. Leaving Impact meant leaving an entire support system.

She was fatherless again, just like she'd been growing up. Part of her remained in denial. How could the man who'd mentored her, who'd taught her how to study the Bible, who'd encouraged her time and time again—how could he be evil? It didn't make sense. Shouldn't things be black and white? A clear villain without a trace of good? But his worn Bible, his emotion-laden prayers, his powerful sermons … the good and the ugly muddled in her brain.

A text notification rang out. She unpocketed her phone and gaped at it. Richard. It'd been hours since she'd heard from him; she'd hoped he'd leave her alone. No such luck.

I haven't the slightest idea what you're talking about. Have you been having those nightmares again?

So, he was going to deny everything? Make her think she was crazy. Early on as his assistant, she'd confided in him about the nightmares she'd had as a child growing up in foster care. Now, he was using them as ammo against her.

Justice had challenged her to be bold and confront him, even if the very idea turned her blood icy. He was right. If Krista and Irene had boldly pressed him about their concerns, she might have left earlier. Maybe avoided some of the fear and pain.

You know exactly what I mean. You let yourself into my apartment last night without my consent.

There. She'd done it. She'd poked the beast. How would he retaliate?

I was on a date night with Natalie last night. Are you feeling okay?

Ugh. She'd get nowhere with him. But at least he knew where she stood and that she wouldn't let this go.

She sat on the springy bed and bounced her crossed leg. Something about this interaction felt eerily familiar. What was it? Another text.

Maybe you hit your head again.

She gasped as the memory came flooding back. Being trapped against Richard's desk. It hadn't been a dream. He'd pressed far too close. She'd tried to get away and tripped. Over what? She squinted, trying to remember. Richard's shoe.

Her jaw dropped. He'd tripped her. Likely given her a concussion. And not gotten her any medical assistance. Her fingers shook as she called Justice. She had to tell him what had happened.

After pouring out her story, she asked him what to do.

"If I were you, I'd press charges for assault."

She sucked in a breath. This was far bigger than she'd imagined. "Can't that wait? I'm not sure I'm ready."

A pause. "You can hold off a couple of days while you process if you need to." His gentle voice calmed her frayed nerves. "Did you ever listen to the other podcasts I did?"

"No." She picked up the fluffy hotel pillow and held it against her chest. "Richard told us not to listen to anything other than Christian music. No TV, radio, social media, or podcasts."

Justice scoffed. "Of course, he did."

How could she have been so naive?

"Please listen to them. I'll send you a link. Their stories might mirror yours in many ways. They might help you see how Richard isolated and manipulated you. Might give you the courage to make that call to the police."

Oh, Lord. I don't want to go down this road.

"I'm scared," she confessed.

"I know. He's a scary man. But it's better to come into the light and let Jesus expose everything than to huddle in the dark where it feels safe. The Lord will be with you every step. I promise."

The truth in his words resonated with her. But she still had questions. "What should I do about Richard's texts?"

"I'd tell him you quit, then block his number. Keep his texts for evidence, but don't let him bully you." He sounded so sure and confident. Would she ever feel that way again?

She'd lost her agency along the way. It might take some time to get it back, to find her voice. "Good advice." *Thank You, God, for sending Justice to me.* She cringed to think of what would have happened if she'd had no one to call. "I'll do that."

Six months after she left Impact, Justice invited Candi into his recording studio—a repurposed large walk-in closet. Their folding chairs sat across from each other, the old classroom desk wedged between them sporting a microphone. Even in the ultra-bright lighting, her complexion had gained color. Her eyes held purpose instead of confusion. He started the podcast like he always did. By introducing her, then asking, "What's your story?"

She breathed deep, then plunged in. As he listened to the truth she'd unraveled from all the lies, his chest filled with pride in her. She was so brave to tell her story. Braver, still, to use her name. The first victim to do so.

No, he couldn't think of her in those terms. She'd been victimized by a predator, for sure, but the woman before him was anything but helpless. She was bold and strong, like David with his stones staring down Goliath.

"I'm speaking out now because I don't want another woman to go through what I did. Richard won't stop unless he's exposed. John 3:19 says, 'Men loved darkness rather than light because their deeds were evil.' But Jesus is the light of the world and that light shines through His people. We must never run from the light. Truth is worth the cost."

Justice broke out in a slow clap. Goodness, he was crazy about this woman. The way she'd walked through the past painful months endeared her to him more and more. Even without a recommendation from Richard, Candi hadn't had a problem finding a secretarial position with a grocery supplier. She'd come to understand that her job in the marketplace was no less holy, no less *Kingdom work* than her job with the church. She shone the light of Jesus at work, as well as in her new apartment complex.

Together, they'd found a new church. The one the Bringer and Reynolds families attended. By all appearances, it was a healthy community, but experience had taught them one never can tell by looking in from the outside. The challenge was keeping their hearts soft while asking difficult questions. Wise as serpents and innocent as doves. They were both growing in that area. At this church, they'd continue to grow together.

From time to time, Candi had reached out to her old friends from Impact. None of them had responded, likely coached by Richard to ignore *divisive* influences. Even Rachel had ignored her. Now that Justice and Candi had worked together to convince the other victims to press charges along with her, hopefully Richard would be found guilty when the case went to court.

Justice wrapped up the podcast and signed off. He gave Candi an encouraging smile as they stood. "You did great. How do you feel?"

She rubbed her hands on her jeans. "That was nerve-racking, but I'm okay. I think I did the right thing."

"I know you did. I'm so proud of you." He leaned close and gently cupped her face in his hands. "You are so beautiful to me. I thank God that He led me to Impact Church so I could meet you."

She leaned into his touch. "At least one good thing came out of that mess. You and me."

"I love you, Candi." His lips met hers in a gentle kiss. She melted against him as his hands threaded through her hair. Her honeysuckle scent wafted to his nostrils. So sweet.

"I love you too," she breathed.

He leaned his forehead against hers, his heart full to bursting. "Marry me." His cheeks heated. He hadn't meant to ask like this, crammed together in his studio, but he couldn't wait another second.

"W-what?" She rocked back, eyes wide.

He fumbled in his pocket for the ring he'd been carrying with him for nearly a week. Pulling it out, he awkwardly dropped to one knee and stubbed his toe on a shoe box. He pressed his lips together to keep from vocalizing the pain. After a deep breath, he looked into her beautiful face and spoke.

"I know it's soon. We can have a long engagement if you want, but precious Candi, please give me the honor of being your husband." He opened the velvet box, revealing a princess cut diamond ring. "I've never met anyone with such tenacity. Your heart for the Lord inspires me to pursue Him even more, and your passion spurs me to look at life through fresh eyes. I want to protect you, honor you, and treasure you all the days of my life. Marry me."

With glistening eyes, she dropped to her knees in front of him and took his hands in hers. "It would be my joy and honor to be your wife."

As he slid the ring onto her finger, he marveled at how God had made beauty from ashes.

Author's Note

I was a new mother of a seven-month-old with another baby on the way when my husband and I felt like God was drawing us to the International House of Prayer in Kansas City, MO. We both quit jobs we loved and moved across the state to what seemed to be a thriving community of like-minded people. People who loved Jesus and wanted to glorify Him. People who believed in the power of prayer. This began our two-year journey as "intercessory missionaries." This meant our (unpaid) job was to pray and worship. What could be better, right?

This season of our lives ended two years later when I had baby number three. (Yep! Three children three and under. We're kinda crazy like that.) But while we moved away from Kansas City, we remained connected to that community. That message. That ideology.

We looked back on that part of our lives with fondness. Our experience was filled with the best people and moments where the Lord met us in powerful ways. I advocated for IHOP-KC. I played the live stream night and day. I bought in.

I had no clue.

In October 2023, everything I thought I knew about IHOP-KC was called into question as accusations of spiritual and sexual abuse against Mike Bickle, the leader and pastor, became public. Enter months and months of untangling. Of questioning. Of tears. Enter more victims (one of whom I knew well) testifying to how he groomed not only them, but their entire families. A group of former leaders joined these women in boldly standing for truth in the midst of a firestorm of opposition, threats, and manipulation. Victims? More like victors.

Across the board, people were shocked as the truth came out. Mike Bickle was the last person most of us would expect. Even people who were close to him were floored. How could most of us not have seen what was truly going on? How could he have duped us so completely? Could we ever trust our judgment again? Thousands of people came through IHOP-KC's doors with a multitude more tuning in via livestream, and none of us saw this coming.

I truly believe the majority of pastors and spiritual leaders are honest, God-fearing people who are laying down their lives for their flocks. Those good shepherds who follow and imitate THE Good Shepherd in the way they lead far outnumber the pretenders. But the pretenders need to be called out. Spiritual manipulation is not okay with Jesus, and it shouldn't be okay with us.

If you've been hurt by any kind of abuse from a spiritual leader, my heart breaks for your pain. You are not alone. Healing from these atrocities is found in Jesus, yes. But also in healthy Christian community. Don't give up on Jesus, and please don't give up on His people. Truth-lovers are out there. Your brothers and sisters in Christ long to wrap arms around you.

This novella is dedicated to the courageous women who have come forward and testified to the truth. May the Lord restore all the years the locust has eaten (Joel 2:25).

In hope,

Sarah

Acknowledgements

Thank you to all the Brave Authors. It's an honor to partner with you. Thank you for not allowing fear to silence your voices.

Thanks to my husband Kevin for providing input on my story and for encouraging me to keep going. Your support means the world to me. Thanks to my children for cheering me on and for your understanding on days when my mind gets lost in fictional worlds.

Thanks to my church and Tuesday night Bible study group. You are a great example of what healthy community looks like and I'm happy to run alongside you.

Above all, thanks to Jesus for empowering me and entrusting me with this sacred call to create with Him.

Other Books

OTHER BOOKS FROM BRAVE AUTHOR BOOKS
Every Life Treasured
Every Captive Freed

OTHER BOOKS BY N.Y. DUNLAP
The Misadventures of Itchy Izzy
Honor: A Christian Romantic Suspense Anthology

OTHER BOOKS BY D. T. POWELL
With Mercy's Eyes

OTHER BOOKS BY SARAH HANKS
The Mercy Series
The Sister in Arms Collection

www.ingramcontent.com/pod-product-compliance
Lightning Source LLC
Chambersburg PA
CBHW071531110726
47908CB00007B/1836